SET IN STONE

K.M. SCOTT

In The Darkness (Project Artemis #1)

After The Storm (Project Artemis #2)

Behind The Scenes (Project Artemis #3)

Hard Work (Standalone)

Books by K.M. Scott writing as Gabrielle Bisset

Blood Avenged (Sons of Navarus #1)

Blood Betrayed (Sons of Navarus #2)

Blood Spirit (Sons of Navarus #3)

Blood Prophecy (Sons of Navarus #4)

Blood Craving (Sons of Navarus #5)

Blood Eclipse (Sons of Navarus #6)

Stolen Destiny (Destined Ones Duology #1)

Destiny Redeemed (Destined Ones Duology #2)

Love's Master

Masquerade

The Victorian Erotic Romance Trilogy

SET IN STONE

The next generation of the Heart of Stone series continues with Tristan and Nina's daughter Tressa's story!

Driven. Sexy. Tressa Stone wants to take over the world. As one of Tristan and Nina Stone's two daughters, she's got the will to do it, and when she does, it won't be because of some man.

But you know what they say about best laid plans.

Killian Brenton has the world in the palm of his hand. The newest quarterback for a New York team looking to get back to the top, he's the toast of the Big Apple and can have his pick of women. All it takes is one look at Tressa and he knows she's the one he wants.

Catching her might be even harder than getting to the big game, but if he does, it will be worth far more than a handful of championship rings.

CHAPTER ONE

TRESSA

TWO HOURS LATE BECAUSE I had to work on the London Richmont redesign project, I rushed around the penthouse trying to find my favorite black stilettos. Had I left them at the house? No, that couldn't be. I'd worn them to some event in the past few weeks since I'd been staying in the city every night.

Summer sat on the couch ready to go because she hadn't gotten waylaid by an overzealous designer hell-bent on having her way. Leaning back, she watched in amusement as I raced from room to room looking for my damn shoes.

"Are you like me and stuff things under your bed when people come over so it doesn't look like you're a total slob?" she asked, stopping me dead in my tracks.

I leveled a stern gaze on her face and slowly shook my head. "No."

Used to how serious I could be, she laughed off my quiet reprimand. "I didn't think so, but I figured it couldn't hurt to mention it."

That no one had been to the penthouse other than

Summer and my parents in so long I couldn't even remember wasn't a detail I felt compelled to mention. I did prefer to keep my personal behavior on the down low, but recently, there hadn't been much to hide. Work had kept me far too busy to be engaging in any of the sexy stuff, except for one night a while ago.

As I marched back into my bedroom to run my foot under the bed just in case my shoes had somehow found their way there, I cringed at how long it had been since I'd been with anyone. Had it really been four months?

Then again, how important was something like sex when I had the world to conquer? I'd have time for all that once I proved to the world that being given the COO position of the Richmont hotel chain hadn't been a mistake borne out of a father's love and good old fashioned nepotism.

My pinky toe snagged on the back of a shoe, and I crouched down in surprise to find my favorite Louboutins sitting on the floor under my bed. I must have kicked them off when I got home that night and they ended up there.

"Found them!" I announced as I slid my feet into the shoes.

"Where?" Summer yelled back with the clear sound of relief in her voice after being forced to wait for me for hours.

"Back in the closet," I lied. "Ready to go?"

I stopped in the doorway and gave her a quick once over while she did the same for me. I could trust Summer to tell me the truth, even if it hurt and even if I lashed out because of it. My brother had not only found a wonderful person to be with, but I'd found a good friend in her too.

"That black dress looks incredible on you," she said with a smile. "Every woman in New York, including me, would kill for legs like yours."

Laughing, I motioned for her to spin around so I could see the back of her to make sure her light green dress looked perfect. "I'll make sure to keep my wits about me then tonight," I joked, and then added, "You look great! That dress is so cute on you."

Summer turned around to face me and shrugged. "I do cute quite well. It's my thing."

I had a feeling Ethan had fallen in love with her far earlier than even she suspected. No wonder. Smart, funny, and cute as a button, she was the whole package. Now all my brother had to do was not mess things up with her and someday soon I might have a sister-in-law and my best friend all in one.

"My brother is very lucky. I hope you never let him forget that."

"He knows," she said with a smile.

"Good. Where is he tonight?" I asked as we made our way to the elevator to leave.

"He's photographing a Great Dane on Staten Island."

"Without his assistant?" I asked, surprised he'd gone without the half of the business that actually handled the animals at the shoots.

"I told him I had a prior engagement to attend," she

explained as the elevator doors opened. "You should have seen his face. I think he thought I had a date or something. He got a look in his eyes like I had told him I didn't love him anymore. I had to explain to him right then and there that I was going to the pediatric cancer event with you and we'd planned it for weeks."

I pressed the button for the lobby. "Keeping him on his toes. Good. Don't let him get complacent with you."

Summer smiled and chuckled like she did whenever I warned her about how to handle my brother. "Don't worry. I won't. I just hope that Great Dane doesn't take his head off. Ethan's not usually the dog whisperer."

As the elevator descended to street level, I secretly hoped my brother didn't end his career as a photographer that night. He'd finally found a way to do what he loved and do it in a way that didn't involve sleeping with women across the world. I didn't know what he'd do if that all came crashing down.

Hearing the worry in Summer's voice, I reassured her. "He'll be fine. Ethan can charm the birds out of the trees. I'm sure one dog won't be difficult for him at all. I'll tell you what, though. If you want to duck out of the event early after we make our presence known, you can do that and take the car service out to join him."

"See? This is why I tell him he's wrong about you. He's convinced you two are mortal enemies," she said as the doors opened to the lobby.

"Not anymore," I said with a chuckle. "When my brother and I stay in our appropriate spheres in this world, I feel nothing but sisterly love for him. It's only when we wander into places we shouldn't that we get into trouble."

"I'll have to tell him that."

"He knows I love him," I said with a wink. "We're just total opposites. Always have been."

And that right there was the absolute truth. My brother would feel perfectly comfortable walking into this charity event tonight more than an hour late, and he'd fully expect everyone would just be happy he showed up. I, on the other hand, knew I'd spend the entire car ride over there thinking of excuses for anyone who asked why I was late.

JUST A FEW STEPS INTO the ballroom at the Stilton Hotel and I couldn't help but be impressed by the work the organizers had done for the event this year. The crowd seemed much larger than in years past. Each May, the Pediatric Cancer Foundation went all out to celebrate their highest donors, of which Stone Worldwide certainly was, but because Summer and I arrived late, we'd missed that portion of the event. I vaguely remembered seeing something about an auction on the invitation, so I hoped we hadn't missed that entirely. While I didn't really travel in antique circles, I thought I might pick out a good piece if I saw something my mother may like.

"I'm going to get a drink. Do you want one?" I asked Summer as I looked back toward the bar.

Her eyes widened and she nodded. "This is

incredible. I thought we were going to be sitting at a table like every awards dinner I've ever had to attend. Is that a runway? What's that for?"

I shrugged but didn't bother to look at whatever she'd become fascinated with. I needed a drink before any fascination could happen for me.

"No idea. White wine?"

Again, she nodded, so I headed off to get us two white wines. Thankfully, the line for the bartender's attention wasn't long, and after pushing through a crowd of people that seemed to suddenly crop up behind my back as I waited for our glasses of wine, I finally reached Summer again.

"Where did all these people come from?" I asked as I handed her the glass.

Still taking in the scene happening around us, Summer shook her head. "I don't know. I guess something big's about to happen."

Something big at a charity event to celebrate major donors? Highly doubtful. I'd attended dozens of these kinds of events, first with my parents when I was younger and then on my own when my father finally decided he could bow out of obligatory events on behalf of Stone Worldwide because I could step in, and never once had anything big happened at any of them. It was always the same, staid event, just at different locations around the city.

Looking at all the people standing around us in the Stilton Hotel's ballroom at that moment, though, I had to admit tonight felt different. I just hoped I wouldn't have to give a speech extemporaneously. I hated those, so I avoided them like the plague. Now that I was there, I couldn't avoid it if it happened, though.

Maybe I needed another drink. Tipping my glass back to finish my first wine, I let it dribble down my throat and then turned to Summer. "Want another?"

She looked at me with surprise. "No. I barely took two sips out of this one. Since when did you become a big drinker?"

"It's been like ten minutes since I gave you that drink," I said with a chuckle. "If you weren't spending all your time people watching, you might want another one too. I'll be right back."

Nearly fifteen minutes and a line twenty deep later, I began walking back to where Summer stood near what I now recognized looked like a dais and a runway. People chattered loudly, making me wonder if I'd missed something. Were they having a fashion show or something tonight? I thought the invitation had said auction, but I'd just glanced at it.

The lights of the crystal chandelier in the center of the room dimmed, and all of a sudden, bright white spotlights focused on the dais at the back of the room. As I wondered what could be happening, people began to cheer and a voice came over the sound system announcing the auction would begin.

All this excitement for what? A rocking chair George Washington may have sat in a few times? A pen Bill Gates may have stuck in his pocket back in the seventies?

With the lights dimmed, finding Summer became next to impossible. Everywhere I turned, I ran into someone and spilled not only my drink but the one I'd gotten for her too. As the crowd roared for something, a man announced over the loudspeaker, "Ready to start big?"

Everyone around me yelled and clapped, so I became disoriented and couldn't find Summer in the sea of people with their arms raised. The screaming grew so loud that the voice of the man running the auction became drowned out. I had no idea why the hell all these people were so excited at a charity auction, but I wanted no part of this craziness.

Raising my arms in the air to salvage at least the half of each glass of wine I held in my hands, I pushed through the crowd toward where I'd last seen Summer and hoped to find her there. Focused on reaching her, I ignored all the madness around me like I'd always had a knack for doing and soon got to her.

"Where did you go?" she yelled as she grabbed a half-empty glass of wine from my left hand.

I leaned down so I didn't have to yell back at her and said into her ear, "This place is crazy. What the hell are all these people screaming about?"

She didn't answer and instead simply pointed at the dais as I realized this was no ordinary auction of boring antiques. Standing there with all the lights trained on him was a man more beautiful than I'd ever seen in my life.

He stood well over six foot and filled out the tux he wore perfectly. My eyes slowly scanned his body from his feet up, and by the time I got to his light brown hair that just barely hit the collar of his white shirt, I'd forgotten there was anyone else in the room but him.

Who was this man?

Then before I could turn to ask Summer, he began walking down the runway and my instant admiration for him quickly cooled. Sure, he was gorgeous, but as he basked in the attention of the crowd of screaming people I now noticed was mostly female, I saw someone who had no problem drawing attention to himself.

Of all the character flaws a man could possess, that was the worst.

Too bad. Other than his being an attention whore, I would have liked to find out more about this stunning specimen of manhood. Disappointed, I wondered what kind of man allowed himself to be involved in a bachelor auction.

Nobody I'd want.

He walked out to the end of the runway and winked at someone, which caused the crowd to erupt again. All it did for me was make me feel more disappointed because up close he was even more attractive with pale green eyes and dark lashes that made him look exotic. For a moment, I fantasized about what kind of perfect body existed under that tux, but that served no purpose. He wasn't anyone I could ever be with.

As he turned to walk back toward the dais, he looked

down at where we stood and suddenly it felt like time stopped. Those incredible green eyes stared into mine, and even as my mind dismissed this man as the attention whore he clearly was, my body reacted quite differently. That familiar ache between my legs I hadn't experienced in far too long and thoughts of how good he'd feel satisfying that ache made me instinctively sink my teeth into my lower lip. He smiled and ran his tongue over his bottom lip, and for a moment, nothing in the world existed but him.

I felt an elbow crash into my side, tearing me out of my imagination, and Summer yelled into my ear, "Oh, my God! Do you realize who you were just giving the eyes to?"

Shaking my head, partly to answer her and partly to get rid of the incredibly sexual thoughts still lingering about what I wanted to do with him, I stood there speechless, not able to say a thing.

"That's Killian Brenton!"

She said that like I should know the name, but it didn't register. Who was Killian Brenton?

Summer's eyes opened wide, as if she'd heard the dumbest thing ever spoken in the world. "He's the new quarterback for New York. He was traded from Miami this spring. He's the biggest thing in town, and you were just checking him out like you wanted to sink your teeth into him."

I waved off her ridiculous comment. There was nothing wrong with appreciating a good looking man, even if he was an attention whore I'd never sleep with.

"Two thousand! Do I hear three? It's for a great cause, ladies!" the announcer said in an amused voice.

Summer leaned over and asked, "Why aren't you bidding like everyone else?"

I shook my head and waved the question away.

"But it's for charity. You don't have to marry the guy."

After I watched him flirt with another woman in the audience, I turned to her and said, "These things aren't even real. No one expects either party to follow through on the deal."

"Then why not bid for him?" she asked, practically goading me to do it. "It's for a good cause."

Clearly, I couldn't deny that, so I raised my hand when the announcer said five thousand dollars. Turning to look at Summer, I smiled. "Happy?"

"Yes. Do you know that he signed a contract for over three hundred million dollars guaranteed and much more in bonuses?"

Three hundred million dollars? For that much, he should just stop parading around like a peacock and simply donate to the charity. But as I watched him interact with the women in the crowd, I saw he was incapable of not being in the spotlight and letting people fawn all over him.

It's a character flaw. He's an attention whore, and that I cannot abide in a man.

I'd met many men just like Killian Brenton in my

time with Stone Worldwide. They believed they were God's gift to everyone on the planet but especially to women. I'd enjoyed proving them wrong whenever I could. They preferred women with few thoughts in their heads who wanted to do nothing more than worship them.

No thanks. I had bigger plans for myself than simply adoring a man for the rest of my life. No matter how gorgeous he may be.

Lost in thought, I didn't see him come over toward us until he stood directly in front of me on the ballroom floor. Craning my neck to look up at him, I couldn't help but be mesmerized by those pale green eyes. God, he was beautiful! He smelled incredible too, and I took a deep breath of air into my lungs, fighting the urge to close my eyes he smelled so good. Was that cologne? I had no idea, but the man was nothing short of delectable.

But why was he smiling like that, like a cat that just ate a canary?

Before I could ask Summer what was going on, he lifted a microphone to his mouth and said in a deep voice that rolled over me like silk, "Congratulations. You're the lucky lady who gets to spend a night with me."

He stood staring at me as I looked up at him speechless and utterly unaware of what was happening. All I knew was I couldn't turn away, or maybe I didn't want to. Whatever it was, this man had an intoxicating effect on me I couldn't explain.

Then he ran the tip of his tongue over his bottom lip

and smiled before turning to step back onto the runway. I watched as he took a bow while the crowd went wild and his words finally sank in. Horrified, I lowered my head because of what everyone would think. How could I have let this happen?

Summer nudged me in the side and asked, "Oh, my God! What just happened there?"

"I don't know," I answered, still shaken by what he made me feel.

"You outbid everyone at ten grand for a date with Killian Brenton!"

Summer's words filtered through the haze in my brain, and I shook my head. "Five thousand, and I have no intention of going anywhere with someone like him."

Summer pointed up toward a big screen behind the stage and the image of Killian with the number $10,000 under him. "You raised your hand when they called for the next bid. I figured you were in the spirit of the evening and decided to be extra generous."

Ten grand. Thank God it was for charity. I didn't care about the money, though. It was only money, after all.

"Five or ten, it's a good cause, right?" I said as casually as I could manage.

"You're going to go on the date with him, aren't you?" Summer asked eagerly. "I mean, I guess you could just say no, but since you paid that much money for a night with him, you might as well."

"I did not pay for a night with that man!" I protested,

needing at least Summer to know that. "It was a charity auction. I would have contributed to anyone asking for a donation to cure childhood cancer, for God's sake."

Ten thousand dollars. How could I have been so lost in thought fantasizing about the delicious and decadent things I'd do with him that I bid ten thousand dollars for a date with a man?

As reality sunk in, I gradually realized everyone near us was staring at me. Jesus. How must all this look? I made a point of living as low-key a life as possible, acting professionally when I stepped out in public, and now I'd succeeded in blowing up all I'd worked for, and for what?

A date with a man. An attention whore. How embarrassing.

I watched as the people around us turned to look toward the stage. I followed their gazes to a huge screen showing a picture of Killian and me looking at each other right before he announced I'd won the bid. Anyone with eyes and a smattering of brain cells could see as clear as day what I was thinking about as I stared at him. I practically had a bubble over my head with the caption, "This man is beautiful. God, the things I would do with him."

My stomach began to churn from the disgust coursing through my body. Mortified, I turned to leave and said to Summer, "This has been fun, but I'm going. Feel free to stay if you want."

I couldn't get out of that room fast enough. With each step, I felt people's eyes staring at me like I was some kind of fallen woman. My head reeled from humiliation.

Summer ran up behind me and said, "You're not staying for the party? You love these kinds of things. What's going on? Are you sick?"

Flustered, I kept walking, my eyes firmly focused on the doors. "No. I'm fine. I just don't feel like doing this tonight."

Summer jumped in front of me in the lobby and stopped me. Smiling, she said, "You're blushing. Oh, my God, you're actually blushing! I've never seen you blush before. What's going on?"

"Stop being melodramatic. I think you've been spending too much time with my brother. I'm not blushing. It's just stuffy in here."

Shaking her head, she grinned like any of this was at all amusing. "No, it's not. It's actually chilly in here. I think they went a little overboard on the air conditioning, to be honest. You're blushing."

"So what if I am? It's not every day I'm publicly humiliated by a perfect stranger in a room full of people I'd hoped to chat up."

"How did he publicly humiliate you?"

I stepped around her and hurried toward the front doors. "I don't want to talk about it. God, who does he think he is?"

Summer rushed to keep up with me. "I think the question is who do you think he is because from where I'm standing, you like him. So are you going to go out with him?"

Again with that damn question. I rolled my eyes in disgust. "For the last time, no. Now let's go. I need some fresh air."

Behind us, the crowd began to cheer again as the announcement that the second bachelor to be auctioned off would be coming up next. For me, I'd had enough of the event already.

We reached the doors, and even though all I wanted to do was get out of there, I looked back and saw Killian standing at the edge of the catwalk staring at me. An attention whore man who craved the adulation of a crowd like that? No way was I going anywhere with him.

CHAPTER TWO

KILLIAN

MY BODY HUMMED FROM A lack of sleep and something else I hadn't felt in a long time. It had been years since a woman made me want her more than for just a quick fuck, and one look from Tressa Stone had me worried that crowd at the Pediatric Cancer Foundation charity event might see the effect she had on me. She practically undressed me with her eyes right there in front of all those bluebloods and society types. I did like a woman who threw caution to the wind, though.

Not that I didn't want to fuck her. You bet I did. How had I lived in this town for two months and not heard about her before? I couldn't decide if she was new money or old, but there was money there, no doubt. She practically oozed wealth. She had that icy thing women with fortunes had going on, but the question was whose money was it?

These ideas swirled around in my brain, among others, like was she as icy as she seemed? I bet she wasn't. She looked like an ice princess, but I knew for a fact she had heat beneath the surface. I felt it right there in that room as we stared at one another. She virtually melted in front of me.

My mind constructed exactly how she looked as she stood looking completely fuckable surrounded by all those people. Dark brown eyes and long dark hair I had a feeling fell exactly the way a woman's hair should when she was on top of me, caressing my skin as she undulated back and forth on my cock, the bottom of her hair teasing my chest with every roll of her hips.

Oh yeah, this date was going to be fun. She'd paid ten grand for me, so I intended on giving her every dime of her money's worth.

I needed to know more about her before our date, which I planned on happening this week. Grabbing my phone, I called my publicist Sherilyn and sent it to the screen on the wall across from my bed.

Her cheery face popped up on the display like always when I called her. I had a feeling I may have interrupted something since her dark blond hair looked disheveled.

"Good morning, Killian. Not that I'm not happy to hear from you, but do you know what time it is?"

Shaking my head, I thought about her question for a moment and came up with nothing. "I have no clue, actually. Were you busy with someone?"

She rolled her eyes and held up a hair dryer. "I was busy getting ready for my day. What are you doing up at five in the morning?"

Then her blue eyes opened wide in terror, and she tossed her hair dryer back onto the bed behind her. "Oh, my God! What happened? What do we need to clean up? Give me the details quick so I can get on it!"

She began to frantically pace back and forth across her bedroom floor, waving her arms in front of her. "Just tell me it's nothing illegal. It's next to impossible to get illegal stuff taken care of on a Sunday. If it's something like that, I'm going to have to roll out some of that big news we keep for times just like this. Let me see. What would work best?"

As she spun out of control right there before my eyes, I sat up in bed and waved my hands to stop her before she ran off to announce to the world that I'd secretly been visiting hospitals or something equally as saintly. "It's nothing like that, Sherilyn. Why are you jumping to the conclusion that I got arrested?"

Stopping to answer my question, she twisted her face into a look of confusion. "Who calls their publicist at five in the morning on a Sunday if it isn't that you were arrested? I know Mike would have gotten you out, but then you'd call me to smooth things over. If it's not that, then what's up?"

Leaning back against the pillows, I folded my arms behind my head. "I want you to tell me everything you know about Tressa Stone."

Sherilyn sat down on the edge of her bed, and her shoulders sagged as she realized she didn't have to start her day in PR high gear since I just wanted some information. Still confused, she asked, "What? Who do you want to know about?"

"Tressa Stone. She paid ten grand at that charity auction for a date with me last night. I want to know all about her. Everything you can tell me."

Looking up, my publicist seemed to search for the information on her bedroom ceiling. When she finally returned her focus to the screen, she shrugged. "I don't know a lot. She comes from a very wealthy family. That I do know. I have no idea of anything about her personal life because she keeps her life very secret. She must because I've never read a single word about her in the gossip pages or on any sites, and as you know, I read them religiously so I can be up on everything. I remember her brother being mentioned in them a lot a while back. He was some kind of photographer. Good looking man, but that's not surprising."

"Well, I want to know more. I need you to find out everything you can about her. I want to be prepared for this date."

Sherilyn shook her head, sending her half-wet, half-dry blond hair swinging around her shoulders. "You know, Killian, those things don't always happen. Everyone involved understands that the important part is giving to the charity. I wouldn't be surprised if she has no interest in going out with you at all."

That sounded ridiculous, especially considering how Tressa looked at me last night. "Trust me. She's interested. No woman pays that much for a date she has no intention of going on. Just find out everything there is to find out about her and get back to me, okay?"

"Okay, Killian. Just don't be surprised when she says no. I'll let you know what I find out."

The screen went black, leaving me sitting alone in bed thinking about Tressa Stone. She wouldn't say no. Christ, if all those people hadn't been around, I had a feeling she would have dragged me to a corner of the ballroom and climbed on top of me right there. I knew how to read women, and that woman wanted me. That I was sure of.

Just daydreaming about fucking her made me hard as a rock. Instead of calling my agent like I planned, I slid out of bed and headed into the bathroom to grab a shower. I wouldn't be getting any more sleep this morning, so why not rub one out and get going on my day?

A LITTLE WHILE LATER AT a time I knew my agent would be awake, I made my second call of the morning designed to help me make my date with Tressa Stone perfect. Mike never let me down, no matter if it was negotiating a contract or helping me navigate my new city. A born and bred New Yorker, he seemed to love giving me suggestions about where to go and what to eat, so who better to ask where to take a beautiful woman on a date?

Dressed in his usual golf shirt and pants, Mike looked like he perpetually was heading out to the links. If he didn't do such an incredible job on getting me the biggest contract for a quarterback in the league, I'd think the guy just spent his entire days goofing around and golfing.

He smiled as his face came into view on my screen

and pointed at me in that way he always did whenever he saw me. "Killian, how are you doing?"

"Good. I need suggestions on where to go to get a good meal. Nothing too loud or popular. I don't want to have to deal with the press. Well, not much anyway."

Mike thought about how to answer for a moment. "Let me mull it over and I'll get back to you. I'm more interested in talking about that charity auction event last night. I saw some pictures already this morning. It looks like you're fitting into this city perfectly."

I ran my hand through my hair and headed over to the window that looked out over the city. Scanning the horizon, I had to admit New York was my kind of place and the weather wasn't anywhere as hot as Miami, thankfully. "I told you I'd be fine. With enough money, I can be fine anywhere. Hell, you could have gotten me the deal with Minnesota and I'd have been fine. Bored to fucking hell and colder than a witch's tit, but fine."

"I hear some woman paid ten grand for a date with you. That's a lot of money for one night."

"She gets to go out with a man who's one of a very elite group of men in the world. Seems about right to me," I said.

"So is that why you want restaurant recommendations? When are you planning on doing this?"

Turning away from the gorgeous view out my bedroom window, I nodded. "I like to strike while the iron's hot, so something this week. I got her number from the organizer last night, so I'm planning on calling her today. So say Tuesday? That's why I need to know where I can take her today."

My agent let out a big laugh. "You do work fast. It's already Sunday morning."

"You didn't see this woman. I would have gone last night if I could have."

"Actually, I did. It's all over the news. You're a hot topic around here, and that charity event is a popular news story every year. Check out the local news. You'll see."

I turned on one of the New York channels and saw Mike hadn't exaggerated. The press had been out in full force, but I hadn't expected this much coverage. I figured New York had more interesting things to concern itself with than some football player hauling in ten grand at a charity auction.

Then I saw the picture of that moment when I walked up to Tressa and our eyes met. Definitely something there. Beneath that perfectly icy exterior, that woman sizzled. I'd bet a good million on it.

"You keep behaving yourself and this town is going to love you. Well, behaving yourself and taking New York to the big dance," Mike said.

I had more confidence in my getting my new team to the championship than I did in my behaving. I'd been a good boy in the time since I moved to New York, but I had no intention of living like a monk for the rest of my life. All behaving and no play made for a very boring Killian.

But I planned to change that with Tressa Stone.

"Well, I can't make any promises about behaving, but you have to admit that charity event helps."

Mike nodded but his toothy grin faded just a bit. "Be careful with this woman. You don't need any problems like that here."

"Like what? I'm single, and if she's single, what's the problem?"

"I don't know her, but I do know the Stone name is important in this city. You don't want to make any powerful enemies here, Killian. This isn't like Miami. New York will chew up a man and spit him out before he knows what's happened. Yes, charity events like the one last night are good, but don't negate all the benefit you get from it by becoming a permanent fixture in the gossip pages."

"Well, you know what Sherilyn says. There's no such thing as bad publicity," I said with a laugh.

But my agent didn't find anything about what I said funny.

"You know my opinion on that. I can get you the world with the talent you have, but if you become a distraction or a problem for your team, I won't be able to get you a deal selling fucking athlete's foot cream, much less anything good."

I could tell any time Mike got hot about a subject when he started dropping F bombs. Since I had no intention of becoming a distraction for anyone other than Tressa Stone, I needed to calm him before he began to get worried I'd fuck up all his hard work.

"Don't worry. I know what my job is here. This whole thing with one woman isn't going to make me lose focus. It's just a date."

Mike arched one eyebrow to show me how skeptical he was about my claim. "I've seen that look before in you. Just remember once workouts start, you need to be all football all the time."

"Have I ever not been?" I asked, knowing the answer to that wasn't exactly no.

But that was when I was a rookie in the league. Now at twenty-nine, I knew I had just a few more years left before it all could slip away in one season. I had no intention of leaving my football career before I wanted to.

"Just remember what you told me when you came to me all those years ago, Killian. You said you wanted one single thing in this world, and that was to play football. As my grandmother used to say, you chase two rabbits and you'll catch neither."

"Got it. You don't have to worry about me, Mike. It's just a date with someone who paid ten grand for some time with me. The least I can do is take her to a nice restaurant."

Mike didn't look convinced. "Yeah. Well, let me think about it. I'll send you over some ideas later today."

The call ended, and as I stood in my bedroom alone again, I thought back to those early days of my career. Christ, I was such a naïve kid. Straight out of college and barely twenty-two, Miami started me halfway through the season when Sterling tore his ACL. Too green to even realize I should have been scared shitless seeing that happen right in front of me on the field, I ran in and huddled up with the players, ready to be the phenom everyone said I was since the first touchdown I threw in college.

By the end of my first season, I could do no wrong. Everything came so easy. Money. Women. Success. And for a few years, life was all I'd ever dreamed of.

Then one day it wasn't. Then one day I was in my late twenties and hurt. Nothing too bad, but bad enough for Miami to want someone new, someone younger. So when New York needed a new quarterback, Mike made the deal and I became the highest paid quarterback in the history of the game.

Now all I had to do was show them I was still the best in the league.

The screen on the wall made a noise to let me know a call was coming in, and I turned to see Sherilyn smiling at me. Her hair didn't look like someone had taken a blender to it anymore, and she wore makeup like she usually did when she worked.

"I'm glad to see you're up and dressed, Killian. I never know how I'm going to find you when I call," she said, blushing as she finished.

I couldn't blame her. More than once here and in Miami, she'd caught me buck naked in bed or standing in front of the monitor. I never had been able to remember that goddamned away message.

Not that it mattered. I imagined she'd seen people naked before me.

"Showered and dressed like a normal person, for once. I don't think I've been up this early on a Sunday when I wasn't playing in years," I said as I sat down on the edge of my bed. "So what did you find out about Tressa?"

Sherilyn looked down at her tablet and scanned the information before looking up at me again. "Tressa Stone is twenty-seven years old. Never married. She has no children. I thought you'd like to know that right off."

"Not married is good. I like kids well enough, so it wouldn't matter to me if she had some rugrats. What else did you find out?"

"She's a member of the Stone family. Very influential family in this city."

"So I've heard."

"She's not a frequent topic in the gossip pages or even on the business page because of her work for Stone Worldwide, her family's company. She's a VP at Stone Worldwide and the newly minted COO of the Richmont hotel chain."

"Nice. What's this company make?"

"There are dozens and dozens of subsidiaries inside the main company. The Stone name is on things from a line of outerwear under the Storm name, a high end restaurant chain under the name brand Harrigan's Chop House, and dozens of other companies. You probably know their Richmont hotel chain the best, though."

I filed all this information away for our date. "So,

she's a business executive? I can see that. She gives off that vibe."

Sherilyn shook her head and frowned. "No, you're misunderstanding. Tressa Stone isn't just a powerful businesswoman. She's also an heiress to a huge fortune. She's set to inherit billions when her parents die, along with her brother and sister, and even now is one of the wealthiest women in all of New York. And the family is old money, not nouveau riche."

"So what are you saying? Someone like her would never lower herself to go on a date with a lowly football player? I'm not exactly a pauper here, Sherilyn."

"I'm saying that maybe she isn't exactly the type of woman you date. Usually, I mean."

The way Sherilyn said that made me wonder if she hadn't told me all she'd found out about Tressa. What was she hiding?

"Is there something you're not telling me about this woman?"

Sherilyn slowly shook her head. "No. You saw her. Does she look like the type of woman who spends her time with athletes? My guess is she's more of a three-piece suit kind of woman who likes men who are like her, if you know what I mean."

I'd known my publicist longer than I knew my agent, so I couldn't believe anything she ever said to me wasn't meant to be helpful. We'd been together through thick and thin from before I even signed with a team, and she'd seen me at my worst and my best. I knew what she was seeing in Tressa Stone, but I saw something else.

Something more than just a businesswoman who projected an icy façade to the world. And I planned on finding out if my hunch about who she was behind that cold mask was right.

"Well, it's just a single date, Sherilyn, so you don't have to worry about me."

"Oh, I'm not worried about you, Killian. I know you. You'll be the same charming man you always are with women, and if she doesn't like that, at least it's just a few hours of your time and it's for a good cause."

"Thanks, Sherilyn. I can always count on you to help me. Talk to you later."

Now that I knew some details about Tressa, it was time to make that date with her.

CHAPTER THREE

TRESSA

AFTER OVERSLEEPING NEARLY TWO HOURS, I sat at the table in my living room and stared out the window that overlooked the city. I squinted at a ray of sun that chose at that very moment to shine into my penthouse, turning away as I prayed my morning coffee would start to do its job. So far, it hadn't done a damn thing to make me wake up, and I couldn't function well until the caffeine kicked in.

The chime from the TV told me someone had made the mistake of thinking they should call me this morning, and I turned to look at the monitor as the person's face came into focus. Ethan. Ugh. Not this morning. Please, God, not this morning.

But he had other ideas.

"Good morning, Tress. How are you feeling on this fine and sunny New York morning? Feeling famous or would it be infamous?" he chirped away with that ridiculous smile on his face.

Wishing my coffee would kick in at that very moment, I mumbled, "I don't have the time to deal with you today, Ethan."

His stupid grin grew even larger. "It's a wonderful day, so why not make time? The birds are singing in the trees, and the newspapers are out with all the news we fine citizens could possible need. Want to see the highlights?"

My brain attempted to figure out what the hell he was referring to, and just as the memory of the charity auction popped into my head, he pointed to the pictures of Killian and me at the charity auction last night that popped up in succession to frame his face on the screen. Each one showed me gazing at the man like some lovesick schoolgirl, or worse, like some horny teenager looking like she wanted to jump him right there in front of everyone in the ballroom.

"I love how you keep things on the down low, Tress. Just how low is that now? I mean, I guess it could have appeared on the front page of the Post and the Times. That would definitely not be keeping it on the down low like you are now with it on Page Six, all the gossip websites, and even on the local TV news."

His teasing made me want to lash out, but I was too exhausted, and honestly, it was all so embarrassing. Ethan had me dead to rights on this mess, and there was nothing I could do about that, so I just snapped, "What are you doing up so early? Did you lose your girlfriend? Did she finally figure out she could do better?"

My brother simply smiled at my sharp attack. His smugness knew no bounds, and justifiably so. He'd waited all his adult life to get me back for all those times

I'd chided him about how he conducted his personal life. I didn't begrudge him this payback. I'd do the same thing myself. I just wasn't in the mood at that very moment to trade verbal jabs with him.

"Summer and I are perfectly fine. I just wanted to check in on my sister who preaches about keeping things on the down low. That seems to be working pretty well for you. I do have to hand it to you, though, Tress. You definitely chose someone perfect for your debut on Page Six. Just wait until Dad sees you standing with Killian Brenton."

I groaned in misery. The thought of my parents seeing me ogling some football player at the charity auction made this morning one hundred times worse. I'd always prided myself on being the consummate professional, and now this would ruin everything I'd so assiduously worked for.

"If I find out you called them about this, I swear to God, Ethan, I will be merciless in my revenge."

He threw his head back and laughed like he was having a grand old time. "They don't live in a cave, Tress. They're going to find out eventually. It's all over the news. One of their friends probably showed them those pictures over breakfast."

Oh. God. The very thought of one of my parents' friends calling them up over coffee and muffins on a Sunday morning just to show them those pictures made me feel like I'd be sick.

And just when I thought I couldn't feel any worse, I

saw my father calling.

"Ethan, go get back to your life and leave me alone. I'm busy."

More laughing at my misery was followed by more taunting. "I've waited for years for this day. I'm not going to let it just go like that. How about we talk about that ten grand you paid to spend the night with Killian? That was how they said it, spend the night, right? I'm loving this down low thing you have going on. You should give lessons on how to keep your private life private, Tress."

"Go to hell."

I hurried over to the TV and ended the call with Ethan to answer my father's. Before I said a word, I immediately assessed how he looked. No frown. Good. No pacing. That was definitely good. When my father was upset, he paced. Maybe he hadn't heard, but then again, if he hadn't, why would he be calling me so early on a Sunday morning?

Plastering a smile on my face, I effected my happiest voice. "Hi, Dad. It's early to see you this morning. Everything okay?"

Oh, God. That sounded panicked, not chipper, like I wanted it to be. Hopefully, he didn't hear the fear in my voice. I had to stay cool. Nothing bad had happened. This whole Killian Brenton thing would blow over by the time Monday rolled around, so I just had to keep things in perspective.

"Oh, yeah. Everything's fine. How was the charity event last night? Did you have a good time?"

My father had never been the teasing type, but his questions sounded oddly taunting, similar to my brother's. Had Ethan already gotten to him? If he did, I would kill him for this. Or even better, I'd torture him. There would be no end to my vengeance.

"It was a very nice event, but they always are. You know how they are. You spent enough years attending them. You haven't spoken to Ethan yet this morning, have you?"

Damn. My words tumbled out of my mouth so quickly my father had to suspect something wasn't right.

My father shook his head. "No. I haven't spoken to him in a few days. Is anything wrong?"

Good. There was my chance to steer the conversation in the direction of my brother. I needed to build on that inherent worry he always had that Ethan had done something wrong.

"No. I mean, you know how he is. You can never tell what he's going to do. One day he's taking pictures of dogs, and the next who knows? That's just Ethan, I guess."

Nodding, my father said, "Your brother has been known to have some wild times. I guess I expect it from him. Now you, on the other hand, I don't expect it from." He stopped talking and pointed to a box at the top of the screen he'd put there as he spoke. "Imagine my surprise to find out my daughter is going out on a date with the new quarterback for my favorite team. You don't even like football, do you? Not that it matters to go out on a date, but you've never wanted to go to a game like your brother and sister."

My stomach dropped to my feet, and I cringed as I looked up and saw the picture of Killian and me staring at each other like long lost loves. Oh, who was I kidding? That wasn't even remotely true. Only I was staring at him like that. At least he hadn't put up the one of me staring at him like some oversexed schoolgirl.

"I think I must have had a reaction to the allergy medicine I took yesterday afternoon, Dad. The pollen has been terrible this spring. Did you see how much of it was in the air this week? I think it made me a little loopy—the medicine, not the pollen—and then I had a few sips of wine right after I got to the event. It must have been that. Honestly, it looks much different than it was in actuality. It's really not a big deal."

Nice job rambling, Tressa. That will convince him everything's fine. Anytime anyone in the history of the world said something wasn't a big deal, those very words told everyone it was so much a big deal.

None of what I told my father sounded even plausible and didn't explain why I was gazing up at Killian Brenton like some pathetic schoolgirl with her first crush. I didn't even have allergies.

God, how was I going to show my face anywhere ever again?

My father smiled sweetly at me like he always did when he saw me worrying about something. "You don't have to explain having a good time, honey. You're a grown woman, and a very competent woman at that. And Killian Brenton is a big deal. I'm not surprised you'd be more than a little impressed with him. The amount you bid to the charity for him all goes to a great cause, so I think you must be feeling pretty good about things."

I wasn't impressed by him. He was nothing more than an attention whore who loved the limelight. That kind of man was nothing but a turn off. I couldn't tell my father that, though, since he didn't see me like that. To my father, I was his overachieving daughter who would someday take over Stone Worldwide. I acted the way I was supposed to, as opposed to my two siblings, and he appreciated that.

So if he knew what had been going through my mind at the moment that picture of me gazing longingly up at Killian Brenton was taken, I'd be too embarrassed to face him.

"It was nothing, Dad. Just some allergy medicine gone wrong. I'm happy to make the donation to the pediatric cancer association, though. At least that went right."

"When are the two of you going out? You did bid on a date with him, right?" my father asked a little too eagerly.

"We're not," I answered, grimacing at how tawdry the whole thing sounded. Thank God it was for a worthy cause. It was truly the only saving grace of the entire situation.

"Why not? He's the talk of the town," my father said with a deep frown, sounding downright disappointed by my announcement that I wouldn't be going out with Killian.

"I prefer my dates to grow out of organic circumstances, to be honest, Dad. I'm sure Mr. Brenton will be fine with my declining his offer. He has other things to occupy his time with, I have no doubt."

"Oh. Well, if you want to do it that way, that's fine. I just think it's a shame you aren't going because if anyone deserves a night out, it's you. I know how hard you work every day. I wish you'd reconsider. I hear he's a great guy."

Ethan had been right. My father did want me to go out with the quarterback from his favorite team. What was it with these men and football that made them think such ridiculous things?

I needed to change the topic or I'd have to explain my dislike for Killian Brenton to my father, something I really didn't want to do now or ever. "I have to go, Dad. I have work I need to get done today, and I'll never finish it if I just sit around all day. Tell Mom I said hi. Are you two just relaxing today?"

Leaving that horrible discussion of my misadventures the night before, my father's eyes lit up, and he smiled. "No. We're coming into the city to take Diana out for lunch. You're welcome to join us. Ethan and Summer said they might come too. We'd love to have you there too."

My sister had recently started leaving the hotel more because of Summer and Ethan's efforts, but I didn't feel right crashing their family time. Diana and I were too different to spend much time together. Every time we did, I seemed to say the wrong thing and upset her.

"I wish I could. Tell Diana I said I'm sorry I couldn't come this time but maybe next time. Tell her I'll stop over to see her this week."

That hopeful look in my father's eyes made my chest ache because I knew as soon as I said those words that I wouldn't go to see my sister anytime soon. I couldn't. Being around her made me too sad because I always thought back to who she was before the accident. It broke my heart to know she'd never be that person again.

"Okay, honey. Have a good day, and Tressa, remember that you deserve to relax and have a good time every so often."

"I love you, Dad. Don't worry about me. I'm having a good time doing what I love, which is working at Stone Worldwide and making it the successful company it is."

The screen turned black, leaving me alone in my misery once more. Feeling a headache beginning to form, I pinched the bridge of my nose and tried to push the memory of those images of Killian Brenton and me out of my mind. So far this day had been utter shit, so it had to get better. Maybe if I took a shower and got dressed. That might make me feel better.

What would really make me feel great would be if someone could invent a way to wipe my mind and the mind of every person in New York of the sight of me looking up at Killian Brenton like I wanted to devour him. That would be perfect.

CHAPTER FOUR

KILLIAN

WHY WERE MY PALMS SWEATY? It made no sense. I'd dated hundreds of women. Well, maybe not hundreds but I'd never had a problem with getting any woman I wanted. There was no reason to think Tressa Stone would be any different. For God's sake, she'd already basically given me the green light the way she looked at me last night. She was probably waiting for me to call at that very moment.

Rubbing my hands together, I took one last glance at the card the woman from the pediatric cancer foundation gave me. Tressa Stone, one date with Killian Brenton. My eyes drifted over her number for the tenth time. For a few moments, I closed my eyes and let my mind linger on that look in her eyes when she was staring up at me. I'd had women check me out before, but that was different.

She was different. And I intended on finding out every way that was true.

I'd take her to one of the restaurants Mike suggested. Maybe the Italian one. Or French. I'd decide once I talked to her. Then we might go for a drive. One of my teammates had told me about this place he bought last year upstate. A nice drive on a gorgeous spring night would set the stage, and then I'd bring her back to my apartment. Or hers. Either would work.

I remembered how she looked up at me when our eyes met. Those dark eyes possessed an intensity I had a feeling I'd enjoy once she was naked and riding my cock. Oh yeah, this was going to be a night she'd never forget.

Eager to get things rolling, I made the call to Tressa Stone I'd delayed for nearly an hour and waited for her face to appear as I wondered what she'd be wearing at barely ten o'clock in the morning. Was she a T-shirt and shorts or silk pajamas kind of woman?

That was easy. Silk pajamas.

A second later, I saw I'd been wrong in my guess. Tressa stood in the middle of what looked like a luxury penthouse in a pair of black cotton shorts and a pale pink T-shirt wearing no bra. Pleasantly surprised, I had to admit even in something as casual as that, she looked incredible. Her dark hair was wet, as if she'd just come back from a swim, and clung to her T-shirt just above her breasts, making the shirt damp so I could see her nipples. Overall, it was quite the beautiful sight I hadn't expected at all.

She stood staring in shock for a long moment before rushing over to grab a white towel off the back of a chair to cover herself. The whole action made me smile at how cute she could be.

"Don't cover up on my account. I like what I'm

seeing."

"How did you get this number, Mr. Brenton?" she asked, clearly flustered as she struggled to cover herself with the towel.

"The woman at the event last night gave it to me since I'd have to call you to arrange that date we're going on."

Shaking her head, Tressa put her right hand up to stop me as she clutched the towel near her neck with her other hand. "Oh, no we aren't. I'll be sending the money to the charity first thing tomorrow, but we won't be going on any date. Sorry you made the effort when it wasn't needed."

"What do you mean we aren't going on the date you paid ten grand for?" I asked with a chuckle. "I'd think any woman who paid that much would be chomping at the bit to make plans."

Clinging to the towel as it threatened to expose her wet breasts again, she shook her head. "No offense, but I thought I was paying five, not ten, but that doesn't matter. It's for a good cause, so all the better. But I have no interest in going out on a date with you, Mr. Brenton."

Was this woman serious? My ego was beginning to feel bruised. Why wasn't she interested in going on a date she paid ten thousand dollars for?

No worries. I knew I could charm her into it. Maybe she was intimidated by my fame. That happened sometimes. "Please, call me Killian, Tressa. For the amount you paid, you can at least call me by my first name."

But even that dose of charm did nothing to make her warm up. Drawing her eyebrows in, she said sharply, "Mr. Brenton, I have to get to work today, but thank you for calling. Please feel free to consider yourself unobligated to have that date with me. I'm sure there are many women who would take my place, so choose one of them. Good day."

With that, she gave me one last glare and that was the last I saw of her before the screen went dark. I stood there in the center of the room in shock. Did that just happen? Last night, the woman couldn't see enough of me as I walked down that catwalk, and this morning, she acted like I was some fucking leper she couldn't get away from fast enough.

Now my ego was more than bruised. Who did this woman think she was? She paid ten grand for a date with the highest paid quarterback in football. It didn't matter if she thought she was only paying five thousand, although I couldn't help but feel that a night out with me was worth more, especially considering all the proceeds went to charity. She acted like I was some fucking janitor who had offended her by asking her out.

Nope. That wasn't going to be the last word on this. No way. Why the hell didn't she want to go out on a single date with me?

Immediately, I called back but got her away message that in a delightful tone I hadn't gotten the pleasure to hear a minute before now told callers that she was busy and couldn't talk at the moment. There was no suggestion to leave a message or ever call back again. I was sure I'd never heard such a dismissive away message before in my life.

What was the problem with this woman?

Frustrated, I stood staring at the dark screen in front of me still stunned at what just happened. Or maybe I was angry. I couldn't tell at the moment. All I knew was I'd never met anyone who could run so hot and cold. This woman wanted me last night, and now she treated me like I disgusted her.

This wasn't over. Tressa Stone wasn't going to have the last word on this. No. I didn't know who the hell she thought she was, but this wasn't over. Not by a long shot.

Irritated, I called my publicist to find out what more she'd learned about Tressa Stone in the past few hours. Her answer? Nothing.

"What do you mean nothing? This woman isn't some kind of ghost, Sherilyn. She's a VP at a major company. She's a member of one of the most important families in the city, and you can't find out a damn thing about her?" I barked as my frustration began to overtake me.

Sherilyn's eyes grew wide at the bellowing sound of my voice. "I'm sorry, Killian. I can't just make up information on this woman. I can't help it if she's kept her personal life very personal. For most people, the first time they've seen a picture of her was this morning. She's just not like you."

"Does she have something against football players, for Christ's sake? She didn't last night, so I don't know what I could have done between then and this morning to change her opinion. We didn't even speak for the first time until five minutes ago."

My publicist nodded in her sympathetic way she thought helped when I got angry. It didn't help, but I appreciated the attempt.

"I don't know why she wouldn't want to go out on the date with you. Did she say if she planned to not give the money to the pediatric cancer foundation too? I can't imagine why she'd do that."

I shook my head as I began to pace back and forth across the room. "No, she's not doing anything like that. The woman isn't a monster. She's also not stupid. Going back on that bid would be a PR disaster for her and her company. No, she's more than happy to pay the ten grand to the charity. She just has no interest in going on the date with me, which incidentally, was supposed to be the prize for the highest bidder."

Sherilyn looked down at her tablet. "Let me see if I can find anything now. Maybe this morning's news blast about her has jarred some tidbit of information loose. Give me a second."

As she scoured her sources, I continued to pace. Maybe she thought she was too good for someone like me. She was a rich girl. That explained the temper tantrum she'd had a few minutes ago. Between being born with a silver spoon in her mouth and being a corporate bigwig, she was probably used to ordering people around.

None of that turned me off her, to be honest. I liked powerful people, and I'd found powerful women made for incredible sex because they were happy to tell you exactly what they wanted. Unlike other men, I appreciated that. It also made for some really hot talk while I was fucking them, just as I suspected it would with Tressa. The spoiled, rich girl thing I could do without, but the allure of a powerful and sexy beautiful woman overruled that character flaw in my mind.

As I marched past her, Sherilyn looked up and smiled. "I did find out something interesting about her father, though. Tristan Stone is a huge New York football fan and has had a box at the stadium for years. There was even talk a few years back that he considered buying the team when it was last up for sale. Keep that in mind if you're thinking about doing anything with his daughter. Your new team wouldn't appreciate you alienating one of the organizations' biggest supporters."

This was good news. Having a family member of Tressa's who was a huge football fan could only help.

I stopped pacing and thought about how to use this information. "Is she close with her father, or is this one of those dysfunctional families where every member is trying to oust the others in some money grab?"

Sherilyn shook her head. "No, I don't think the Stones are like that. Every picture I'm seeing with her father they look happy. She's worked at Stone Worldwide since college and all through her graduate school years when she was earning her MBA. From what I can gather, she's the heir apparent to the company since neither of her siblings work there."

"Okay, then. This will be my plan: Get in tight with Dad."

Sherilyn scowled at me. "Don't be so cynical. I've met Tristan Stone on a number of occasions. Despite his reputation for being a shark in business, nearly everyone likes him. He lost his entire family in a plane crash when he was young, and I hear there's some family tragedy with one of his children. His wife is some kind of artist, if I'm remembering correctly. I don't see why how her father feels about football changes anything anyway. She's a grown woman, Killian. If she doesn't want to go on that date with you, maybe you should just gracefully accept that and back off."

I looked at her through squinted eyes, not believing what I was hearing. "No way. This is a matter of pride now. The woman basically acted like she was too good for me. Nope. We're going on that date. I have no intention of having people at that charity asking me why the date isn't happening and why the press they're expecting isn't happening."

"Fine, but I don't understand what you plan to do with the information about her father and how he's a fan of the team."

"Let's say I like to know everything that's going on around me, on and off the field. Send me the information about where I can find Tristan Stone tomorrow."

Without missing a beat, she said, "Oh, that's easy. The thirty-fifth floor of the Stone Worldwide building in Midtown. I'll send you the address."

That she knew the man's exact location so quickly impressed me. "Do you carry that kind of information around in your head?"

Sherilyn laughed. "No. Well, I guess yes. Before I became a publicist, I was a reporter on the business beat. I interviewed him at his office a few times. Unless something's changed, he'll be in his office tomorrow morning like he always is."

"Good. Send me the address. Oh, and let's see what my new employer might have to offer one of the team's biggest fans, okay? I wouldn't want to go see him empty-handed."

Sherilyn nodded and began making a second call even before our call had ended. "I'm on it. I'll let you know what I hear."

"Good. Make sure it's something impressive."

The picture went dark as I continued to pace back and forth across the room. A little visit with dad tomorrow morning would do the trick to soften her up. Since her father was a huge fan of the team, she'd see that living up to her end of the deal regarding our date was the least she could do.

I winced at the reality that I had to do any of this to get the woman to go out with me, but a deal was a deal, and I had no intention of looking like some fool who could reel in ten grand for a charity but couldn't get someone like Tressa Stone to have dinner with him.

After all, who the hell said no to dinner with a star quarterback?

CHAPTER FIVE

TRESSA

MONDAY MORNING I AWOKE WITH the singular hope that the world had forgotten about me with that damn Killian Brenton. I'd been the name on everyone's lips all day Sunday, enough that I couldn't even leave the penthouse to go out and enjoy the nice May weather. After the fifth or sixth time I saw the pictures of us, I turned off the TV to spend the day working from my bedroom.

But even that didn't stop the day from being devoted to what happened. I ended up fielding calls from people far and wide, some of whom I hadn't heard from since high school, because my picture had been in every paper, magazine, and gossip site up and down the East coast. Why they all seemed so damned interested baffled me.

I walked out of the Richmont to start my workweek only to find the press and their cameras lurking around on the sidewalk waiting for me. A few of them yelled questions about my relationship with Killian, to which I wanted to yell back, "There is no damn relationship! Go away!"

Thankfully, I was able to duck into the car the service

had waiting for me at the curb and drove away before they could descend upon me like a swarm of locusts. However, I ran into a group of reporters outside the Stone Worldwide building when I arrived to work, which meant I had to dash through the lobby in four inch heels to get to the elevator. As I tried not to break my ankle racing across the marble floor, I silently cursed that bastard Killian Brenton.

I hadn't planned on a run so early in the day, especially in my favorite work shoes. A few of the paparazzi had gotten pictures, but I had a feeling they hadn't expected me to tear off like I did.

As I rode up in the elevator to my floor, I couldn't believe all of this nonsense had been added to my life because of that man. I already hated him, and I'd only known he existed on the planet for less than forty-eight hours!

How did people live like this, being hounded by photographers day and night because of who they were with? I'd never even had a full conversation with him that any of these people knew of, and still they hurled questions at me about the nature of our relationship.

The very idea made my stomach roil. That man and I would never be anything to one another. He was an attention whore, pure and simple, and of all the things I hated in people, that was the worst. Attention whores thought the world revolved around them. Their narcissism never failed to make them truly ugly on the inside, no matter how impressive the outside was.

I couldn't deny that he had something I liked. More than liked. Fine. Something I really liked and possibly would have desired.

So he was stunning. All right. He was. The man was gorgeous from head to toe. I'd never seen any man in the world who looked so sexy in a tux. Most of them looked like overstuffed penguins in tuxes, but Killian had worn his in a way that told me what those black pants and white shirt were hiding was nothing less than perfection.

So what? So I ogled him. I did. I'm a grown woman who knew a good looking man when I saw him. Was it a crime to appreciate beauty now? I had no idea why everyone was making such a big deal about how I looked at him. Some of the articles said it was a look of love. Love! God, everyone in the world was so melodramatic.

I liked what I saw and didn't hide it when I checked him out. Period. Full stop. That's all it was.

As for Mr. Brenton, I'd been very clear with him about how I felt about this date I'd won. No thanks. Why would I go on a date with a man like him? So I could listen to him drone on about how important he was and how much money the team paid him just to come to New York?

I'd pass, thank you. The idea that someone playing a game was paid three hundred million dollars made me question the sanity of anyone associated with that sport, but that was neither here nor there. I didn't need to sit through a meal listening to him brag about how worthy he was to receive that amount of money to throw a ball down a field.

The elevator doors opened as my phone began to ring, tearing me from my thoughts about that man. I looked to see my father calling.

"Hi, Dad. What's up?"

"Can you come up to my office?"

This was exactly what I needed to get my focus back. My father and I would discuss something—maybe he wanted a progress report on the redo of the Richmont in London—and I'd get back to being my normal self instead of this distracted mess I'd turned into in the past two days.

"Sure, Dad. I'll be right up," I happily answered.

I'd even take some talk about his time with my mother and Diana yesterday. Not normally my favorite topic of conversation, at least it would get my mind off Killian Brenton and the upheaval he'd brought to my once idyllic life.

My father's assistant smiled at me as I walked across the black marble tile on the thirty-fifth floor where the executive offices were at Stone Worldwide. Although I'd been made a Vice President and the COO of the Richmont hotel chain, I chose to stay in my office on the twelfth floor where I started with the business for now, even though my father had offered to have the executive suite completely redesigned to accommodate me. My father would retire someday, and I'd be here soon enough. He deserved to be the only Stone on this floor until that day.

"Good morning, Tressa," Brenda said in her low voice.

I nodded and smiled as I wondered if anyone else ever found the way she sounded jarring. "Good morning. It's a beautiful day, isn't it?"

"It is. Your father is waiting for you. There's coffee in there, but I can bring in tea, if you like."

I waved off her suggestion. "No, coffee's great. Thanks, Brenda!"

Opening my father's office door, I walked in feeling great and then instantly felt like someone had sucked all the air out of my lungs as I stopped dead. Standing there in front of me, I saw Killian Brenton with my father talking and laughing like they were the best and oldest of friends.

Son of a bitch. What was he doing here?

For a moment, the memory of what I did to Ethan with Summer flashed through my mind and I finally understood why he still to that day called it an ambush. The difference, though, was that he cared for Summer even then. I didn't even like Killian Brenton.

I needed to get the hell out of there and quick. "Oh, I'm so sorry. I didn't realize you were in a meeting. I'll come back later," I said as I turned to leave, grabbing the handle to open the door.

Before I could escape, my father said, "Tressa, please don't go. I believe you know Mr. Brenton."

Closing my eyes, I wished the floor would open up and swallow me whole at that very moment.

Unfortunately, it didn't, so when it became obvious I'd have to stay and be professional, I turned around, all smiles for the two of them. "Not really. We've only met once, but it's very nice to formally meet you, Mr. Brenton."

Killian smiled and walked over to shake my hand. He seemed to glide across the floor and reached me in two steps. Seeing him up close like this, I realized how much bigger than me he was. I'd never stood next to a professional athlete, other than at the auction, and I couldn't help but admit Killian was impressive. Even in jeans and a basic white dress shirt, he looked incredible, and what I'd guessed about his body hidden beneath that tux had been one hundred percent correct.

In fact, it wasn't just his size that was impressive. Somehow, in the light of my father's office, he looked even better than he had at the charity event. His gaze focused on my face, his green eyes studying mine so intensely that I was thankful my father couldn't see how this man looked at me.

I silently pleaded for my face not to show how uncomfortable I felt at that moment, praying I wouldn't blush so my face turned beet red. God, he smelled incredible, just like he had that night. Once again, I had to fight the urge to take a deep breath in and close my eyes to revel in the scent. What was that? Something musky with a hint of citrus? Was there vanilla in there too? Whatever it was, it made him practically intoxicating.

"It's a pleasure to get to finally meet you somewhere we can talk without hundreds of people standing around us. I wanted to thank you for contributing such an incredible amount to the pediatric cancer care organization. They've joined forces with me this year to promote the cause to as many people as we can. Normally I wouldn't be caught dead at a bachelor auction, but I'll do anything I can to get people to give to cure cancer in kids."

Damn. I couldn't be rude to him after that little speech. Was that for my benefit or my father's? I wasn't sure, but I plastered a smile on my face to show my graciousness.

"I'm always eager to help out worthy causes, Mr. Brenton, and I can't think of a worthier one than curing cancer in children."

Our eyes locked, and I couldn't help but think his pale green eyes with those dark lashes were stunning. A woman could get lost in those eyes, and for a moment, I did. But then I remembered how he acted at the auction, strutting up and down that platform while all those women hollered at him and he ate it up. The man standing there in front of me in my father's office was no different simply because there were no screaming crowds adoring him. He was an attention whore, a playboy, the kind of man I actively avoided.

"Please, call me Killian. May I call you Tressa?" he asked in that deep voice of his I didn't want to like, not even a little. Except I did and more than a little.

From behind him, my father's gaze met mine, and he nodded eagerly, like my giving this guy my permission to be nice to me was important. Feeling like I didn't have a choice, I said, "Of course."

My father walked over to join us and said, "Killian came here to thank us for our donation and to invite us to a benefit the team is holding next weekend. I'd love to go, but your mother has me booked for a trip to see your Aunt Jordan and Uncle Gage in Palm Springs from Friday to Monday. I'm sure you can go alone, Tressa, can't you?"

I loathed when my father played matchmaker. I knew he always had the best of intentions, but I still felt uncomfortable whenever he did it to me or either of my siblings. I'd watched him do his Cupid act with Ethan half a dozen times when we were in high school, and my brother hated it each time. My father had only tried it on me one time with some guy from Cornell in my junior year of college, and that date had been the worst of my life. I couldn't even remember his name, but I distinctly remembered he drank more than any guy I'd ever met, much to my father's dismay that night when I arrived home in a cab. Now he wanted to try a second time, and I doubted this attempt would end up any better.

As much as I wanted to say no, my father giving me that look that said he really wanted me to do this made declining impossible. So I forced myself to give Killian my best smile and said, "I'll see what my schedule looks like. I'm sure it will be delightful."

I only ever said the word delightful when whatever I was being forced to do was anything but delightful. My father knew this as well as anyone, and over Killian's shoulder I saw his expression change to that hopeful look he wore whenever he wanted his kids not to disappoint him. I was used to seeing him look like that with Ethan and even Diana, but rarely ever me.

Damnit. I'd barely been formally introduced to Killian Brenton and already my father was giving me that hopeful face like he did with my sister and brother who routinely disappointed him. So far nothing Killian brought to my world had been good.

"I look forward to seeing you there, Tressa. Are you a football fan like your father?"

Arching my eyebrow in disgust, I shook my head. "Not really."

My father quickly said, "Tressa works so much I doubt she's gotten to be a fan of anything much in the past few years."

While the two men in front of me joked about how everyone was busy, I felt my disgust for Killian grow by the second. Now he had my father making excuses for me when it came to not liking football? Since when did that make a damn bit of difference?

"Well, please excuse me, but I have work to get back to."

"Please, let me walk you out," Killian said before I could turn to escape. Pressing his hand to the small of my back, he said, "It was great to meet such a supporter of

New York football, Tristan. I look forward to seeing you again."

"Of course, and thank you for the wonderful offer to attend the event. I'll have to make sure I ask Tressa all about it."

As Killian gently guided me out of the office, I looked back at my father and gave him the death stare I'd only used on others in business negotiations before. I didn't appreciate my own flesh and blood serving me up for this Cro-Magnon's delight.

The door to my father's office closed, and I immediately moved away from Killian's hold. Spinning around, I shook my head as I glared at him. "I'm not sure what all of that in there was, but I don't like it."

Before I could continue, Killian tugged on my arm to move me. "Unless you want to have this discussion in front of your father's receptionist, I suggest we continue our talk somewhere else."

I looked back and saw Brenda quickly try to make it seem like she hadn't been listening to every word we'd said. Furious over the way this fool had already made me look in front of two people I knew, I stormed away toward the elevator.

Killian caught up with me just as the doors opened and I marched in. Before I could press the button for my floor, he pushed his finger into the button that stopped the elevator from moving.

"Now, let me explain."

Cutting him off, I tried to push him away so he

didn't stand so close, but I couldn't budge him. Christ, was the man made of bricks?

"No, let me explain, Mr. Brenton. I don't like people manipulating one of the people I love more than life itself simply to further their goals. I'm sure your agent or your PR person did a little digging and found out my father loves football. I'm sure you know he's had a box at the stadium for as long as I've been alive. Maybe longer. So you thought you could just waltz into his office and sweet talk him so you could get to me. Well, forget it. I'm not interested in going on any date with you. I had the money sent to the charity this morning, so the transaction is complete. Now if you don't mind, I have work to get to."

Killian simply grinned, like anything I'd said could be misconstrued to be something even slightly amusing. "Why don't you want to go out on this date with me? I'm a decent looking guy. I've got money. Not as much as you, but a good amount. I've been the toast of the town since I arrived in this great city, so what's the problem?"

"Right there. I have no interest in a man who can't get enough of the press taking his picture. You're an attention whore, Killian, and that is the last thing I want in any man I spend time with."

"So you do like the way I look," he said, stepping forward so the space between us shrunk to almost nothing. "I thought you did Saturday night, and I'm usually pretty much on the mark with things like that."

I liked the way he looked—way too much for my own comfort. He had a presence about him that emanated power like no other man I'd ever met. It had an intoxicating effect on me, and that was nothing to say of what he made me feel when he stared at me with those incredible eyes of his. Then there was his mouth. His lips were nothing less than inviting and made me wonder what they'd feel like against mine. They looked soft, and something deep inside me craved to know just how they felt on my mouth…on my skin…between my legs.

Yes, I definitely liked how he looked far too much already.

Get it together, Tressa. Remember why you didn't like this man in the first place.

Right. His ego. It made wanting to even stand there with him for another minute impossible.

Twisting away from him, I pushed the button to get the elevator to move again. "You're perfectly fine, and I'm sure many women appreciate how you look, Killian. I just don't want to go out on that date with you."

"We're making progress," he said from behind me in his low voice that made me instinctively close my eyes. "You called me by my first name. I liked the way it sounded coming out of your mouth too."

My eyes flew open as I realized I was letting myself be seduced by him. Oh. My. God! This man was infuriating!

I turned around and glared at him. "Does this work on other women? Are there really females who think this thing you do is charming?"

A slow, sexy smile showcased his beautiful white teeth and perfect mouth. "I don't know if they think it's charming, no. It has been known to work on women, though, charming or not."

"Well, it's not working on me."

That was a lie. I knew it. He probably knew it too.

"Not even a little?" he asked, staring deeply into my eyes.

God, all I wanted to do was get out of that elevator without saying something I'd regret. I wasn't sure if he had some ability to hypnotize with those gorgeous green eyes, but whatever he was doing with them as he stared at me, it was working.

I couldn't let it.

And then just when I didn't think I couldn't stand him looking at me that way a second longer, he opened his mouth again and broke the spell.

"I'm not a man who gives up easily when I see something I want, Tressa."

The elevator punctuated his statement with a ding, like it was announcing the end of a round of boxing, and I snapped back at him as the doors opened, "I am not a thing. That was your first mistake. I don't give second chances after a mistake like that. Good day."

I marched out of that elevator with the silent approval of every woman who had ever wanted to tell off some smug guy who knew he was hot and used it to get whatever his heart desired. I felt his stare on me as I walked to my office and didn't look back, even when he yelled down the hall to me.

"Tressa, remember what I told you. I don't give up easily. We will have that date."

No, we won't, Killian. This time you lose.

CHAPTER SIX

KILLIAN

AFTER MEETINGS WITH THE TEAM all day, I headed back from the stadium with Tressa on my mind. Our encounter in the elevator on Monday morning showed me she had fire for sure, but that fire wasn't fueled by dislike for me, by any means. I didn't know why she didn't want to admit to liking me, but nothing I'd seen so far had given me anything but a green light with her. I'd never shied away from a challenge before. I wasn't about to start now, especially with the promise of something so incredible if I conquered it.

I checked to see if she called since I'd sent her flowers earlier. Nope. Sitting back, I watched as the lights on the highway flew past the car and wondered why she hadn't at least sent me a message to thank me. I'd never met any woman so difficult, but after what I'd felt when we were in that elevator together, I couldn't give up getting her to go out on that date.

Maybe the flowers hadn't been delivered. A quick check on the florist proved that wrong. They'd been signed for by the woman herself.

So she wanted to play hardball. Okay. I could do that too. I'd hoped she'd come around on her own, but I wasn't above going low to get what I wanted.

Time to go in for the kill.

A few seconds later, I was looking at Tressa standing in the living room of her penthouse. As always, she looked gorgeous, even dressed in a loose blue dress that hid what I imagined was an incredible body. She frowned when she saw me, so I knew didn't have much time to get out what I wanted to say before she'd end the call.

"You again? I think you'd be considered a stalker now."

"Well, this is a serious call. I'd hate to have to tell the organizers of that event the other night that you refuse to go on our date. Would that be considered fraud? They did advertise that the winning bidder would go out on a date with me. I think that's sounds a lot like fraud."

I watched with pure enjoyment as Tressa's mouth dropped open. I'd found her soft spot.

"It's not fraud. Don't be ridiculous. God, you are a piece of work, Killian Brenton."

Putting on my best sad face, I continued, "The rules charities have to follow are pretty serious. Charges of fraud could get them shut down. I'd hate for that to happen, wouldn't you? They help so many kids with the money they get people to donate. That's not going to be easy to make up, and I think we both know cancer isn't just going to stop because they go out of business."

Tressa's shoulders sagged and she hung her head.

"You're not going to let this go, are you?"

"No."

Looking up, she seemed almost defeated. I saw it in her dark eyes. I didn't want to see her like that. This was never about beating her at something.

"Why? Why does this mean so much to you? I already sent the charity the money I bid. What does it matter if we go out on a date or not?"

For a moment, I didn't know how to respond. Her frustration with this whole thing confused me. It was just a date, and I knew she liked me just as much as I liked her. Why did she still want to fight me on going out for one damn dinner? Leaning back against the driver seat, I turned to watch the cars as mine passed them and figured now was the time to be serious with her.

"This charity means a lot to me. My foundation works with them to help in the fight against pediatric cancer. I wouldn't usually let myself be auctioned off, but for this charity, I'd do anything."

Tressa nodded and then sighed. "Can this date be somewhere low key? Please?"

I shook my head no. "The PR is important to helping them bring in more money."

"You're the one everyone wants to see, Killian. Not me," she said in a pleading voice.

"Seeing me with a beautiful and successful businesswoman who's from New York would be impressive, Tressa. You're no fool. You know this."

After a moment of hesitation, she finally relented.

"Fine."

Success! I knew she'd give in and go on our date. Even though I wanted to celebrate, I controlled myself and coolly said, "How about tomorrow at eight? I'll pick you up. Just tell me where."

"The Richmont Midtown," she said flatly.

"Great! Cheer up. It'll be a good time. We'll have dinner and a few laughs."

She nodded and then the screen went black. I had to admit I felt good. I knew she'd agree. Thankfully, I'd made reservations earlier that day. It always paid to think positive.

JUST LIKE BEFORE I CALLED Tressa the first time, my palms suddenly grew sweaty as I pulled up to in front of the Richmont hotel at quarter to eight Wednesday night. I'd been playing football since third grade, and never once had my palms gotten sweaty before or during a game. In fact, I couldn't remember any time I had sweaty palms other than when I called her for the first time and right now.

"Stay cool, Killian. It's a date, not a lifetime. One night, and if things go to plan, a night that will end with this woman in my bed. Nothing to be nervous about," I said to myself in the rearview mirror as I checked out how I looked one last time.

I looked good, so now it was show time. Tressa walked toward the car dressed in a knockout red dress as the press that had been hanging out around the hotel for days began to rush her, so I quickly jumped out of the car and ran up to her.

Putting my arms around her shoulders, I shielded Tressa from the reporters already swarming around. "Enough. The lady is just trying to go out to dinner, and you guys rush her like she's holding the secret to life here. Give her some space."

"Are you two dating?" one young guy with a camera yelled out from behind another reporter busy sticking his phone in our faces to get a comment.

"How long have you been together? Miss Stone, does this mean you're leaving Stone Worldwide? Killian, does this mean you're off the market?"

Tressa's head spun toward the reporter who asked about her quitting her job, but I pushed him away and said in her ear, "Don't even listen to them. They ask questions that don't make any sense sometimes. Just ignore them."

"Why would they think I'm quitting Stone Worldwide? Who would have told them that?" she asked pointedly, clearly thinking I'd had something to do with it.

"It's nothing. Don't worry. Just get in and you'll be fine."

I opened the passenger side door and held off the reporters as she got into my sports car. Satisfied I'd been able to protect her and still have the press get their pictures, I smiled at the reporters to give them a good shot.

"Thanks, guys. She's not used to all of this, so try to take it easy on her."

One woman with glasses yelled as I walked around the car to open the driver's door, "Does this mean you're off the market, Killian? Are you still single?"

I simply waved and flashed them a smile before getting in and driving off. All they really wanted was a good picture to put with whatever they planned to write about anyway, and I knew my part in all of this.

Looking over at Tressa, I saw she truly didn't like the attention of the press. Her frown told me our run in with them had started our date out on the wrong foot. No worries. I'd fix that.

"Sorry that got a little wild back there. I'm glad I was around to protect you, but remember, they're harmless."

She turned to look at me as her frown grew deeper. "Protect me? You're the reason they're out there day and night in the first place. If you would have just left me alone and not insisted on going on this ridiculous date, I would have never had to deal with them at all."

The car stopped at a red light as I said, "To be honest, they're out there because of the picture someone took of you looking up at me at the auction. I didn't have anything to do with this. It's because of you, actually."

I heard something like a growl come out of her at my explanation. Not exactly fixing things. I had to switch gears, so I said, "I think you're going to love the place I picked out for dinner. My agent tells me great things about it."

"Where are we going?" she asked, only slightly less infuriated than she was a moment ago.

"The National Club."

My car took that as an opportunity to inform me of the important details about our ride. "Dinner reservations are for eight, sir. I'll call ahead and let them know you're on your way and to have the valet look for the closest spot near the building as it's going to rain in approximately two hours and thirty-one minutes."

Tressa looked at me and arched her eyebrow. "Approximately? I think your car doesn't understand the meaning of that word."

I smiled, and the car answered, "I understand every word in every language known to man, Miss Stone. I simply like to be precise whenever I can be. I don't want you to get wet on your date with Mr. Brenton. We will arrive at the National Club in fourteen minutes. Please sit back and enjoy the ride."

The light turned green, and with that, the car continued on its way as I turned in my seat to face Tressa. "So have you ever been to the National Club?"

"No offense, but your car is a know-it-all. I turn all that off, and more often than not when I drive, I actually perform the act."

I couldn't help but be charmed by this woman. Even cranky, she had a way about her that made me want to be around her. At the moment, she looked downright unhappy to be there with me, though, but that would change.

"I like an old-fashioned woman. It seems like nobody drives anymore."

"Well, I do. My brother does too, along with my father. My mother never liked driving after an accident she was in years ago, so she was more than happy when self-driving cars became available."

"You are an interesting woman, Tressa Stone. I want to know more about you."

For the first time, she smiled. "Why don't you ask your car? I have a feeling it can find out anything you like about anything in the world."

I shook my head and laughed just as the car began talking again. "Sir, Miss Stone is twenty-seven years old. She is the daughter of Tristan and Nina Stone. She is one of the few people on the planet who can say they're a fraternal triplet. Less than one percent of the population is a triplet, according to the latest information from the National Center for Health Statistics. Her brother's name is Ethan, and her sister's name is Diana. Tressa is named after her paternal grandmother. When she was four, she—"

Leaning forward, I quickly pressed the button to turn off the sound of the car. "Enough of that. Since you're an old-fashioned girl, I'll learn about you the old-fashioned way."

Amused, Tressa chuckled. "Then you won't learn much since this is going to be our one and only date. I think you're going to have to go back to talking to your car on this one."

"We'll see. I'm hoping to impress you with my charm so you'll at least smile in the pictures the press gets. You're truly a beautiful woman when you aren't scowling."

"And when I am?" Tressa asked sharply as her expression instantly returned to unhappy.

I studied her face for a moment and smiled. "I'd guess most people would say you're intimidating, but I have a feeling you're more frustrated with things than unhappy."

She rolled her eyes and sighed in disgust. "Frustrated, huh? Typical man. I bet you think if I just had a dose of your magical penis that I'd be a perfectly happy woman, don't you?"

"No. All I meant was you know what you want out of the world, and you work hard to get it. When those around you don't work as hard, you get frustrated."

Tressa looked away and after a moment quietly said, "Oh. Well, color me embarrassed. I'm sorry I said all that."

"No problem. I'm tough. I can handle it."

As she stared out the window, I knew for sure now she was definitely not disinterested in me. No woman mentioned a guy's cock if she hadn't thought about it at least once. I had a feeling I was exactly the kind of man Tressa Stone would enjoy. Men had let her down because they weren't strong enough to handle her. But I was, and I intended on finding out just what it took to make her happy.

"So you're a triplet?" I asked, just realizing what the car had said minutes earlier.

For a moment, Tressa didn't answer, and I figured I'd have to keep asking her questions in the hopes of starting a conversation both of us might enjoy. But then she turned to face me and gave me a little smile.

"I am. Two girls and a boy."

"I thought triplets were always identical. I guess I learned something today," I said with a chuckle.

"No, not when there aren't all the same sex. My brother meant we'd be fraternal instead of identical."

"So do you and your sister look the same and he just looks different?"

My question made her genuinely laugh, and even though I knew she was laughing at me, I didn't mind because for that moment, she didn't look like she wanted to slap my face or bark at me anymore. She looked happy.

"No, it doesn't work that way either. My sister looks like my mother, but my brother and I resemble my father more, as I'm sure you noticed when you were there with us the other day. I'm just the female version of Tristan Stone. My brother could be his twin."

"I've never met anyone who was a triplet. That makes you unique, Tressa."

She shrugged like that didn't mean much. "I think I'd rather be unique because of something I've done after I was born."

"Twenty-seven years old and already the COO of a major hotel chain? That makes you pretty unique. VP at a successful company like Stone Worldwide too? Again, pretty unique, and trust me, I know about being unique.

I'm one of only a handful of people on the planet to do what I do at my level."

Narrowing her eyes, she stared at me and asked, "Your car didn't tell you all of that, so how do you know about me?"

"Maybe I asked it about you on my way to pick you up."

"Did you?"

I didn't want to lie to her, so I shook my head. "No. I asked around. I wanted to know about the woman who paid ten thousand dollars for a date with me. By the way, I promise to make it worth every penny."

My answer made her blush. "I swear I thought it was just five thousand. Every time you say that number, I sound more and more ridiculous."

"Why?"

As the car stopped in front of the National Club, she winced like what she had to say made her uncomfortable. "No self-respecting woman would pay that much money for a date, Killian. I looked desperate."

"You looked like the most beautiful woman in the room, Tressa. Trust me. There's nothing desperate about you."

For a second time, she blushed, and I had to admit this side of her made me like her even more.

CHAPTER SEVEN

TRESSA

THE MAÎTRE DE AT THE National Club escorted us through the main dining room of the restaurant dimly lit with candlelight and wall sconces. As we walked past other diners already at their tables, I saw their reaction to Killian as he followed behind me, his hand gently brushing my arm as if he was protecting me somehow. Their gazes passed right over me and then they smiled up at him and said his name, while others pointed and whispered about his being new to town and how much the team paid for him. I looked back and saw him smiling in return like he truly enjoyed their attention.

When we were finally seated at a secluded table near the rear of the restaurant, I couldn't help but notice that Killian had chosen the chair with his back facing all those people who'd just adored him as he walked by. While he scanned the menu, I sat transfixed by how much they actually cared about him being there with them.

"Does it ever bother you to feel people's eyes on you?" I asked as I watched one man point in our direction.

Looking over his menu, Killian shook his head. "No.

It's just something you get used to. They're like the press. I figure if I wasn't doing something right, they wouldn't give a damn about me or what I do."

"I don't think I'd ever get used to it. The fact that people keep turning around and looking at us seems so intrusive."

Killian lowered his menu and flashed me one of his stunning smiles. "They're probably looking at you."

Suddenly, I felt completely exposed. Holding my menu up in front of me to hide everything from my eyes down, I said, "Why? Because of those pictures everyone plastered all over the papers and online?"

"No. Because you're gorgeous and wearing that dress."

I looked down at my red dress that I'd bought for last year's Christmas party at work. I'd debated on wearing something that showed a little cleavage since I didn't want to give Killian the wrong idea, but as I stood in front of the mirror modeling it earlier that evening, I loved how it looked next to my dark hair and how it always made me feel beautiful.

Now I wondered if I'd made a mistake.

"Is there something wrong with my dress?" I asked, happy to be hidden behind the menu.

He shook his head and smiled again. "Not as far as I can see. You do understand people stop and look at beautiful women, right? I can't believe this is the first time in your life you've been stared at by strangers because of how you look."

"That's not who I am, so I have no idea what you mean."

Lowering his menu, he leaned forward and whispered, "Tressa, these people aren't looking at me anymore. My back is to them. If they're staring over here, it's because of you."

"You're just trying to make me think that we're similar, when it's obvious we aren't. If I was alone at this table or with any other man, no one would give us a second thought. They're looking at you, and you love it."

His response to my indictment of him was to shrug. "Any idea what you're going to get? I hear the swordfish is great here. I'm not much into that, but my agent raved about it."

Killian's sudden change in conversational topics caught me off guard. I'd planned on keeping him on the one about him being an attention whore, but he didn't seem to want to talk about that anymore.

Not that it mattered. It didn't change the fact that he loved the attention and I hated it.

We sat in silence staring at our menus until the waiter arrived to take our orders. As I watched Killian order steak and asparagus, I couldn't deny this felt like any other date I'd ever been on. I even had to admit that it was probably better than any I'd been on since he was definitely more attractive than any man I'd ever dated.

After I ordered and we were once again left alone, the silence returned. Not that I'd expected we'd have much to say to one another anyway. We had nothing in common, and he was a football player.

"So tell me more about this old-fashioned streak you have."

I looked across the table at him and tried to determine if he was making fun of me, but he seemed sincere. I didn't know why he wanted to know much of anything about me since this whole date was just the fulfillment of that auction so the charity could never be guilty of defrauding anyone.

"I'm not sure there's much to tell. I actually drive cars instead of letting them drive me. I guess my use of phones would be considered old fashioned since I would prefer not seeing the people I'm speaking to most of the time."

"Why's that?"

"Because I'm not superficial. I don't judge people on what they look like. I judge them on what they do and how they act."

Killian leaned back and leveled his gaze on me. "See? We're not that different, you and me. I'm the same way."

Somehow I doubted that. I would never admit it to him, but I looked up some of the women he'd dated in the past few years. Every girlfriend was stunning, each one more gorgeous than the last.

When I didn't respond to his ridiculous claim, he continued. "I judge people on their abilities. On the field, a player is valuable if he does his job well. Off the field, people's behavior dictates whether or not I spend time with them."

As much as I wished I could let that go, I couldn't.

Something about this man brought out the fight in me.

"So the women you've spent your adult life surrounded by were carefully chosen based on their behavior and not on their looks? I'm sure they're all deep thinkers and people working to change the world, right?"

Instead of taking the bait, Killian simply smiled. "Women are different."

"Oh? Why is that?"

"Because maybe I don't get to meet many deep thinkers and women looking to change the world."

I didn't know how to respond. The way he said that sounded strangely disappointed, like he wished he did meet more women like that. I doubted that, though. Women who dedicated their lives to intellectual pursuits and to changing the world would have no place in Killian Brenton's life. How would they look for the camera?

"What made you go to the charity event the other night? You've already made it perfectly clear that it wasn't to meet me, so what was it?"

"I go to those kinds of things all the time. I like to support charities whenever I can."

"Me too. My foundation works with the pediatric cancer organization. It's one of the charities I support. I bet you didn't think I did that, did you?"

I saw in his expression he was sincere and not just lying to impress me. What I didn't understand is why he was bothering.

Leaning forward, I looked him straight in the eye and said, "Killian, let's lay our cards on the table. You don't have to make me like you. That's not necessary. You wanted this date to happen, and it is. I'm guessing it was some kind of conquering thing you athletes have in your DNA that made you practically blackmail me to come tonight. Or maybe it was an ego thing. You couldn't handle the idea that any woman wouldn't be interested in going out with you. Whatever it is, you don't have to work to impress me. After tonight, we'll never see each other again, so relax and have a few drinks. Maybe go talk to your fans. I'll be fine here. Really."

He said nothing for so long that I wondered if something in his brain had short-circuited and he couldn't speak anymore. I watched as he nodded like he understood and then leaned forward so our faces nearly met in the middle of the table.

In the dim light, I saw a sparkle in his green eyes that seemed entirely out of place with what I'd just said to him. Maybe he hadn't understood me.

Then he spoke and I was the one left speechless.

"Tressa, at first I thought you were simply beautiful but shy. Then I decided you were a nasty bitch, plain and simple. Now I see neither of those were entirely right. You're beautiful, you have a streak of bitch a mile wide, but you're not shy and you aren't nasty. I'll admit my ego was a bit bruised when you refused to go on our date, and yes, I manipulated you to come here tonight. I'm guilty of those things just like you're guilty of all your faults. That said, I know what I saw when you looked at me Saturday night. I wasn't mistaken then, and I'm not mistaken now.

I don't know why you want to pretend you aren't attracted to me, but as I told you already, I don't give up when I meet someone I want."

My heart beat wildly as the words came out of his mouth so calmly yet so forcefully. No one had ever spoken to me like that. It wasn't rude or offensive. It was simply strong and straightforward, and I couldn't help but like Killian more than even before.

And it didn't escape my notice that he'd changed his way of talking and I wasn't a something he wanted anymore but a someone.

Killian Brenton and I would never be anything romantically, but I couldn't deny he'd impressed me. He wasn't just a pretty face and a great body.

"So now that we got that out of the way, maybe we can enjoy ourselves?" he asked with a sexy smile that made my stomach flip.

"Okay. I can appreciate someone who's a straight shooter like me."

The waiter brought our food, and for the next hour while we ate, I genuinely had a good time there with him. I hadn't expected him to be smart or funny, but after we both said what was on our minds, it felt like a wall had come tumbling down between us.

And then some reporter with a camera showed up on our way out to the car and everything changed.

Chapter Eight

Tressa

"Killian, you seem to be taking New York by storm. A new team, a new city, and now a new girlfriend. What do you want your fans to know?"

I instinctively stepped away from the blond woman and her photographer, leaving Killian to deal with them. It felt like they'd been lying in wait for us while we enjoyed our dinner inside the National Club. We'd had such a good time during the last hour that I'd forgotten who he was, but no sooner had this woman approached us and her cameraman began taking pictures, he morphed into the same old person I'd suspected he was all along.

An attention whore.

He answered her questions with a flirtatiousness that made me wish I was anywhere else in the world than there at that moment. His cute way made her ask more questions, and all the while I wondered if he even remembered I was standing next to him.

It was like he couldn't get enough attention from this stranger he'd just met when we walked out the door. As the seconds ticked by, I found myself turned off by him once again. I didn't know why it disappointed me because he was exactly what I thought he was from the moment I laid eyes on him strutting around on that catwalk, but it bothered me.

I'd let myself think he wasn't this preening fool so eager to pose for pictures and talk about himself incessantly, and I felt stupid.

When the blond woman turned to ask me a question, I pushed past her with barely a smile. "Excuse me."

Thankfully, she didn't care enough to ask any follow up questions or chase after me. When I reached the car, the valet kindly opened the door for me so I didn't have to stand there waiting for Killian. He finally joined me after I sat waiting for a few minutes, and as we drove away, I simply stared out the window watching the cars we passed by.

"I have to admit I was a little surprised when that reporter approached us."

Without bothering to look at him, I said, "I don't know why. Wasn't the whole point of the date to get press for the charity? I guess I should be thankful you didn't invite them to the table to have dinner with us."

"I made sure to tell the maître de that we weren't to be interrupted. I knew you didn't want to deal with that. I slipped him some money to make sure he took care of business," Killian answered, sounding quite pleased with himself.

What may have been a nice gesture before now felt like another manipulative ploy. As much as I liked the

Killian I'd spent the last hour talking to, I didn't like the version of him I'd seen outside the restaurant and nothing he could do would change that.

I'd gone on the date I paid for. Now I just wanted to go home.

By the time the car pulled up to the Richmont, I couldn't wait to get away from him. When he asked if I wanted to go for a drink, I shook my head and opened the door to leave.

"Thank you for a nice dinner. Goodbye, Killian."

I heard him say something, but I didn't stick around to find out what. The disappointment I felt nearly overwhelmed me. I'd been foolish to question my gut feeling about him, and as I hurried into the hotel, all I wanted to do was be alone.

As I rode up in the elevator, tears welled in my eyes. I didn't know why because I'd never wanted to like him in the first place. But for a little while there, I'd let myself think he was the kind of man who I could be with and who would want to be with me.

We were too different, though.

The doors opened and I walked out into the private hallway outside the penthouse. Taking a deep breath, I let it out slowly, hoping all my likes and dislikes concerning Killian Brenton left with it.

From behind me, I heard a sound and turned to see him walk out of the elevator. Stunned he'd followed me, I was even more surprised when he asked, "What's the problem? We had a great dinner, and I know you enjoyed the conversation. Why are you all icy again?"

My disappointment and sadness evaporated, replaced by anger. How dare he fucking call me icy simply because I didn't want to smile for the camera or give some cute answer to that reporter's idiotic questions?

I spun around to face him. "I bet you think every woman who isn't draped all over you like a bitch in heat is icy. Well, let me help you out, Mr. Brenton. You aren't that wonderful that I should warm up at all for you."

Opening the door to go inside, I couldn't believe when he walked in behind me. Stunned at how presumptuous he was, I said, "What…that wasn't an invitation."

He didn't answer and stepped forward toward me so there was no space between us. "You know you were having a good time. Why are you in such a hurry to get me to leave?"

"What on earth could you possibly want from me now, Killian? There are no cameras here to memorialize this moment."

Suddenly, he appeared to understand and smiled. "Ah, the press bothered you. It couldn't be avoided. You know that."

Hating how obtuse he was acting, I shook my head as I prepared to set him straight. "No. The press doesn't bother me. They have a job to do, and they do it. I admire that, in fact. It's how you crave attention that bothers me. I don't like men who are attention whores, and you're the biggest one I've ever met. I'm sure there are women who don't find that to be a character flaw, so why don't you go find one of them?"

"I guess I could lie and tell you that dealing with the press is just part of my job, but the truth is I like being me. I like that the press follows me around because of who I am."

"Good for you. I suggest you go find them and leave me alone," I said before I turned to walk away toward my room.

"What is it with you? So I like being famous. What's so wrong with that?"

Fine. He wanted my opinion. Now he was going to get it. I spun around and stared into those gorgeous green eyes so he'd know I meant every word that was about to come out of my mouth.

"What's wrong with it is someday you won't be. The press and the cameras will be gone, and then what will you be? A man is only worth what he inherently is. What are you on the inside, Killian? What are you when the cameras and the press and the throngs of adoring fans are nowhere to be found?"

He looked like I smacked him across the face. He didn't seem to know how to answer my questions. That didn't surprise me. Sadly, though, I already knew the answers.

But then he walked over to where I stood and shook his head. "I saw the way you looked into my eyes the other night. I saw the way you reacted when I told you the truth at dinner tonight. You love the idea of a powerful man finally being able to handle you. I'm guessing no man ever has. Whatever I am to the rest of the world, I'm exactly what you want when it's just the two of us."

"Fuck you, Killian. Fuck you and your superficial bullshit celebrity nonsense. Go find yourself a woman who thinks you're something because I don't."

For a moment, it felt like time stopped. We stared each other down like two opposing fighters each refusing to give up, and then he slid his arm around my waist to pull me to him, holding me tightly with his hand firmly against the small of my back. Before I could protest, he leaned down and pressed his mouth to mine in a kiss that made my head swim and took my breath away.

I should have pushed him away. He'd barged into my home and into my space. I'd never said I wanted him to kiss me like that. Men needed to get my permission to get something as intimate as a kiss from me.

But I didn't want to push him away. I wanted to inhale how incredible he smelled so my mind would forever remember this moment. I wanted to feel his lips on mine as he kissed me like no man had ever kissed me before. I wanted him to take me in his arms and give me what I'd wanted from the first moment I saw him.

Even more, I wanted exactly what he said. A man who wasn't too weak to handle me. Every man I'd ever dated had been too weak. When I opened my mouth, they grew small. I wanted someone who could meet me eye to eye and not flinch when I was strong.

But even more, I wanted someone who would be strong when I couldn't be. The way Killian made me feel made me think he could be that kind of man.

His tongue teased mine with the promise of future delights, making my pussy run wet with desire, and a tiny mew of need escaped my throat. He slid his hand down over my ass and pulled me into him, tilting his hips forward so his cock pressed against my abdomen. So much bigger than me, he threatened to overwhelm my body with his if we continued standing there in the middle of my living room.

Breaking our kiss, I tried to form a coherent sentence as my mind reeled from how much I wanted him. Motioning toward my bedroom, I mumbled, "Let's go in there."

He had other ideas, though, and in one swift movement he pushed my dress up around my waist and lifted me up to straddle his hips. I tried to slip off my panties, but his hand holding me to him made it impossible. Never had I hated wearing the damn things so much as at that moment.

Killian's gaze drifted down my body, and he smiled. "Little red silk bows? Do they untie, or am I going to have to rip these beautiful underwear off you."

His green eyes danced with delight, like he relished the idea of tearing off my clothes. I shook my head and reached for the bow on my left hip, but he covered my hand, stopping me.

"No. Let me."

Tugging on the end of the silk bow, he unraveled it instantly. In seconds, my white silk panties with the adorable red bows I'd bought especially for tonight ended up on the floor beneath me.

He lifted his head and looked into my eyes. "I like them. I'd like them even more in black."

I felt like I was melting there in his arms. "I don't have them in black. I got them a while back and don't think they even carry them anymore," I lied.

Why I lied about something so insignificant I didn't know. At that moment, all I truly knew was I didn't want to talk about my underwear. I didn't want to talk about anything.

Leaning in, he nuzzled my neck and whispered against my skin, "Even better would be if you wore nothing."

The feel of his lips brushing the shell of my ear made a rush of need race through me. I felt him moving his free hand beneath me, and I prayed to God he was unbuttoning his pants.

He gently sunk his teeth into my earlobe, sending my body into overdrive. I dragged my nails across the nape of his neck and moaned, "Oh, God..." as I arched my back. What was taking him so fucking long to get his pants open and his cock out?

"Someone's eager," he groaned as he finally unzipped his pants and I felt his cock press against my ass.

I rolled my hips in an effort to speed up what Killian clearly wanted to drag out, but he stopped me by pulling my body to his and holding it there. I knew he wanted me as much as I wanted him—his rock hard cock was evidence of that—so why was he taking so long?

"Look at me, Tressa," he ordered in a low voice tinged with as much need as I felt.

I did as he commanded and saw in his eyes the sparkle I'd seen a minute before when he asked about my panties. I stared into them and felt myself get lost in the pale green color I'd never seen in anyone else's eyes before.

"There's that look I saw at the auction. I knew I wasn't wrong," he said low and deep, his voice resonating against my chest as he pulled me to him.

He hadn't been wrong. I wanted him like I'd never wanted any man that night, and I wanted him even more now. In those seconds as he held me to his body and we gazed into one another's eyes, he saw the truth of how I felt about him.

"No, you weren't," I admitted quietly in a voice barely above a whisper.

"What do you want, baby?" he asked, grinning as I tried my hardest to fight against his strength and roll my hips to feel his cock against me.

He knew exactly what I wanted. My wet pussy rubbing against his stomach told him. The look in my eyes told him.

And yet still he asked what I wanted.

"Is this some kind of triumphant conqueror thing for you? You knew I wanted you from the moment I saw you, so now that you have me in your arms, you want me to say what I want so you can feel like you won?" I asked playfully, not bothered at all to tell him exactly what I wanted from him tonight.

The corners of his mouth lifted ever so slightly, and he repeated his question. "What do you want, Tressa? Tell me."

I felt his hand stroke the full length of his cock beneath me, as if he needed to remind me what my reward would be for finally admitting the truth to him. Leaning forward, I ran my tongue along the outside of his ear and grazed my teeth against his earlobe.

Dragging my fingernails lightly over the back of his neck, I whispered, "I want you to fuck me. I want to feel that cock of yours you've been teasing me with fill me. That's what I want, Killian."

I didn't care that my voice verged on pleading with him to fuck me. Never in my life had I sounded like that with anyone, but it didn't matter. This man had something that made me want to lower my defenses, and I wasn't even afraid of my vulnerability.

The muscles in his neck and shoulders twisted, and a second later our foreplay ended. He stuffed his hand into my hair and tugged my head back so we once again faced once another. The look in his mesmerizing eyes was different now. Gone was the sparkle of delight, replaced by a stare of pure, unadulterated need. Now I'd see the truth of who Killian really was.

He staggered over to the wall and lifted me a few inches higher before lowering me down onto the tip of his thick cock. I clung to his neck in anticipation of finally getting what I'd wanted since the moment I first saw Killian Brenton.

Watching me intently, he slowly entered my body, inch by delicious inch, until there was no space between us. A tiny whimper escaped from between my lips when he finally filled me, and he stayed still, merely watching me for a moment.

"I'm not hurting you, am I?" he asked sweetly and began to ease out of my body.

"No. Don't stop," I answered, urging him with my words and my body to return to where he'd been so I could feel completely full once again.

Our bodies joined, and once more, it felt like time stopped. But that ended quickly, and Killian groaned low and deep like some wild animal before kissing me hard as desire overtook him.

And then he began to fuck me. His mouth devoured mine as he plunged his cock into me over and over. Each time he entered me, he touched a spot that sent my body to a place I'd never felt before. After just once, I craved that feeling more than my next breath. Each time his cock left me, I eagerly pushed down to have him back inside me. I didn't care that I looked too enthusiastic or that I might want him more than he wanted me. I'd always worried about that when I had sex with men before, but with Killian, all those fears disappeared, replaced by the most incredible sensations my body had ever experienced.

He fucked me like no man had ever fucked me. God,

he fucked me better than I'd ever read in any magazine or book. I didn't know if it was his size or that once he began in earnest, he fucked like a man with the singular goal of making me come, but whatever it was, he made my body surrender to his every thrust like it was made for him to do as he chose.

It wasn't just what he did with his cock, though. Everything about him focused entirely on me. With each moment, I wanted more of his attention. The feel of his hands on my body worshiping me as they held me so I didn't fall. The sound of his voice when he murmured my name into my ear like the word held meaning for him. The taste of his lips as he feasted on my mouth like it held something necessary for him.

No man had ever acted like this with me. I reveled in him and how he made me feel like the only person in the world who mattered. I hadn't expected it and couldn't really understand it considering how he usually acted, but I couldn't get enough of it.

I couldn't get enough of him.

And then just when I didn't think I could feel any more incredible, my release raced through me and I tightened my legs around his waist to keep him from moving out of me again. I wanted to feel every wonderful inch of his cock inside me when I came.

My pussy milked his cock through my orgasm, and Killian moaned low in my ear, "Fuck, you feel so fucking good."

I didn't know how long my body enjoyed what he'd

given me, but finally, my thighs began to hurt from squeezing him between them. As I eased them open a tiny bit, he gently pressed me against the wall one final time and came, his body sagging against mine as he held me in his arms.

We said nothing to one another while we stayed there in that place in the corner of my living room as the tremors from our lovemaking still rolled through us. Killian nuzzled my neck and let out a sigh of contentment against my skin. I gently ran my hand across his shoulders, feeling the thin sheen of dampness, and kissed next to his ear.

"That was nice," I whispered, knowing that was the understatement of the century.

He lifted his head and flashed me a sexy smile that told me he knew how much nice undersold what we'd just done. "Definitely nice."

God, I was in trouble. Not only was he gorgeous and sexy, but he succeeded in the one thing no man ever had. I wanted more than just one night with this man.

CHAPTER NINE

KILLIAN

SLOWLY, I OPENED MY EYES and looked around as my brain woke up and tried to figure out where the hell I was. Looking down my body, I saw Tressa's dark hair spread out over my chest and stomach. Below that, her gorgeous long legs intertwined with my tanner legs, making us look like two parts to a single whole.

Our date definitely had gone better than I thought it would, and I'd had pretty high hopes for it. As usual, we'd had sharp words for one another, but after that, holy fuck. I'd thought it would take to at least the second date to get her into bed.

Not that I had a problem with us fucking on the first date. We were both grown adults, so why not? It was just that she fought me so much just to get her to go out to dinner that I thought she'd fight me more on getting her clothes off.

As my memories of the night before began to filter through my brain, my cock got hard. That thing she'd done with her tongue. Fuck. I needed to experience that again for damn sure.

Pushing her hair back to see her face, I had to admit she really was incredible once she let her guard down. I hadn't thought she'd turn out like that.

Her eyes opened and she looked up at me sweetly. Still so beautiful, even first thing in the morning.

Then her expression changed, and her dark eyes grew wide. "Oh, my God. How did this happen?"

I smiled down at her. Definitely the same Tressa. "Well, I kissed you and you kissed me back and our clothes fell off. From that point on, it was just nature."

Tressa covered her face. "Don't make jokes. This isn't funny. The press is going to know you stayed here and I'm going to have to deal with questions all day. Oh, my God! What time is it?"

She rolled off me to look for her phone, but it wasn't on the nightstand. The sight of her perfect ass made my cock grow even harder. Reaching over, I slid my hand around her waist to pull her back.

"I think you should bring that beautiful body back here so we can continue what we left off with when we fell asleep."

Leaping out of bed, she hurried around her bedroom looking for her phone. Folding my arms behind my head, I watched her and loved how sexy she looked running around naked.

"I don't think the sun's even up yet, so I'm sure you're fine," I said as she bolted out of the bedroom.

She returned a minute later with her phone in her hand, shaking it in the air. "Four calls missed already! I can't believe I let you convince me to sleep with you last night."

"Just curious. What part of what I did convinced you? You know, for future reference. Was it the kiss or something else?"

"Stop making jokes. As the Chief Operating Officer of the Richmont hotel chain, I'm responsible for every hotel around the world. There could be a problem in one of the London locations. They called twice already."

I patted the bed next to me and smiled. "Come back over here. You can call them from bed, can't you?"

Just then, Tressa looked down and her eyes grew wide again. "Ugh! I have to get dressed and get to the office."

She rushed off to the bathroom, so I followed her and found her turning on the water for a shower. Leaning against the doorframe, I watched, loving what I saw, and asked, "Are you always this stressed out after a night of incredible sex?"

Turning to look at me, she let her gaze run from my head to my feet and frowned. "Please stop asking me questions. I might have a crisis on my hands, and you're standing there with the world's biggest hard on."

I glanced down at my erect cock and smiled as I looked back up at her. "I don't know if it's the world's biggest, but thanks for the kudos. Seriously, are you usually this stressed out in the morning? You're not going to make it to thirty if you keep it up like this."

"Please let me take a shower so I can get to work," she said as the water began spraying from the showerhead.

She stepped into the glass shower and wet her hair as I watched her, impressed with how beautiful she truly was. She really did have to relax, though. The woman had only been awake for less than five minutes and already she was functioning at prime stress level.

I followed her into the shower and grabbed the shampoo bottle off the shelf. Tressa opened her eyes and looked up at me with an expression of pure exasperation. "You don't know how to take no for an answer, do you?"

"You haven't told me no since last night. Now turn around so I can shampoo your hair."

"Shampoo my hair?" she asked, obviously surprised by my offer.

I squeezed some of her orange shampoo that smelled like citrus and coconuts into my hand and began to work it into her long brown hair. "Yeah."

Leaning around her, I saw her smile as I gently massaged the shampoo into her hair and scalp. "Then I'm going to do something else to take the edge off."

"And if I say no?"

I kissed her cheek and continued to shampoo her hair. "You won't. Now relax. You're going to like starting your day like this so much you're going to be begging me to take showers with you every morning."

"You think so?" she said with a chuckle.

"I know so. Stop fighting this. You know you like it, so just let yourself enjoy it."

She started to say something in response but stopped and leaned back against me instead. As much as I loved the feel of her body pressed to mine, it made shampooing her hair impossible, so I gently pushed her off my chest and turned her around to face me.

"I promise once I'm done here we'll get back to that," I said with a smile as I smoothed her hair off her forehead.

"Should I close my eyes or are you good enough that I can leave them open?" she asked with a smile.

"Better close them. I don't think sex with a crying woman is a good thing."

She followed my instructions and giggled. "So women don't routinely cry when you're fucking them, Killian?"

I tugged her hair and tilted her head back to kiss her. "No, and I would think you'd already know that since we've already had sex nearly four times."

Tressa's eyes flew open just as a stream of shampoo rolled down from the top of her head. "Eyes closed," I said before pushing it off her face.

"Sorry. But I don't understand the nearly four times. By my count, it was only three. The first time out in the living room and the second and third times in my bed. Where's number four coming from?"

"You started sucking my cock but fell asleep. Don't worry. I'm not holding that against you. Okay, time to rinse."

She opened her eyes and smiled up at me. "You're a very bossy hairdresser, sir."

I stepped around her and waited as she moved under the water. She really was beautiful, even with her hair soaking wet and with no makeup on her face. When she finished, she opened her eyes, pushed her hair back, and looked down to avoid my gaze.

"This isn't exactly the way I want anyone to see me. I must look like a drowned rat."

Reaching out, I snaked my arm around her waist and pulled her to me so her body pressed against mine. "You look as gorgeous as you did last night. Next up is conditioner."

"Conditioner?"

I pointed at the bottle on the shelf next to us. "Conditioner. You wouldn't have it here if you didn't use it."

"I'm just confused at how you know anything about all of this."

Squeezing a glob of conditioner into my palm, I smiled before rubbing my hands together. "My mother had a salon when I was a little boy. Ready?"

Tressa looked down at my hands and shook her head. "That's not going to be enough. My hair is way too long and needs about five times more."

I slid my hands over her hair down to the ends. "Trust me. This is enough."

She stared up at me in disbelief as I began to massage the conditioner in. "You are a very bossy hairdresser for sure."

"Shhh. I'm working my magic here."

"I guess I'll just have to keep myself busy some other way," she said with a giggle as she reached out and palmed my cock.

The feel of her hand stroking up and down my shaft felt so fucking good that I forgot what I was doing. My hands stilled in her hair for a moment, but when she cupped my balls and gave them a gentle squeeze, I grabbed a handful of hair and tugged as need coursed through me.

"Enough conditioner. Rinse," I bit out.

With a pout, she let go of my cock and stepped under the water to do as I ordered. A minute later, she was finished and we could get down to business.

"Now as for that stress relief I promised."

"Let me guess. A deep conditioning treatment."

Her teasing made me smile. I ran my hands down her sides and cupped her ass. "I don't think I've ever heard it called that, but we can use that for our secret code."

"Why do we need a secret code?"

I leaned down and nuzzled her neck, nibbling on her skin. "You never know. We might be in public somewhere when the need to fuck you comes over me."

"Mmmm…so we're going to be in public now? I don't see how that will work since cameras follow you everywhere," Tressa said as she slid her hands down over my abs to palm my cock once again.

Lifting my mouth from her neck, I kissed her lips. "I'll make sure they don't. Deal?"

She looked up at me and smiled. "Deal."

"I should warn you that the need to fuck you will be happening quite often."

"Oh? You can see into the future?" she asked as she

slid her hand from the base of my cock to the tip.

Fuck, her touch made it nearly impossible to think straight. Enough of this playing games.

I lifted her up and held her over my ready-and-waiting cock. She wrapped her legs around my waist, eager for what I was about to give her, and slid her arms around my neck. Steadying my feet on the wet tile, I lowered her down onto me and gave my hips a single thrust, filling her completely.

Tressa moaned softly, and I saw in those beautiful dark eyes how much she loved this. For all her fighting and iciness, the truth of who Tressa Stone was could be found in her eyes as she rolled her hips each time I pushed my cock into her perfectly tight cunt.

She truly was unlike any other woman I'd ever been with. As difficult as she'd been before last night, as soon as we kissed, everything else but desire melted away in her. The transformation shocked me at first since I'd suspected she wanted me but never thought the woman beneath the feisty façade could be so sensual and yet so sweet.

"Oh, God…don't stop," she whimpered in my ear in that voice that bordered on begging and made something deep inside me want to make her mine.

I couldn't have stopped, even if I wanted to. The need to please her took over my mind and body, and I pumped into her in search of that moment when she'd whimper as her orgasm raged through her and her cunt milked my cock to my own release.

She rode me as much as I fucked her, the two of us

desperately needing to come. Our eyes fixed on one other with an intensity I didn't recognize from anyone I'd ever been with. In hers, I saw desire and passion and something else I couldn't place.

Was it fear? Why would she fear me?

As I watched her bite her lip as her body began to give in to me, I saw whatever that was in her eyes disappear, replaced by pure satisfaction as she came hard on my cock. The feel of her walls squeezing me pushed me over the edge a moment later, and I buried my face in her neck.

We stood there in the shower, the water hitting her back as I sagged against the cool tile wall behind me. My eyes remained closed, and I reveled in the pleasure we'd given one another and how good she felt in my arms. Tressa gently ran her fingertips across my back and shoulders, softly stroking my skin while she sighed in contentment.

"That was…incredible," she said quietly before kissing my cheek.

I lifted my head to see her smiling. I liked seeing her like this. Relaxed. Happy. Satisfied.

"See? I told you it would relieve your stress."

Looking away, she blushed so adorably I couldn't help but be charmed. We'd had sex in half a dozen positions and shared the most intimate parts of one another since last night, and my lame joke about sex as stress relief embarrassed her.

"What?" I asked, needing to know why she blushed at

that.

Tressa lifted her head and met my gaze. "Nothing. We better get out of this shower or we're going to be pruney for days."

I kissed her, letting my lips linger on hers to avoid ending our time together so soon, and then lowered her to the tile floor below. She quickly turned off the water and opened the glass door, grabbing a white Richmont hotel towel to cover herself before handing me one.

"If you need more than one, there are more in the cabinet over there," she said, pointing toward the vanity and tall cabinet on the other side of the room.

She hurried out of the bathroom, leaving me standing there in the shower alone wondering where the woman I'd had sex with last night and again a few moments ago had gone. The Tressa Stone who'd fought me every step of the way since the first time we met in her father's office seemed to have returned, but I had no idea why.

And I had to admit I was disappointed.

I dried off and wrapped the towel around my hips before heading out to her bedroom. I found her combing her hair as she sat on the bed. Taking a seat next to her, I said nothing but waited for her to speak.

Finally, she turned to look at me and said, "I can't sit around here all day. I have to go to work."

"Nobody's stopping you."

"You're stopping me. You keep making me want to stay," she answered with a cute smile.

Reaching out, I touched the ends of her hair and

kissed her softly on the shoulder. "Then stay. Tell all those people who think they should be bothering you twenty-four hours a day that you're taking a day off."

The smile faded from her face and she shook her head. "I can't. That's just not who I am."

"Is that why you're back to icy Tressa?"

Her mouth turned down into a deep frown and her eyes filled with sadness that made me instantly regret my words. "Please don't describe me like that. I would think after all we did that you'd know I'm not icy."

"I didn't mean that as anything bad. I just noticed something changed in you after we finished in there."

Tressa shook her head, but the sadness remained in her eyes even if the frown left her face. "Nothing changed. I'm the same person I've always been. And you're the same person you are."

That sounded ominous. I didn't like where this was headed.

"Whatever we are with the rest of the world, we're pretty damn good when it's just the two of us, don't you think?"

"Can that ever be enough, though?" she asked, cutting to the heart of things like always. "You're famous and those cameras and the press aren't going anywhere. I don't want to live my life on the gossip sites with strangers dissecting the look on my face or the clothes I wear or if you really care about me because of the way you hold my hand. I'm the wrong kind of woman for that."

"I told you. I'll make sure that won't happen."

Tressa turned her body to face me and I saw that promise wouldn't be enough. "You love being famous. You told me that last night. You like being someone the press follows around. I won't ask you to give that up."

I took her hand in mine and brought it to my lips. Kissing it, I looked at her and smiled. "You don't have to ask me to give it up. I'll have that and when it's just us, they won't be around. I'll make sure of it. Trust me. It's not as big a deal as you think. Today, I'm a big story in this town. Next week, someone new will come along and I'll just be the quarterback for New York. It really happens that fast."

The look of hope that had flickered in her eyes for a moment dimmed, and she asked, "Then why hasn't it happened already? You've been in the league for years."

"Because I never had a reason to not look for it until now. I'm twenty-nine, though, and my days as a quarterback for any team are numbered. I think it's time I look for something else."

"And I'm that something else?"

I'd never lied to any woman before, and I didn't want to start with Tressa. "Here's the thing. If you haven't heard about my past already, you will, so let me tell you the truth. There have been a lot of women, but none who made me think of them more than the game. Until you. Now maybe it's because I've met you late in my career, or maybe it's because you're you. I don't know. And I don't know what's going to happen with us. All I know is from the moment I first saw you at that auction, I haven't been able to stop thinking about you."

"I can't live my life in a fishbowl, Killian. I hope you understand that."

"You won't have to," I said and then pulled her onto my lap. "It's not like I'm going to impress you with dinner at fancy restaurants and public things like that. You'll get the private Killian that no one else gets."

Looking into my eyes, she asked, "Will that be enough for you?"

I chuckled and kissed her. "Trust me. From what I've seen so far with you, I'll have more than enough to keep me busy."

Tressa's cheeks blushed that pink color that made her look sweet. Whatever happened with us, I liked the challenge of making her happy enough that she felt comfortable letting this side of her come out. I had a feeling she didn't do that for most people.

CHAPTER TEN

TRESSA

AFTER A LONG DAY AT work, I arrived back at the penthouse to find a bouquet of twenty-four red roses in a crystal vase waiting for me on my living room coffee table. I lifted the small, white envelope out of the flowers and smiled when I read the card.

Redeemable for one shampoo.

This thing with Killian could never work out. I knew that. I knew our differences were too much for either one of us to overcome, no matter what we told one another. Still, I couldn't deny the man did something no man had ever accomplished.

He made me happy. I hadn't realized how much I wanted that until he came into my life. I couldn't deny I had a good time with him last night. He was incredible in bed, and when there was no press around to take his picture, he was attentive like no other man I'd ever met. He also could handle me and rocked my body like no one else ever had.

I closed my eyes and remembered how I felt in his arms. An ache formed between my legs as the memory reminded me of how he knew just what to do to please me.

But it was useless to think about what might be when it couldn't be. He wasn't going to change who he was, and I wasn't going to change who I was. We were just too different.

I should call him to thank him for the flowers. No, that would be a bad idea.

What was the point? We'd talk, he'd make me want to see him again, and that just wasn't something I should do.

He was going to eventually call, and I didn't want to intentionally avoid him by putting on the away message again. After the time we'd spent together, he deserved better than that. Maybe I could go out. The press had left the front of the hotel, and I had a feeling I had Killian to thank for that. So I could go somewhere.

But where? Summer was on location with Ethan taking pictures of Kiki Anderson's prize show dogs out in LA, so she wasn't available. Prize show dogs. How ridiculous. But I had to give Ethan credit. For all the doubts I'd had about him, he was a natural businessman, after all. He'd turned something he cared about into a viable business.

That business, however, kept my best friend on the other coast at the moment. I couldn't go see my parents, even if the drive out to the house might do me some good. One problem. They both knew about Killian, and I had no doubt that the entire conversation would be about him. That was the last thing I needed.

The idea of going to see Diana crept into my brain, and I instantly dismissed it. We hadn't spent any time together in ages. What would I say to her?

I walked over to the window to look out over the city as guilt began to fill me. She was my only sister in the world, and I never saw her, even though we lived in the same hotel.

Turning away from the world outside, I glanced up at the TV. He'd be calling soon. I felt it, like the time we'd spent together had made us close enough for me to know how he'd react to my not calling to thank him for the flowers.

Without thinking about where I was going, I left the penthouse and a few minutes later found myself standing outside of my sister's door. Not even a suite, it was just a regular hotel room. I'd never understood why she insisted on living there.

Don't do that, Tressa. She's been through enough. Don't say the wrong thing and upset her. She wants to live here, so leave it alone.

I knocked on her door as doubt about what I was doing began to make me want to leave. I didn't, though, and when the door slowly began to open, I made sure to put a smile on my face.

Her reaction to seeing me wasn't what I hoped, though. Tears filled her blue eyes as she asked, "What happened? Is it Mommy or Daddy?"

Immediately, I put my hand up to stop her from

jumping to the wrong conclusion. "No, nothing's happened. Everyone's okay."

Diana's fear and sadness that I'd bought bad news were replaced with a look of confusion. "Then why are you here? You never come to see me."

Anyone who thought I was the only Stone who could be blunt was seriously mistaken, but I deserved that. Forcing myself to smile, I said, "I wanted to talk to someone. Any chance you have some time for your only sister?"

She returned my smile with one that lit up her entire face. "Of course, Tressa. I always have time for you. Come in."

I walked into her room and a feeling of disgust washed over me. The Richmont had suites she could choose from. As the daughter of the owner and the sister of the COO of the Richmont hotel chain, she could have her pick. Yet still she insisted on living in this regular hotel room.

As I looked around at the light tan walls every basic room in the hotel had, Diana said, "Please, sit down."

Turning around, I saw her already seated on the couch, so I sat down at the other end. All that space between us made me feel like we were strangers.

"What's going on that you wanted to talk about?"

"Oh, nothing much. Just thought it would be nice to catch up."

Diana smiled sweetly. "Even though Summer and Ethan have been taking me out a lot more lately, I don't leave this hotel room much, Tressa, so this is going to be a short conversation on my part."

I couldn't help but look around the room and frown. "Why aren't you in a bigger room? Didn't Daddy tell you how much nicer you'd feel in a suite?"

"I know this hotel has suites. It has a penthouse you've been living in for the past few months too. I like this room. It's cozy, and it's mine."

The defensiveness in her voice made me hang my head. As always, I'd said the wrong thing, even if I did have the best of intentions. "I didn't mean anything bad. I just wondered if you'd like more room to move around in. That's all."

"It's okay, Tressa. I'm happy here. Daddy told me about your big news. Congratulations!"

Oh, God! My father had told Diana about Killian. Had he been going around telling everyone? "It's not that big a deal. Really. Whatever he said, take it with a grain of salt."

"I think you're downplaying it. Becoming COO of the Richmont hotel chain is a big deal."

Relief washed over me, and I burst out laughing at my mistake. "Oh, that. Thanks. I'm proud of what I've accomplished with Stone Worldwide."

We sat silently for a few moments before Diana asked, "Then why were you minimizing it?"

"I wasn't. I just got confused about what you were referring to."

"What did you think I meant?" she asked, leaning

forward, curious.

Figuring my sister wouldn't tell anyone, I said, "I thought Daddy had told you about this guy I bid on at a charity auction the other night. We had our date last night."

Diana's mouth dropped open and she stared at me. "I've never seen you like this. What's his name?"

"Killian and what do you mean like this? How am I acting?"

Diana smiled and shook her head. "Like you like him. Like you like him a lot, in fact."

I waved my hand to dismiss that immediately. "No, I don't. It's nothing big at all, in fact."

"Then why are you blushing?"

Touching my cheeks, I felt them heating up against my fingertips. "I am not. It's just hot in here. Why is everyone in this family so convinced I'm always blushing?"

"Because you are. You like this Killian. Is that why you wanted to talk?"

I shrugged and shook my head. "There's nothing to say, really. He's nobody special. Just a guy I had to go out with. We went out and that's that. We've got nothing in common, so it can't go anywhere."

"Oh, okay," Diana said quietly like she was disappointed. "I was hoping you'd come to talk about a guy. You've never talked about any with me."

"That's not true. Remember Corey Adams? I talked about him day and night in eighth grade. I'm embarrassed to think how much I talked about him, in fact."

"Eighth grade? That was over a decade ago. I meant since we became grown adults who didn't spend our time talking about how gorgeous some boy looked in his corduroys."

Her memory of Corey's corduroys made me giggle. "I did have a thing for those corduroy pants he wore. What were they grey or brown? Either way, I doubt it was a good look for anyone, including poor Corey Adams."

Diana didn't answer, and the way she stared like she was studying me made me nervous. "Why are you looking at me in that funny way?"

"It's so nice to hear you giggle like you used to. I've missed that."

"I've never been much of a giggler, Diana. You were always the one who giggled."

She nodded and gave me a tepid smile as I thought about the last time I giggled before now. Killian. He made me giggle. He said such silly things sometimes. How could I not giggle at him?

"I've missed you, Tressa. We used to be so close."

My sister's words hit me square in the chest, like someone pressing on my heart. We were close. Never as close as Ethan and she ever were, but I always knew I could tell her anything and she'd understand. I missed that.

"We still are," I lied in a voice full of forced cheeriness. "Things just got busy. That's how life is, but we'll always be sisters, no matter what. Nothing changes that."

"I guess."

Diana's expression morphed into the one she always made when she was upset. Ever since we were children, whenever she was sad, she pressed her lips tightly together and drew in her eyebrows toward her nose. It never failed to make every one of us want to do whatever we could to make her happy again.

I always screwed up like this. This is why I rarely came to visit her because I ended up saying something stupid that hurt her feelings. I didn't mean to. I never meant to hurt my sister. I just didn't know how to behave around her.

Hoping to cheer her up, I blurted out, "Would you like to see what Killian looks like?"

It didn't take even a nanosecond to regret saying that. I knew if she saw me staring at him up on her enormous TV screen that she'd know I liked him more than I wanted to admit to her or anyone else.

But Diana's eyes lit up with excitement at my offer, and she jumped up off the couch to turn the screen on. "Yeah! Definitely. What's he do for a living? Is he an executive like you?"

"No. He's an athlete. A quarterback."

My sister's mouth dropped open in shock. She had every reason to be surprised. I'd never dated anyone other than businessmen and executives. Even in high school, I had no interest in the jocks everyone loved, including Diana. Killian definitely wasn't my type.

"A quarterback? The new one for New York? I read about him. He's supposedly just what the team needs."

She sat down next to me as I stared at her, confused how she knew all this. Turning to face me, she said, "What? Don't you remember Daddy taking Ethan and me to the games when we were kids? I don't know everything about the sport, but I know New York needed a quarterback and Killian Brenton is supposed to be how the team plans to get back to top form."

"Then you know what he looks like already, so we don't have to find a picture," I said, grabbing the remote from her hands.

She took it back from me and pointed it toward the screen hanging on the wall in front of us. "No way. I want to see this man you say you bid on. Like for a date? How much did you pay?"

"It was for a charity, so please remember that, okay? It's not like I'm in the habit of paying men to date me or anything."

Diana grinned at my pained explanation. "Got it. So how much was your winning bid?"

"Ten grand," I admitted sheepishly.

Her smile disappeared as a look of shock registered on her face. "Ten thousand dollars! Even for charity that sounds like a lot for a date. Where did you two go?"

I felt my cheeks getting warm again and knew I was blushing. Looking away, I said, "The National Club. It was nothing big."

As I attempted to hide my obvious interest in Killian,

Diana said to the TV, "Pictures of Killian Brenton, quarterback."

A second later, dozens of images of the man popped up on the screen. Some with women, some alone, some with him in a tux, some of him in his Miami uniform. He looked phenomenal in all of them.

"Tressa, he is gorgeous! Are his eyes green? Wow, those are beautiful eyes. Are they as nice in person?"

I lowered my head so I didn't have to look at all the pictures of the man who had rocked my world multiple times last night and this morning. "They're pretty nice. The green is very light, like a color I've never seen in anyone's eyes before."

"And his tanned skin makes them even more beautiful," Diana said as she stood up to walk over to stand in front of the TV. Looking back at me, she smiled. "He really is a gorgeous man."

"Yeah. He's all right. I mean, he wears a tux pretty nicely. You know how most men looked awkward in a tux? He doesn't," I mumbled.

"I see. You look pretty incredible in this picture I found too."

My stomach sank at her mention of how I looked. That meant she'd found one of the pictures of the two of us at that charity auction event. Dread filled me, and I covered my eyes with my hand. "God, that isn't the one where I'm looking up at him like I want to devour him, is it?"

"No. Look. It's a nice picture of the two of you. He's

looking down at you and you're looking up at him but not like you want to devour him. It's more like you want to know more about him. Tressa, I promise it's not bad. Look."

Lowering my hand, I focused on a picture in the upper left hand corner of the screen my sister pointed to and realized I'd never seen that shot before. Unlike all the others the press had circulated, this one focused on Killian's point of view instead of mine. He looked stunning as always, but I saw in his eyes something that said maybe he hadn't exaggerated when he told me that morning that from the moment he saw me he couldn't stop thinking about me.

"Yeah, well that's him," I said in my best casual tone, hoping to hide how much I liked that picture and what it told me.

"When are you seeing him again?" Diana asked as my eyes scanned the rest of the pictures on the screen. Whether he was in his uniform or in a tux or anything in between, the man never took a bad picture.

And as that thought went through my head, another one did too. How many women had he been with? Had he been photographed with every single one? In front of me, I saw no fewer than ten of his ex-girlfriends, each one stunning as they hung off his arm.

"Tressa, did you hear me? When are you seeing him again?"

I moved my head so I didn't focus on all those women and looked at my sister. "I don't know. Probably never. It was just a charity thing, you know, so I did my part and went out to dinner with him."

Diana returned to her seat next to me on the couch and tilted her head like she couldn't believe what I'd said. "I don't understand you. I've never even seen you two together, other than that one picture, and it's obvious to even someone like me who is as socially backward as they get that you like this person. Why are you acting like you don't care?"

"We're just very different. What's the point of trying to date? Look at the man. He's an attention whore. I'm the exact opposite. I keep my private life private."

My sister didn't buy my excuses. Shaking her head, she said, "You're not the exact opposite of him. I am. You are a normal woman who's had incredible success in business. People know your name, Tressa. They may not want to take your picture every time you step outside this hotel, but you're well-known in this city and around the world. So what's the real reason you're acting this way?"

There again was that bluntness we shared. Even Ethan didn't get to me like Diana could with her candor. No one else had a way of cutting to the truth like she did.

Well, no one other than me.

"I haven't been successful with men, Diana. At some point, I just figured out that I'd have people I slept with from time to time and that's all I'd ever have when it came to relationships. I don't think Killian Brenton is going to be any different."

She took my hand in hers and gave it a gentle

squeeze. "Maybe he could be if you let it happen. You don't have to push everyone away, Tressa. He could be the guy who has just what you want in a man, but you'll never know if you don't give him a chance."

Everything she said made sense. I hated that, but it was the truth. Nothing I could say would change that.

Diana lowered her head and added, "I know you probably are thinking that I'm no one to give advice since I don't have anyone in my life. That's true, but so is the fact that you don't have to push people away, Tressa."

"You don't either, Diana."

She looked at me, her eyes full of tears, and smiled. "That's nice of you to say, but I don't have any of the things you have going for you. You're beautiful, smart, successful, and confident. If you want Killian Brenton, you can have him. I know you can."

I didn't know what I wanted when it came to Killian. All I knew at that moment was my sister had no idea how great she was.

"Well, I better get going. I have a ton of work to do. You know how I am. Work, work, work," I said awkwardly as I stood to leave.

She followed me to the door and touched me on the arm. "Come back again, okay? I like seeing you, Tressa. And don't work so much that you don't have fun."

Taking her in my arms, I hugged her close and felt that sense of happiness I'd missed from her. "Maybe the two of us could go out sometime like you do with Ethan and Summer?"

Diana smiled and nodded eagerly. "I'd like that."

"Good. We can do whatever you want, okay?"

I turned to leave and heard her say, "Next time I'm going to ask for details on Killian, so you've been warned."

In a flash, my face heated up from a blush, and I looked back to see her smiling. For all that had happened, Diana wasn't as awkward and strange as she thought she was. She was just a normal person working through some things. I'd forgotten that for too long.

CHAPTER ELEVEN

KILLIAN

TWO DAYS. IT HAD BEEN two days since I last saw Tressa. I'd kissed her long and deep before walking out the door of her penthouse and missed the feel of her next to me before I reached the elevator. Then I'd sent her two dozen red roses I knew she'd received since I already checked with the florist.

I'd never called fucking florists to check on flower deliveries. Then again, I'd never had to. No woman had ever gotten flowers from me and not called for two days. Hell, no one had ever gotten flowers and not called five minutes later to thank me, usually with an offer I couldn't resist.

Not Tressa Stone. Nope. She received the flowers the day I ordered them at eleven-fifty-eight. I knew she'd worked all day, but even assuming she didn't get back home until that night, she'd still had those fucking roses for over thirty-six hours by now and I hadn't heard a damn peep out of her.

I'd called her no less than four times in that thirty-six hours too, each time getting her away message. That infuriating away message that made me want to throw my fucking phone off the edge of my balcony.

She couldn't be avoiding me. No way. Not after the night and morning we had together. She had a good time. I knew it. A man knows when a woman is into him. There'd been no faking orgasms with Tressa. I'd made her come until her thighs shook. She had a good time.

We both did. Fuck, we both had an incredible time. I knew there was a soft side to her, and I got to see it in all its glory that night and in the shower that morning. She was open and sweet and downright submissive at times, while at other times she was practically ravenous in how much she wanted me.

I hadn't been able to think of anything but her since. If I didn't know better, I'd swear she'd possessed my mind. The memory of how she felt beneath me and how she sounded when she whimpered right before she came haunted me.

And yet she was able to not call me at all. She knew I'd called and she'd gotten the flowers. What was with this woman?

I tried to call her again, and again I got that damn away message. Pacing back and forth across my living room, I forced myself to think of anything but Tressa Stone. The first game I played in the pros. The day I was drafted by Miami. My first game in college. Those were the memories I always went to when I needed to focus. All showed I was a winner who'd been blessed time and again in life.

Yet this time, none of those helped. My mind kept drifting back to the other night with Tressa at her penthouse. Why the hell was I so obsessed with this woman? She wasn't the most beautiful woman I'd ever been with. For fuck's sake, I'd dated supermodels, actresses, and beauty queens.

I stopped in front of the glass doors that led out to my balcony and stared out at the lights of the city. This had nothing to do with how she looked. Tressa was a knockout from head to toe. She rivaled any of the women I'd been with.

No, this had to do with something else she had that other women didn't. I could find a woman who wanted me anywhere I looked. She made me work for every second I got with her, but even though I loved a challenge, this was beginning to piss me off.

Fuck. I needed to get my mind off her or I'd end up going crazy. Needing something to distract me, I called Sherilyn. As usual, she answered immediately. If only Tressa was like my publicist that way.

"I was just about to call you. I need an answer about that premiere for Athena's movie. I was supposed to tell her people if you were coming two days ago."

Athena's new movie. I wanted to fly out to LA and spend the night with my ex at some stupid premiere for another one of her movies like I wanted to rip my arm off and beat myself with it. The first few times were sort of fun, but after a while, movie premieres all became the same.

"When is it?" I asked, wondering if a quick trip out of town might help me clear my head.

"Tomorrow night. I know it's Athena, but you know how she loves having you on her arm at these things. It doesn't hurt you either to have the public see you at events like this. I know you've got a lot going on here in New York with the team, but it would only be a quick flight out, a few hours at the premiere and after party, and then a quick flight back."

New York to LA was never a quick flight, no matter what she wanted to say. Even worse was flying out there and then practically turning right around and flying back to the East coast.

Then again, I could use a change of scenery. I was supposed to go to that event I told Tristan about, but since Tressa clearly had no intention of attending, I didn't feel like showing up either.

"Fine. Tell them I'll escort her to the premiere. I don't want to spend more time than I have to out there, so forget the after party and be sure to get me on the first plane back after the premiere. Make sure she knows I can't stay too."

Sherilyn beamed a smile and nodded. "Of course. I'm so glad you're attending this premiere, Killian. I think it's a good promotional move for you. It keeps you in the public eye, and it shows you and Athena are still close."

"We aren't still close," I said, rolling my eyes at the thought that Athena and I felt anything now. "She just knows I make her look good since her last two boyfriends were drugged up wastes of space. If she had a decent man in her life, I'd never hear from her again."

My explanation of the true relationship between my ex-girlfriend and me seemed to disappoint Sherilyn, and she twisted her face into a grimace. "Well, it keeps you in the public eye, so that's a good thing."

"Make the arrangements and send me the information."

"Great! I will. By the way, how did your date go with the woman who won the auction the other night?"

Sherilyn's chipper voice suddenly irritated me. I opened my mouth to vent my frustration but decided against it and simply ended the call. Even though she knew me better than nearly anyone else in the world, I didn't need her trying to make me feel better about the whole situation. That would only make things worse.

I returned to pacing for another fifteen more minutes and then tried Tressa one more time. At the first sound of her voice on that fucking away message, something snapped in my brain, but instead of tossing something through the TV, I decided I needed to take matters into my own hands.

AFTER A QUICK KNOCK ON her door, I waited for Tressa to answer it, reminding myself to stay cool and not let her see how much she'd gotten to me. The fact that I'd taken the chance and come over even though I knew she was avoiding me already made me look a little more eager than I liked.

She opened the door a crack and glared at me with a look of disgust. Not exactly the response I'd hoped for after the night we'd shared.

Without saying hello, she said, "How do you make it past security? I pay people to make sure no one gets up here."

"Your security guard is a football fan. I was on his fantasy team last season and made him a fortune. I could have talked him into selling his mother for that," I said with a smile.

"Ugh. I'm really busy, Killian."

I noticed she hadn't returned to calling me Mr. Brenton anymore. That was progress. Not that she should after the all night fuck session we'd had.

Leaning in toward her face, I asked, "Did you like the flowers?"

She drew her eyebrows in and sighed. "Yes, I did. Thank you."

"I just wondered since I never heard from you after they were delivered."

Looking down toward the floor, she mumbled, "I was busy."

We stood there in silence for a long moment before I finally said, "I feel sort of stupid standing out here in the hallway, Tressa. Can I come in?"

"No."

Suddenly, jealousy filled me, and I craned my neck to look around her to see if she had another man in there with her. "Why?"

"Because I can't spend another night with you like last time. That's why."

Her answer made all the worry ebb out of me. Smiling, I said, "Another night like last time?"

"Please, Killian. This isn't going to work. I'm not really the kind of woman to just have one night stands with men, and I'm definitely not a woman to have a relationship now."

The way she pouted when she said that made me want to kiss her through that tiny crack in the door. "That doesn't leave much room for you to relax and have a good time."

"I don't have time for either, to be honest."

"I get it, Tressa. You have a world to conquer. But there has to be some time when you leave work and let yourself have fun. Trust me, I had to learn that the hard way."

She didn't answer me, so I nudged the door open a bit more. "You know you like having fun, Tressa."

For a moment, I waited to see how she'd react and then gently pushed the door open a little more. She didn't fight me and reluctantly stepped back to let me in.

"This will never work between us."

Stopping just inside the door, I kissed her. "It already has worked pretty damn well. Neither one of us is looking for forever, so why can't we enjoy ourselves for a little while?"

"Because a little while turned into an all-night marathon last time," she said with a skeptical look in her eyes.

"I was doing my best to impress you since it was our first time together," I said, chuckling at how hard she wanted to make this on the both of us.

Tressa closed the door and turned her back to me to walk away. "I don't know why you keep trying with me. We're as opposite as opposite could be. Polar opposite, actually."

Following her into the living room, I found her sitting on the couch. Nothing that indicated she'd been working sat nearby, like a tablet or computer or even her phone. I didn't see any paper or a pen either.

"Busy, huh?"

She scowled and folded her arms across her chest. "Why are you here, Killian?"

Leave it to Tressa to cut to the chase and jump right over all the sweet talk I had planned. Fine. Somehow we'd returned to being blunt, so that's what she'd get.

"Because it's not nice to receive gifts from people and not say thank you, Tressa."

My scolding tone irritated her even more, and she stood up to walk away from me. "Don't speak to me like I'm a child. That might work on other women you know, but it won't work on me."

"Then don't act like one. That might work on other men, but it definitely doesn't work for me."

Even though I enjoyed this kind of verbal sparring with her, the way she spun around and glared daggers at me told me she didn't like it as much. Without any emotion, she pointed toward the door and said, "I'm really busy, Killian. I think you should go."

Fuck. With every word she spoke, it was like I could see another layer of the wall around her going up. What the hell was wrong? We'd had a great time together the other night. What had changed since then?

Maybe verbal sparring wouldn't work tonight. Maybe I needed to use another tactic with her.

I walked up behind her as she stood staring out the window and gently wrapped my arms around her. Resting my chin on her shoulder, I said, "You're clearly not busy, Tressa, so what's going on?"

She took a deep breath in and blew it out in a rush before her entire body sagged beneath me. "I'm not the right kind of woman for you. I don't know why you don't see that."

"Isn't that for me to decide?"

Closing her eyes, she hung her head. "We're too different. Why won't you admit that?"

I squeezed her in my arms and nuzzled her neck. "I'm not worried about our differences. I like our similarities a lot more."

Tressa turned in my hold and looked up at me with worried eyes. "What similarities exactly are you talking about? The only thing we have in common is that we're good together in bed."

"You say that like it's a bad thing."

My joke fell flat, and she returned to scowling at me. "I'm not the kind of woman to be some guy's fuck toy.

Sorry. It doesn't fit with my personality."

"That's not what I think of you, Tressa."

Folding her arms across her chest, she shook her head. "Then what do you think of me? You said you couldn't stop thinking about me ever since you saw me at the auction. What does that mean? You saw a woman you wanted to sleep with and that was your goal? Well, you achieved the goal, so why do you keep coming around?"

I took her face in my hands and knew I had to tell her what I'd realized on the ride over there. I didn't really understand it myself, but it needed to be said and she needed to hear it.

She looked up at me with fear in her eyes as I tried to find the right words for what I wanted to tell her. I had a feeling she'd heard a lot of bullshit lines from guys before me. Maybe that explained why she ran so hot and cold. She'd figured out from them that letting a man know she cared for him got her hurt, so she intended to hurt first so she never had to deal with that pain again.

"Have you ever thought one thing, but then when the time comes and you're given everything you want, you see that you wanted something else?"

Talk about saying nothing in as many words possible.

Her eyes grew wide as what I wanted to say came out all wrong. "What?"

I'd gone from verbal sparring to verbal fumbling in just a few sentences. I needed to find the right words before she slapped me across the face and threw me out of her life forever.

"Wait. That wasn't what I meant. Let me try again. I thought I couldn't stop thinking about you because you were gorgeous and the way you looked at me that night made me want you. Then I thought I couldn't stop thinking about you because you wouldn't even call me to say thanks for sending you flowers. Neither of those are true, though. I don't know why you've gotten under my skin, but you have and I can't think of anything else but you. And I don't mean just sex with you. I mean you, Tressa. The way you look when I joke around. That cute way you blush at things. The way you giggle at things I say."

"So this isn't about you just coming here because you want sex?"

I shook my head, still pretty amazed at that fact myself. I'd never been the decent guy type when it came to women. Tressa was different, though. I didn't know why, but unlike her, I didn't feel the need to examine that question.

"No. I'm not going to lie. The sex is phenomenal, but that's not the only reason I want to be around you. Now if you'd stop fighting me at every turn, we could have a good time, sexually or non-sexually."

The look on her face told me she still didn't believe me, so I took her hand and led her back over to the couch. I expected some kind of resistance, but thankfully, she didn't argue. We sat down and I moved her so she could lie back against my chest while we talked.

Leaning forward, I moved her hair over her left

shoulder so she wasn't resting on it. "Comfortable?"

"I guess," she answered tentatively, like she expected me to begin undressing her at any moment.

Not that I wouldn't have been all for that, but instead, I wrapped my arms around her and leaned back against the couch cushions to relax. I couldn't remember the last time I just sat and talked with a woman once we'd slept together, but it felt nice to be there with her and not have the expectation of anything but some conversation.

"So how was work today, dear?" I asked with a smile.

Tressa sighed. "Horrible, but thanks for asking."

Moving my hands up, I began massaging her shoulders, which were as tight as drums. As I attempted to ease the stress out of her body, I said, "Horrible isn't good. Want to talk about it?"

Another sigh made her body sag against my torso. "No. Maybe. I don't know. I'm sure you have no interest in hearing about the problems I'm having with a designer who thinks she knows best and who's being overpaid for having taste in her mouth and that's it."

"I'm all ears. We're just hanging out here trying to relax, and if that means telling me about this horrible designer, then do it. Whatever makes you feel better."

Tressa turned her head to look up at me. Still suspicious, she narrowed her eyes and asked, "Is this some kind of new seduction technique of yours?"

"Nope. Just me giving you a chance to vent after a bad day. Want me to start first? I sent flowers to a beautiful woman and do you know she never even sent me a message to say thanks?" I said with a smile.

Her expression softened and her eyes grew wide. Smiling, she said, "She sounds like a complete and total bitch. You should forget about her. You know, other fish in the sea and all that."

I shrugged and shook my head. "If only I could. I don't know what this woman has, but I can't get her out of my mind. It's maddening, to be honest. I'm just going to have to keep trying to convince her that I'm a good guy."

"Maybe she doesn't deserve you. I mean, if she isn't even polite enough to say thank you when someone sends her flowers, maybe she isn't worth it."

Pressing a kiss to the top of her head, I felt her soft hair caress my lips. "She's worth it."

For the first time since we lay down, she squeezed her arms against mine and smiled. "Well, if that's the way it is, I'm sure she'll warm up to you eventually. Some people just take longer than others."

"That's fine. I've got nothing but time."

Looking away, Tressa asked in a voice barely above a whisper, "What about all the other women, though? Maybe you'll want to spend your time focusing on one of them instead."

So that was the problem. Or part of it. I had a feeling a woman like Tressa Stone had layers of resistance to someone like me.

"As much as I'm sure it would surprise the world, there aren't other women to focus on. Just the beautiful woman who seems to hate my flowers."

She didn't respond for a long time until she finally said, "She doesn't hate them, and she doesn't hate you. She's just difficult."

"I'm not sure difficult is the right word. I have another word for her. I think of her as challenging, and there's nothing I like more than a challenge."

I felt her body tense up against mine and knew I'd said something wrong. A second later, Tressa pushed herself up off me to stand up. I didn't know why she was running away since we'd been having a pleasant conversation, but I planned to find out.

Following her into her bedroom, I found Tressa standing near the window that overlooked the city. I walked up behind her and tried to slide my arms around her, but she pushed me away.

"What's wrong?"

She shook her head and wouldn't look at me, turning her back so I couldn't see her face. The truth was I had no idea what I said, but at least I knew I'd said something wrong. Silently, I gave myself points for that.

"I don't know what I said or did, but can you at least tell me so I don't have to spend the rest of my life wondering how I fucked up?"

"I'm not interested in being some goal for you to reach, Killian. That just makes me sound like another notch on your bedpost."

"I don't have a bedpost, and even if I did, I can't imagine cutting a notch into it even once, forget multiple times."

My lame joke meant to get a response did just that, and she turned around to face me, her expression twisted into a look of disgust. "This isn't funny to me. Why do you have to make a joke when I'm being serious?"

"Because I want to see you smile."

"I don't want to be a challenge to you, Killian. Challenges are things you overcome."

"You'd rather be thought of as difficult?"

Tressa looked down toward the white carpet on the floor and shrugged. "This is why I'm not a good fit for you or anyone, for that matter. Maybe there's no word to describe what I am. Maybe I'm just a bitch like I said before."

I took a step toward her and then another. Opening my arms, I brought her to me and hugged her tightly. "You're so focused on fighting this thing between us. I don't know why, but you'll tell me when you want to. Until then, I'm not giving up on you. Just giving you fair warning."

She tilted her head up and gave me a tiny smile. "I'm always going to be difficult. I just am. I want to believe you're an okay guy, but my experience with men says otherwise."

God, I had no idea what she'd gone through with men before me. I could only imagine. Weak-ass men afraid of strong women were everywhere, unfortunately, and in her dark eyes, I saw she'd had more than a few run-ins with that kind of asshole guy.

I wasn't one of them, though. For all my faults, I wasn't the type of man who feared a strong woman. Exactly the opposite, in fact, and I planned on proving that to her in spades.

At the moment, though, all I wanted to do was make her happy. "Well, first things first. I'm way better than okay. I would think the reviews of our night together show that. Secondly, I do cute romantic things like send flowers. That's got to be a sign I'm more than okay. I guess if I went out and picked them that might be more impressive, but I have a feeling if I stole my neighbor's flowers, she'd call the cops. That's another point in my favor. I don't steal flowers."

As much as she fought it, a smile lit up Tressa's beautiful face and she giggled in that adorable way I couldn't help but love. This difficult woman who insisted on putting me through my paces and pushed me away over and over giggled at my stupid jokes.

"You say the silliest things. You know that?" she asked as she cradled my face in her hands.

"I'm disarming. It's one of my best traits."

I leaned down and pressed my forehead to hers. "And I'm not going to give up on you, so you're just going to have to find another way to deal with me."

Chapter Twelve

Tressa

Crossing my legs in front of me, I sat on my bed and scanned the designs for the London Richmont hotel the designer sent a few minutes before. As my eyes roamed over the images, I ground my teeth in frustration. I hated each one more than the last. All she could think of was remaking the hotel with a retro design. The woman couldn't talk about anything else since she joined the project.

The problem was I didn't want it to look like something out of the 1950s. I flipped through the pictures again. The furniture looked skimpy and boxy, and what was with those wooden spindle dividers that hung from the ceiling cutting up the lobby area and that enormous red lamp that looked like some horrible swollen tentacle lurching out into the middle of the seating area?

I should have never agreed to let her show me anything retro. Christ. Of all the decades she wanted to emulate, why that one?

Disgusted, I set my work aside and closed my eyes. This meant we'd have to have another meeting so I could explain once more what my vision for the hotel redesign was. Hopefully, she'd listen this time and not ignore every point I mentioned in favor of wretched pinks and yellows, geometric prints, and hideous lighting.

I could have simply hired someone to handle this, but I wanted to do it myself, even though I was the COO. I wanted to put my mark on the Richmont chain. Now I wondered if that had been a mistake.

Pushing all the hassle with the designer out of my mind, I took a deep breath in and tried to relax. All of this would work out. I just had to make sure she knew what a Richmont hotel should look like and how the chain presented itself. Once she understood that, everything else would go smoothly.

At least I hoped it would.

Relax, Tressa. You can handle this.

I smiled as the thought of what Killian would say to me at that moment popped into my head. He'd make some stupid joke so I'd smile or say something cute to make me giggle. Even when I wanted to remain upset, he knew how to lighten my mood.

That thought led to another. I shouldn't have let him in last night. One night was enough.

Who was I kidding? One night was never going to be enough. I knew that from the minute he kissed me the first time. The man had the ability to make my head swim with just a single kiss. And that said nothing about how he made me feel during sex.

God, I didn't want to think that way. I wanted to

believe we wouldn't work out. We were so different, so how could we?

But that wasn't the truth. The truth was I enjoyed being with him. When it was just the two of us, he was a great guy. But when the cameras were around? I hated that kind of publicity, and the fact that he loved it bothered me.

I leaned back against the pillows as the memory of the last time we were together settled into my mind. No matter how hard I made it for him to get close to me, he didn't give up. I walked away, and he followed. I pushed him away, and he came back with his arms open wanting to hold me.

He wasn't going to give up, and I loved that. I didn't want to admit it to anyone, even to him, but I secretly wanted him around.

As I got lost in thought about Killian, my phone rang. My heart skipped a beat at the idea that it might be him, but one glance and I saw it was Summer calling.

Without saying hello, she asked in a voice full of concern, "Tressa, what's going on?"

"Nothing I'm working. Why? Is something wrong? Are you and Ethan okay?"

My mind instantly traveled to the idea that Ethan had fucked up. If he did something to break them up, I was going to march right up to his apartment and let him have it. Or maybe he was hurt. Animals weren't like humans. Maybe one of them attacked him.

As my brain raced with every conceivable stupid thing

my brother could have done, Summer said, "Everything's okay. Ethan's fine, and I'm good. I'm just wondering how things went with Killian the other night. I never heard back from you after I returned home from the shoot."

I breathed a sigh of relief before answering her question. "They went," I said.

"That's not much of an answer, but if I didn't know better, I'd swear I can practically hear you smiling. You had a good time, didn't you? Is he nice?"

Nice? No, nice wasn't exactly the right word to describe Killian Brenton. Other words came to mind, though.

Sexy. Fucking incredible in bed. Distracting.

"I don't know if I'd call him that," I said with a chuckle. "We had a good time, though."

My comment was met with silence for a long time before Summer squealed, "Oh my God! You slept with him, didn't you? I can hear it in your voice. That's the sound of a woman who had great sex with a gorgeous man!"

"Don't be ridiculous."

"You did! Just admit it. It's not like I'm going to ask about the personal details, unless you want to give me them, of course. It's okay. You're two grown single adults. Why can't you have sex?"

"Please stop. I swear you and my brother are two of a kind. Is there nothing off limits with you two?"

"I won't tell anyone, Tressa. Not even Ethan. I just think it's great that you had a good time. That's all I was saying."

"Well, it's not a big deal. Two people had dinner and a nice time. It happens all the time."

Summer didn't seem to be buying my dismissal of the whole Killian thing, though. "Sure, although you two aren't just two ordinary people. He's a star quarterback for a New York team that's looking to have their best season in five years, and you're the COO of Richmont Hotels and a VP at Stone Worldwide. Not exactly just two people."

"Well, I have no idea if any of that makes a difference. It was all for a good cause anyway."

"Yeah. The pediatric cancer foundation. Definitely a good cause, although I don't think they expected you to sleep with Killian," Summer said with a giggle.

"God, you're so much like Ethan! This conversation is over, and don't tell anyone about this, Summer. Promise."

"I promise, Tressa, but no one would have an issue with this anyway. You're allowed to be happy. I think most people would say you've earned it."

Summer sounded so much like Diana it was scary. "Well, I have to earn my salary by working, so I'll talk to you later."

I ended the call and tossed my phone off to the other side of the bed. I loved being friends with Summer, but sometimes she could be so silly. Then again, it would have been nice to be able to tell her about my time with Killian. I hadn't had a good old fashioned gossip fest with another female in a long time.

Grudgingly, I returned to the redesign of the London Richmont hotel, making detailed notes on exactly how I wanted the hotel to look. A few minutes later Summer called a second time, and now she sounded frantic.

"Hey, how did you and Killian leave things after your date and whatever else you did?"

"I told you I didn't want to talk about this, and don't you ever say hello when you begin a call?"

"Hello. I'm just wondering if you two decided anything."

"Decided anything? No. But I have to admit I am enjoying seeing him."

"So you've seen him more than just that date for the charity?"

I finally relented and shared the details with Summer. "Yes. Okay. Yes. You're right. We slept together. More than once. God, I didn't realize how much I wanted to share this with someone, so I hope you're not going to get all provincial or anything on me. As you said, we're grown single people, right? Why can't we have a good time? And yes, I know he's a huge attention whore, but we're not doing anything in public, so it will be fine."

My confession was greeted with silence for so long that I wondered if Summer was still there. Nervously, I said, "Of all people, I didn't think you'd be so judgmental about all of this. I expected you to be more supportive."

"Uh, Tressa, are you watching TV right now?"

"No. Why? What does that have to do with what I

just told you?" I asked as I searched the bed for the remote control.

"I think you better turn it on. Go to the Premiere channel," Summer said in a tone that sent a chill racing down my back.

Oh, God. Please don't let him be telling people about us on worldwide TV. Please, God. He seemed to understand how much I hated the spotlight. He wouldn't do that. Would he?

Afraid of what the answer to my question could be, I asked Summer, "Why? What the hell channel is the Premiere channel? Is it a sports channel or something? Is Killian on a sports talk show or something?"

"It's up in the low three thousands," Summer answered in a somber voice. "Thirty-one twelve."

I pressed the numbers into the remote and a moment later on the screen, up popped Killian with a stunning platinum blonde. Tall and willowy, she had the most perfect breasts I'd ever seen, and they were practically spilling out of the black evening gown she wore. I had no idea who this woman was, but they looked beautiful together, like they were made for one another.

Then a thousand questions raced through my mind. Where were they? Why was Killian dressed in a tux and with this woman? Who was this woman? Clearly, they knew one another well, if the way she draped herself over his arm was any indication.

"What am I looking at, Summer?" I asked, hating how much hurt hung off each word.

"I don't know. Who is she? This is the movie premiere for One Lucky Day, some movie about a guy winning the lottery and then having some horrible things happen to him. She's in the movie, I think."

None of that answered the real question I had about the scene playing out in front of me.

"Is this live?" I asked, unsure why that would matter.

"Yeah, I think so."

With each passing moment, my stomach twisted into a knot as I watched Killian walking the woman down a red carpet, basking in the attention as photographers took pictures of him and the beautiful actress hanging on his arm. I knew I shouldn't be jealous. Why would I be jealous? We had no commitment between us. I'd made it perfectly clear to him that I didn't want anything like that.

Then why did every moment I watched him with that woman make me feel like someone was hollowing out my insides?

Swallowing hard, I forced myself to sound like this didn't bother me at all. "The man can wear a tux. I'll give him that. And whoever she is, she can wear a black gown like nobody I've ever seen."

"Maybe they're just friends," Summer suggested, but it sounded like a sad attempt to be helpful.

"I have to get back to work. I'll talk to you later."

Summer began to say something, but I ended the call without another word as I stared at the TV screen in front of me. Killian looked happy with all those people clamoring to get his picture or his date's picture. Whichever it was, he looked right at home in that scene.

I watched for a few moments more before turning off the TV. I had no idea if this woman was just a friend of Killian's, like Summer said, or if she was something more serious. It didn't matter.

Or did it?

Slowly, my disappointment and sadness turned to anger that he'd been cheating on this actress with me. I'd seen her with him in some of those hundreds of pictures I'd found. She was someone he'd dated before.

Or maybe they'd never broken up? Regretting every moment I spent with him, I chastised myself for ever giving him a chance.

You should have gone with your gut, Tressa. Why did you ever doubt yourself?

CHAPTER THIRTEEN

KILLIAN

THE REDEYE FROM LA TURNED out to be even worse than I thought it would be. Three hours seated next to some guy who smelled like he'd bathed in twenty dollar cologne and in front of a woman who quietly sobbed the entire time from the moment the plane took off to the moment the plane landed in New York. I'd tried to relax and get some sleep, but between his smell and her sadness, it wasn't happening.

Stepping off the flight, I squinted at the daylight and inhaled a deep breath of fresh air, thankful to be away from that guy. Sherilyn had arranged to have a driver waiting for me, and I found him standing outside the terminal. At least that would be good. I could count on her for that.

I slid into the back seat of the black Town Car while the driver talked about it being a nice day in the city, according to some weather forecast. Interrupting him, I said, "Take me to the Richmont hotel in Midtown."

As the car rolled toward its destination, I thought about trying to call Tressa again but decided against it. I'd called her three times before getting on the plane, but each time I'd gotten that damn away message of hers.

I couldn't help but wonder why she hadn't answered. When we saw each other the night before last, we hadn't even had sex. We spent the whole time talking, and I thought we had a good time. I thought I'd finally succeeding in showing her I wasn't just some attention whore athlete, and even more, I wasn't some asshole guy like the ones she'd dated before.

So why that goddamned away message again?

The car ride felt like it took forever, but we finally reached the Richmont and I jumped out of the backseat as I yelled back at the driver, "I'll be back in a few minutes!"

I saw the night security guard who let me up to the penthouse last time, so I flashed him a smile and made a beeline for him. A few well-placed words and if Tressa hadn't left for work yet, I'd be upstairs to see her in a matter of minutes.

"Hey, Charlie! Do they keep you here 'round the clock?" I asked with a laugh, only half kidding.

He responded to my lighthearted teasing with a stony look and gave me his prepared speech like last time. "I'm sorry, sir. I can't let you go up there."

Time for the charm offensive.

Pulling the slightly overweight man aside, I patted him on the back like we were long-time friends. "Charlie, I get that she has you telling everyone that, but she doesn't mean me. Trust me. I'm guessing it just slipped her mind."

The security guard looked around to make sure no one was nearby and then whispered, "She gave everyone orders to not let you or anyone up there, but I'm going to tell you the truth. Miss Stone isn't here. She had the car service take her away in the middle of the night around three a.m."

Three in the morning? Why would she leave at that time? Instantly, my mind went to another man.

"Where'd she go?" I whispered, sure he wasn't lying to me but also sure I had no idea why Tressa would go out in the middle of the night.

Unless it had to do with some guy.

"That I don't know. It was all very hush-hush. All I know is she isn't here anymore."

"Was she going to her office?" I asked, hoping that was the answer and not that Tressa was spending the night with some other man.

Charlie shook his head. "I don't think so. She had a bag like she takes when she's going on a trip."

A trip? Granted, we weren't at the point in our relationship that we told one another everything. I hadn't told her about my quick trip to the West coast, so maybe my gut feeling was misplaced. The problem was I couldn't shake the idea that something was wrong.

"Any idea when she's scheduled to come back?"

The security guard shook his head. "No idea. She just came down at right after eight o'clock last night and told us no one was to be allowed upstairs, including you, and then she came down again at three this morning with her bag. She got into a car waiting for her and left."

Quickly, I seized on that car as jealousy coursed through me. "Was it the usual car she uses from the car service or was it someone's car, like someone she was traveling with?"

Holding his hand up like he wanted to stop me from jumping to the wrong conclusion, Charlie smiled. "She got into a car service vehicle like she always takes. In fact, the only other car I've ever seen her get into is yours, Mr. Brenton."

"Okay. Thanks, Charlie."

As I turned to leave, he gave me a pat on the arm to console me. That was what my life had come to because of Tressa Stone. Now security guards pitied me.

By the time the car dropped me off at my apartment, I didn't know if I felt angry or disappointed. I still had no clue as to where she went, and even though I couldn't think of a single reason why she'd be avoiding me this time, I had a sneaking suspicion something had happened to change her mind about me.

Had she tried to contact me while I was in LA? I checked my phone and found no calls from her. Since all calls were directed to my cell, she wouldn't have gotten my away message. I wondered if she'd come over with the idea of surprising me. That didn't sound like Tressa at all, but a quick check with the security in the lobby of my building and I crossed that idea off the list of possible reasons she'd be upset with me.

After a quick shower, I called her office and her assistant gave me a very vague answer that she wasn't in today. If anyone knew where Tressa was, it was that woman, but her very businesslike way told me she wouldn't be offering any additional information on her boss's location. When I asked when she'd be back, the woman claimed she didn't know.

So much for that route. I ended the call and had to admit that I shouldn't have expected anything more from Tressa's assistant. She was as cold as her boss appeared to be.

No worries. I had another way I could get around the assistant's stonewalling. Why not go straight to the top and ask Tristan Stone where his daughter was?

The woman who had been all smiles the day I was there to see the man in person tersely told me to hold and then left me waiting for nearly five minutes. Finally, she came back and transferred the call to her boss.

"Killian, how are you doing? I saw on the news yesterday that you guys might be getting another wide receiver. That could make New York practically unstoppable, don't you think?" Tristan asked in the same jovial way as when I'd met him in his office.

That felt like a good start. I had no idea why everyone else at Stone Worldwide was so icy this morning, but at least Tristan seemed his usual self.

After discussing how a wide receiver would shore up the offense and make the team a powerhouse, I segued to the real reason I'd called him. "Sir, I called because I'm trying to find Tressa. We've been seeing each other, and I just want to make sure she's okay."

"You two have been dating?" Tristan asked, clearly surprised.

I hesitated for a moment to call what we'd been doing dating since I doubted it would technically be considered that, but then I answered, "Yes. We've seen each other a few times this week. When I returned from LA this morning, I found her gone and no one seems to want to tell me where. I've called her a few times, but it always goes to her away message."

"That sounds like Tressa is avoiding you, to be honest, Killian. Only you'd know why."

But I didn't.

"I honestly have no idea. We did have a misunderstanding after our first date, but we cleared that up a couple days ago. I don't know what could be wrong."

"Well, as much as I wish I could help you, I think my daughter is the one to deal with. I will tell you this. She's not in the country at the moment, but I expect her to return within the week. If I talk to her, I'll be sure to tell her you've been trying to contact her."

Disappointed, I thanked him for his help, but just before I ended the call, he said, "If it helps, Tressa isn't treating you any differently than anyone else, Killian. This is how she is when she's upset about something. She's been like this since she was a little girl. I don't know what could be the problem, but this isn't unusual for her. Give her time. I bet she comes around."

I thanked him again and tossed my phone onto the kitchen counter in frustration. Where the hell could Tressa be and why was she avoiding me this time?

Knowing that she routinely did this to others, even her family members, didn't make me feel any better. For fuck's sake, we'd had a good time the other night. What did I have to do to make this woman understand I wasn't just some dick like other men she'd known?

After becoming more and more frustrated by the whole damn situation and pacing for an hour, I made sure all my calls would go to the videophone and sat down to watch some TV. I didn't have to be at any meetings until afternoon, so hopefully, I could find something to take my mind of Tressa.

A few minutes later, I heard the familiar noise alerting me that I was getting a call. My stomach tightened and my heart skipped a beat as I hoped it would be Tressa, but it wasn't.

Disappointed, I sat back as Sherilyn showed up on the screen all smiles. "How was the premiere?"

I shrugged. I'd completely forgotten about the premiere until that moment. "Good, I guess. The movie was shit, but I pretended I liked it. I have a feeling Athena knows it's bad, though. No need to pile on when someone's down."

"You looked good, Killian. Black tie affairs always work for you. I have no doubt when you're done with football that modeling or even acting is in your future."

I stared at her utterly confused. "What do you mean? You weren't there, were you?"

"No," Sherilyn said, laughing as if anything I'd said was funny. "We have this thing called TV now. I saw you on the Premiere channel. I'm still amazed they have an entire channel dedicated to movie premieres and after parties. But then again, there are thirteen game show channels, three channels dedicated to dogs, and an entire channel for needlepoint, so why not? To think people used to think fishing shows were ridiculous."

"What the fuck are you talking about?" I asked as the idea of a channel for needlepoint ran through my head. Who the hell would watch that?

"The Premiere channel. Are you okay? That flying out and back in one day must be messing with you."

"What channel is this Premiere channel?"

"Thirty-one twelve. They're going to be replaying the whole One Lucky Day premiere and party around the clock, I'm sure. You can see. You looked great. Athena did too, but she always does."

I pressed the buttons on the remote to go to the channel, minimizing Sherilyn into the corner of the screen. Two women dressed in black gowns and talking about who attended some party appeared in front of me.

"How much of it do they show?"

"Everything. I can't believe you've never heard of this. It's been around for a few years now. I've seen you at a couple of them on that channel. They start with the stars walking down the red carpet, and then if you pay, you can see the film right when it premieres. Then they have a team of people who mill about at the after party interviewing the guests."

Just then, I saw the beginning of the One Lucky Day premiere show. I watched as the star of the movie and his girlfriend walked down the red carpet and posed for pictures. Then right behind them I saw Athena and me walk toward the press. At least now I knew why Tressa wasn't answering my calls.

Then I heard the commentator say, "It looks like Athena Rogers and Killian Brenton are as close as ever here tonight for this premiere. I have to say they always made a gorgeous couple."

Fuck. Tressa had seen this and jumped to the logical conclusion that I was even worse than just an attention whore athlete. Thanks to these assholes and their comments about Athena and me, she thought I was with another woman.

I began pacing again as the commentator continued talking about useless shit like who the designer of Athena's dress was and who designed my tux. Who the fuck cared about those kinds of things?

"Sherilyn, I need to find out where someone is. Any ideas on how to do that?"

"Uh, here or international?" she asked.

"Out of the country. I don't know where, though. Left in the past few hours."

Sherilyn nodded. "All pilots have to file flight plans. If you know where the flight left from, assuming the person is on a plane, that could be one way. Which airport?"

"I don't know. I need you check all of them. I'm guessing it's a Stone Worldwide private jet she took. I need you to find out where Tressa Stone went."

Sherilyn stared at me, clearly confused about all of this. "Why don't you just call her?"

"I tried. She's not answering my calls. I keep getting her away message."

"Maybe she's sleeping. Not everyone keeps the hours you do, Killian."

"I want you to find out where she went, Sherilyn."

Still confused, she shrugged. "Okay. Give me a little while. I'm not even sure flight plans are public. I'll do what I can."

"Good. Find out as soon as you can and get back to me."

I ended the call and sat back on the couch. Tressa saw me with Athena and jumped to the wrong conclusions. Of course she did. With the way Athena was hanging all over me, like she always did, most people likely thought we were back together even without that jackass reporter talking about it.

As I sat there waiting for Sherilyn to call back, my mind moved from how much I hated this fucking Premiere channel to how much I hated the fact that I had to keep chasing after Tressa. Every time I wanted to see her, I had to fight tooth and nail to get to her. She had to be blackmailed into going out on that damn date she paid ten grand for. Then I didn't even get a thank you for the flowers, and when I went to see her, I had to charm the damn security guard to get to the penthouse. And after all that, she still kept me standing out in the fucking hallway where I practically had to beg her to let me in.

Why did she have to be so damn difficult?

A few minutes of that shit and I had to reel myself in. The truth was I liked Tressa, and the work I had to do to be with her wasn't anything more than I'd ever done with anyone else. True, most women didn't make me work so hard to see them, but the drama and bullshit I had to deal with once we were together were just as difficult to deal with as the hassle Tressa put me through.

And when I finally did get to be with her, I had a good time, and not just with the sex. When she let down her guard, she was fun and even sweet. I liked that. I didn't understand her dislike of the public eye, but getting to be around her privately made up for that.

I'd never shied away from a challenge, and Tressa Stone was just that. I wasn't ready to give up on her quite yet.

Sherilyn called back a half hour later, and I knew instantly she hadn't been able to find out what I needed to know. "No luck. She didn't fly out of any airports in the area. Maybe she went on a cruise?"

"Doubtful. Okay, thanks."

The screen went dark again and I closed my eyes. Where could she be? I didn't have a clue, so I had no choice but to wait until she returned home. I just hated not being able to tell her that what she saw wasn't what she thought she saw.

CHAPTER FOURTEEN

TRESSA

THE CAR ROLLED DOWN MANHATTAN'S streets on the way to the Richmont hotel as I prayed to God Killian wouldn't be waiting there for me when I arrived. After such a successful trip to London, the last thing I wanted on my return home was to deal with him after what I saw on that ridiculous Premiere channel.

Pushing the memory of him and that blonde with the most perfect breasts I'd ever seen out of my mind, I focused on the London redesign. I'd expected to have to fight with the designer, but as soon as we sat down and I calmly explained in the nicest terms how I hated her American midcentury designs for the hotel, she thankfully agreed and we started fresh by discussing exactly how I wanted it to look.

If only every facet of my life could work so smoothly.

I took a deep breath in and closed my eyes as I let it out slowly. *Don't think about him. Don't. You made a mistake, but now you're going to fix it and be done with Killian Brenton.*

The car stopped and the driver said, "The Richmont,

miss. Would you like me to help you with your bag?"

Opening my eyes to thank him for the offer, I saw a nightmare awaiting me outside the car. Dozens of reporters milled about in front of the hotel. Damnit! Why were they here? Did that mean Killian was inside waiting for me? How could he know I was returning now?

I didn't answer the driver and opened the car door to see the press rushing toward me. I barely stepped onto the sidewalk before they swarmed, yelling out questions like a crazed mob, all of them about the same topic.

Killian Brenton.

"Tressa, are you and Killian dating?" one asked as I began to push through the crowd.

I kept my head down and my bag in front of me to carve a path through them. I wanted to answer their questions by announcing how much I wasn't dating goddamned Killian. I also wanted to tell each of them to go away and leave me the hell alone.

None of that came out of my mouth, though.

"Is it serious? How long have you been together?" another one yelled as I passed by him.

I cringed at the description of us as serious. Hadn't any of these vultures seen him with that blonde woman just a few nights ago?

Just then, one of them yelled out, "Killian was just with his ex Athena Rogers the other night at the premiere of her new movie. Did you know they're seeing one another again? How does that affect your relationship with him?"

My heart sank at each word. Was I considered the other woman he was cheating with, or was I the foolish girlfriend who didn't realize she was being cheated on? Both sounded horrible, and under my breath, I cursed the moment I laid eyes on Killian.

I finally reached the glass front doors and saw the portly security guard named Charlie waiting just inside. Opening them for me, he did his best to chase away the reporters, stopping them as they tried to get into the hotel lobby.

"Miss Stone, I'm so sorry you had to return home to this. I promise you not a single one of them will get into the hotel, though."

Spinning around to face him, I glared at him and didn't even try to hide how furious the scene outside had made me. "No one is to be allowed upstairs, and that means no one! And if a single one of those reporters or anyone else gets up to my penthouse, you'll be fired quicker than you can say your name! Got it?"

The man's round eyes opened wide and he nodded quickly. I turned on my heels and marched over to the elevator to take me to my home. I'd planned on relaxing tonight, but I had something else to attend to now, and I didn't want to wait until I cooled down.

As the elevator passed each floor, I grew angrier and angrier. Balling my free hand into a tight fist, I pressed my fingernails into my palm to keep my rage at a fever pitch. When the doors finally opened on the top floor, I stormed out toward the penthouse, throwing my bag onto the couch before I turned toward the screen on the wall next to me.

"Call Killian Brenton now!" I demanded and waited impatiently as the piece of electronics did its job.

A few moments later, he appeared on the screen looking as pleasant as always. But I wasn't in the mood for pleasant. In fact, I doubted I'd be anywhere near pleasant in the next week.

"Tressa, I'm so happy to see you."

I held up my hand and shook my head. "Don't speak. I'm not listening. I am, however, furious about the mob of reporters outside my hotel crowding me as I return home from a business trip and asking me questions about the two of us dating. You did this, didn't you? I couldn't have been clearer about how I felt about being in the limelight, and still you told one of them we were dating, which we aren't. Why? Why would you do that? What purpose did it serve?"

He flashed that sexy smile that I couldn't resist, which only frustrated me more. "I guess we haven't done much of what dating entails, but you wouldn't want reporters to be asking if we're fucking, would you?"

"I hate you. Do you know that?"

Killian shook his head and smiled even more broadly. "No, you don't."

"Despise you. That might be more appropriate. Loathe you. Yeah, that feels right. I loathe you for what you've done. Goodbye, Killian."

He leaned forward so his face was all I could see.

"Which thing do you loathe me for? I'd like to know just for future reference."

God, the way he looked at me with those green eyes. No. I shouldn't look at him. I needed to focus on my loathing of him.

"I just told you. There are reporters outside my damn hotel bothering me. I can't even leave, for God's sake! I'm trapped here, and it's all because of you telling them we're dating, which I feel the need to repeat, we are not. We. Are. Not."

"Oh, okay. I thought it might have been for that whole movie premiere thing, which you know would mean you don't hate me at all but like me an awful lot. At least that's what it would look like, you know, if you were loathing me for that. Which you aren't, I guess."

My cheeks began to heat up, and I turned away so he couldn't see my face. "I'm not having this conversation with you. I don't know what you're talking about, so you're making no sense. You better get whoever you told we were dating to retract that right now."

"So the loathing isn't about the movie premiere? Good, because that was just me doing a friend a favor."

I spun around to see him staring at me and grinning. God he was infuriating! "I don't care what or who you do, Killian Brenton. Actually I do care what you do. Tell whoever you have to that we aren't dating right now so I can leave my hotel room."

"I had a feeling you cared. You come off like some kind of ice queen, but I know what's smoldering underneath that cool façade, Tressa. I've seen the real you, so I knew you cared. But it wasn't anything to worry about. Athena isn't anyone to me anymore. We're just friends, and she asked me to attend her premiere with her. Nothing else to say."

What was wrong with this man? Hadn't he heard a word I'd said? And what kind of name was Athena? Did parents who named their children after Greek goddesses know ahead of time their daughters would look like that blonde Killian had hanging off him just a few nights ago?

God, my mind was racing! This man made me crazy. None of that mattered. All that mattered was Killian getting those damn reporters with their cameras out from in front of my hotel.

"You're not paying attention, Killian. I don't care who you do or what she looks like, goddess or gargoyle. I only care about the reporters outside my hotel waiting for me to comment on what you told them, so tell them the truth right now."

He leaned back away from the camera and folded his arms behind his head like this was a casual talk we were having. "I'll tell you what. How about I come over and tell them in person? That way no one can misquote me. What do you think of that?"

Hanging my head, I sighed as the frustration began to make my head pound. "That will only make them think we're together, which we aren't, Killian. There are a million other ways to let them know we aren't dating. Use one of those."

"I don't know if there are a million. Maybe a dozen. That might be an overestimation, actually."

Clearly, he wasn't taken this or me seriously, so there was no point in continuing this conversation. "Fine. Goodbye, Killian."

Before he could utter another idiotic syllable that would only make my head hurt more, I turned off the videophone and the screen went black. I stood there staring blankly into space as my frustration and misery overwhelmed me. Covering my face with my hands, I tried not to be upset with everything that had happened—seeing Killian with that women named after a Greek goddess, having to travel to London and back in three days, coming home to a swarm of reporters waiting for me, and finally dealing with the man who had been the cause of all my misfortune since the moment I saw him—but it was no use.

My life was a mess, and it was all his fault. I hated him. Loathed him. Yes, that was better. Loathing sounded more righteous, and if anyone had a reason to be righteous about Killian Brenton and the havoc he wreaked on people, it was me.

Since I was now trapped in my own home, I had to do something to relax before the stress of all of this made the top of my head blow off. Stomping into the bathroom, I ran a bath and poured nearly an entire bottle of bubble bath into the tub.

Just as I stripped down to my bra and panties, I remembered I hadn't put the away message on. Fuck. I didn't want to have to deal with Killian calling back, or even worse, my parents asking about my love life.

Which I didn't have with Killian Brenton anymore, as much as that made me even more miserable to think about.

So I marched out to the living room and fixed the only problem I could before stomping back to the bathroom and slamming the door behind me. I tossed my bra and panties aside and slid into the tub to cover myself with bubbles up to my chin, and when the water nearly came up over the sides of the tub, I stretched my foot out to turn off the water with my toes.

"God, give me the strength to get through this madness and come out the other side still standing strong," I mumbled as I sank under the water completely.

An hour later, I still loathed Killian, but at least my headache had subsided. Hoping to take my mind off him and everything about him, I sat down on my bed and closed my eyes to do that yoga thing Summer claimed helped relieve stress. It had never worked before for me, but I was desperate, so I slowly breathed in and held the air inside my lungs before letting it out slowly and counting to ten each time. I couldn't deny that it calmed me a little, but every thought that filled my empty mind was about Killian.

And people wondered why I rarely dated. This was why. Romance meant nothing but misery for me. Always had and always would. I just needed to accept that and acknowledge that I'd be alone for the rest of my life.

That idea made me wince, throwing off my breathing and making my stress come rushing back. I didn't enjoy living alone. That morning when I woke up and saw Killian there with me in bed hadn't been bad. It had been sort of nice, actually.

But maybe some people were meant to be alone. I freely admitted to being a difficult person to deal with. Perhaps that meant being alone.

I didn't want to think about any of this tonight.

A knock at my door tore me out of my thoughts. Hopefully, some food would make me feel better. It had taken the kitchen long enough, though. As I walked toward the door, I told myself not to bark at the person with my dinner. I wasn't angry with them, and the restaurant was busy at this time of night.

I opened the door and there standing in front of me wasn't a member of the hotel staff but Killian smiling at me.

"Oh, my God! I'm going to have to fire that security guard. Do you realize you just made that man unemployed?" I asked as I moved to shut the door in his face.

Killian stuck his foot into the space to stop me from closing the door. "I'm here to take you away from all the madness. And you can thank the security guard because he's making sure the reporters stay out front while we sneak out the back."

This man had lost his mind, and if I wasn't careful,

he'd make me lose mine too.

"I'm not going anywhere with you. Go away. You've lost your mind if you think I'm going to spend another minute with you. Goodbye."

He leaned in toward my face and said, "You keep saying that word, but I'm not hearing that you really want me to go."

The way he looked at me made it difficult to focus my justifiable anger at him, but I had to. Avoiding his gaze, I said, "I do really want you to go. Since I first laid eyes on you, you've been nothing but trouble. I don't need this in my life. I had a perfectly good life and now it's all upended because of you."

Killian propped himself against the door frame and smiled confidently. God, he was cocky. "You do need this in your life. Admit it. You and I have a good time together."

Now I had to look at him because he was clearly not understanding what I was saying. Maybe if he saw my true feelings in my eyes, he'd finally get it. "We do nothing but have sex, Killian. Do you think you're the only man on Earth who can give me that? Your ego needs a check."

Lifting his hand in front of my face, he lifted one finger and then two. "One, that's not true. We had a great time just hanging out and talking the last time we were together. And two, while there are other men with cocks on this planet, they aren't me and my cock."

"You're ridiculous. Stop talking about cocks. I'm

furious with you, so the last thing I want to think about is any of your body parts.”

“I had a fan tell me once that I had great calves. Maybe you want to think about them instead?” he asked, clearly making fun of me and how upset I was with him.

“Enough!” I yelled before walking back into my room. “I can’t do this with you anymore. You’re driving me crazy.”

Killian followed me and came up behind me to wrap his arms around my shoulders. Nuzzling my neck, he said, “I want to drive you away from this place. Come with me.”

He certainly didn’t lack focus or persistence.

“I can’t.”

“Yes, you can.”

I turned in his hold and looked up at him. As much as he made me crazy, I couldn’t deny that I liked having him around. And my body had already kicked into overdrive with just a single touch from him.

But I couldn’t forget why I’d been so happy to fly away the other night.

“I don’t want to feel things for you, Killian. Do you understand that?”

Hurt flashed in his eyes, and he shook his head. “No, I don’t. Why do you want to deny you like me as much as I like you?”

“Do you know what it felt like to sit here on my bed and watch you and that woman walk down that red carpet the other night? I know I had no right to be upset by that, but I was. I don't want to feel that way, and you made me feel that."

He stroked my cheek and leaned down to kiss me softly on the lips. "Athena is just a friend. Actually, she's not even that. We used to date but broke up a while ago. She needed someone to walk the red carpet with her at that stupid premiere. That's all it was. I flew out just in time to do that and flew back the same night on the red eye. What you saw on that stupid show was literally all we did together."

None of what he said sounded like a lie, but the problem was worse than him possibly not telling me the truth. Just feeling that way meant there was the real risk he could hurt me.

I hung my head as all the frustration of the past few hours ebbed out of me. Pulling me into his arms, he held me to him, and as much as I hated to admit it, I felt good for the first time in days.

Killian kissed the top of my head and whispered, "I'm sorry you had to see that and you thought I was just another asshole guy. I didn't know if we were at that place where we told one another things like when we're leaving town."

Looking up at him, I said, "We weren't, and that only made what I was feeling worse."

"Well, I'm sorry anyway. Let me make it up to you. Come with me tonight."

My defenses melted away as he stared down at me with those beautiful eyes and smiled like I was the most important person in the world to him. "Where are you taking me?"

"Anywhere. Everywhere. I've got a car, and we've got the open road."

"I have a job, Killian. Don't you have one too?"

"I do, but I can take a few days away with the only woman I want to spend time with. As for your job, you're an executive at your family's company, so I can't imagine you can't take a few days off too."

Nothing seemed to tamp down his enthusiasm for this plan of his to get away. "I don't have any makeup on and my hair's a mess."

He shook his head. "Doesn't matter and no it's not. Anything else?"

"It does matter to me. I have nothing packed."

Killian kissed me on the forehead. "Then you put on some makeup, and I'll pack you a bag. Don't be surprised if all I pack are socks, though."

I looked up at him and rolled my eyes. "You're insane."

"You have five minutes starting now."

When I didn't move, he leaned down to kiss me and whispered against my lips, "Four minutes and fifty three seconds."

This was crazy. I couldn't believe I was going to run off with Killian for a few days. I'd never done anything like this in my entire life, but something about how carefree he was made me want to do it.

And my gut wasn't telling me no. I just prayed it wasn't making a mistake this time.

Chapter Fifteen

Tressa

Just before midnight, we drove up a long driveway to an enormous old pale blue house on a secluded road in the Catskills. All the way there, we talked about what Killian had done in his career, and I found myself giggling at more of his silly jokes. I'd driven upstate countless times, and never before had I enjoyed it so much.

He parked the car and leaned forward to look out the windshield at the old house. "I hope it has running water."

"I wouldn't worry. You'd be surprised at what these older homes have going for them," I said, knowing from my childhood how houses like this held great possibilities.

Killian looked at me in surprise and then nodded. "That's right. You're an old fashioned girl. I forgot."

"I don't necessarily like houses like this more than my penthouse, but I grew up in one of these older homes. They have some really interested things to them."

"Since I grew up in an apartment above a grocery store in Nebraska, I wouldn't know about that kind of thing," he said with a wink.

"Well, look for cold spots in places and creaky floorboards that make sneaking up on people next to impossible."

"Aren't cold spots signs of paranormal activity or something like that?"

The serious look on his face told me he hadn't been joking. Rolling my eyes at the idea of supernatural cold spots, I laughed. "Not that I know of. Mostly it just means that the house is old and poorly insulated."

He shrugged at my purely logical answer and leaned over to kiss me. "Well, if we find one, I promise to keep you warm. Of course, it is May, so I don't think there will be a lot of cold spots tonight."

"I guess I'll be on my own to fend off any chills then," I teased.

Shaking his head, he kissed me quickly before turning to get out of the car. "No way. I'll be on the job keeping you warm. Don't you worry."

I moved to follow him and saw he had other ideas. Racing around the front of the car, he opened my door and bowed. "You have to give me a chance to be a gentleman," he said with that sexy smile of his.

He took my hand and helped me out as he explained whose house we were looking at. "It's one of my teammates'. He's one of those people who's all about old things. Houses. Cars. You name it. He bought it last year and offered it to me when I said I wanted to get away. He didn't say anything about what it looks like on the inside, so brace yourself. It could be rough."

I scanned the outside of the blue Colonial style home and had a feeling the inside would be beautiful. There was something about houses like this that held up against the test of time.

"You might be surprised. People pay good money for homes in this area. I'm guessing this has at least four bedrooms and at least a couple acres of land. But I'm a little surprised one of your teammates bought a house all the way out here. It's not exactly a place for a young guy."

Killian took me by the hand and walked toward the front door. "Darius mentioned something about liking how quiet it is here. From what I can see, there's nobody nearby, so it's probably deathly quiet most of the time."

As we walked into a dark entryway, I nudged him in the side. "I'm guessing you aren't a big fan of silence since you called it deathly quiet."

"Not in a pitch black house where I can't seem to find the damn light switch I'm not. Every horror movie I've ever seen has had this exact scene. If I can't turn on the light in about three seconds, we're out of here. We can stay at that motel we saw on the road on the way up."

I clung to his arm as the two of us walked in tandem toward the wall and Killian felt his way in search of the light switch. I hoped he found it before the time was up because by the looks of that motel, I had a feeling we'd be spending the night with a family of roaches sleeping on top of a bedspread that likely had stains from someone's murder still on it.

"Found it!" Killian yelled out just before a light above

us turned on and brightened up the beautiful foyer we stood in.

"Hey, this is nice. I like all the wood," he said as we swiveled our heads to look around at the home we'd walked into.

"Let's see the rest of the place. I bet it's beautiful."

We walked into a room to our right that looked like a sitting room or living room. Killian's friend hadn't furnished it with much other than a grey couch and a white wingback chair, so it looked pretty empty. The lack of even a rug highlighted great hardwood floors, though. Like in the foyer and hallway, woodworking all along the walls with wainscoting decorated the room, but in here, it had been painted white instead of remaining the original dark wood.

Killian looked around and said, "It feels like a farmhouse. Or what I think a farmhouse would feel like since I've never been in one. Let's find the kitchen and get a drink."

After walking through what seemed like a dining room that had nothing but a single old wooden chair placed in the corner, we reached a kitchen that instantly took my breath away. Unlike the other rooms we'd seen so far, this one had been completely modernized with stainless steel appliances, including a chef's stove, and a black granite countertop that made the white painted wood cabinets stand out stunningly.

I stopped just inside the doorway as Killian headed directly for the refrigerator. "Wow."

Peeking his head around the door, he smiled. "Now this is what I'm talking about. I can do old if a house has a kitchen like this. And even better, Darius made sure the fridge is stocked. Check it out!"

Killian hadn't exaggerated. Looking in, I saw enough food to feed an army. "Are we going to be joined by other people? That's a lot of food."

He turned around holding a bottle of red wine in his hand and flashed me a devilish smile. "No one but the two of us for as long as we want to stay. Time to find a corkscrew and get this getaway started."

"I thought it already started. You know, with the drive up?"

As he rummaged through drawers to find the corkscrew, he laughed. "No. That was getaway foreplay. This is the real thing. Where the hell does he keep the damn corkscrew? He has wine but nothing to open it."

I began opening cabinet doors to help in the search, but a minute later he announced he'd located the all-important corkscrew, lifting it high above his head as he said, "Found it! It was in a drawer with those holder things you use to hold ears of corn and are shaped like ears of corn."

Killian poured us both a glass of wine and as the first sip slowly eased its way down my throat, I felt my body warm. I didn't know Darius, but he knew good wine.

"So, tell me where did you fly out of when you went away?"

I hadn't expected that to come out of Killian's mouth

after he took his first drink of wine. What a strange question. "That's odd. I don't think I've ever been asked that."

Killian leaned against the countertop and took another sip of wine. "Well, I like to think I offer firsts in a number of areas."

"Teterboro. My company's private plane always takes off from there. Why?"

"Because my publicist couldn't find any flight plan for any plane from Stone Worldwide flying out of the New York area. Where's Teterboro?"

"I have to tell you that's got a very strong stalker vibe to it that right there. Why would she want to know that?"

He took a sip of wine and placed his glass on the countertop. "Because I wanted to know it and I asked her to find out."

This conversation was making me uneasy. "Why?"

"Because I wanted to know where you went so I could find you there."

"And do what exactly?" I asked, challenging him.

"Surprise you at your hotel. I'd think by now that you'd be almost expecting that from me."

"Yes, a whole week of knowing you and I'm already used to the unexpected from you," I said with a smile as I secretly thought to myself that it had crossed my mind that he'd try to visit me in London.

"Were you disappointed I didn't show up?" he asked in that cute way that told me he wanted to hear I missed him.

But I didn't want to give him that. Not yet.

"I was furious with you, so you should be happy you didn't show up."

He walked over to me and stopped to place his wine glass on the island in the center of the room where I'd been standing the whole time. Leaning down, he kissed me softly on the lips and smiled.

"Well, you know that you shouldn't have been furious with me, so are you disappointed now that I didn't show up in London?"

"I don't even know how to make heads or tails of that, Killian. I think you might be certifiably crazy."

He looked up like he was thinking about how crazy he actually might be and then looked down at me, shaking his head. "I'm not crazy. Well, maybe a little, but only about you."

When he said things like that, I couldn't deny that just being around him made me happy. Something about the way he didn't seem to need to ever hold back on what he felt or said made me want to be that free. I couldn't be, not yet at least, but I wanted to be.

Turning away, I took a drink of my wine and pretended to study the room around us. "I'm sticking with my original diagnosis. You're crazy. My own crazy stalker. I can't decide if that scares the hell out of me or makes me chuckle."

Gently, he took my chin between his thumb and forefinger and turned my head to face him. "You know, not that I'm a stalker, but you pretty much make it so hard for a man that he has to resort to basically stalking you just to get you to see him, Tressa."

"Maybe that's just my way to weed out men who aren't worthy."

Killian smiled and took the glass of wine out of my hand. "Good to know I pass the test."

"Don't you think you're jumping ahead of things?" I asked as he slid his arm around my waist and pulled me to him.

"No. I believe in thinking positively. I have no doubt I'm passing all your tests."

"Do you go into everything in life like that?" I asked, amazed at how confident the man always was. Did nothing ever make him doubt himself?

Nodding, he grinned, his eyes sparkling as he gazed down at me. "Yeah. There's no other way to be. If you have the goods, then all you need to do is use them to the best of your ability and you'll succeed every time."

"I can't decide if you're confident or cocky."

His hands slid down from my waist to cup my ass, pulling me toward his body so I felt his already hard cock press against me. "Cocky is thinking you're good when you're not but you can bullshit your way through it. Confident is knowing you're good because you are. I'm confident."

"Too confident, I think," I murmured against his ear as he dipped his head to nibble on my shoulder.

He looked up and faked a hurt expression. "How could you say that? Haven't I proven more than once that

I'm the best at what I do?"

"Are we talking about football or something else?" I asked, loving how he played along with my teasing. "Because if we're talking about something else, I'm not sure I'm ready to reward you with the title of best."

His hurt expression melted away, replaced by a sensual look that told me my time for teasing him had ended. "Then I'm just going to have to prove it to you tonight so you know who you're dealing with."

Scooping me up in his arms, he threw me over his shoulder and began walking through the house as I protested. "What are you doing? Where are you taking me, Killian?"

"Watch your head," he said, completely ignoring my questions, as he walked through the doorway to head for the stairs.

"Put me down! I can walk on my own," I said, lightly pounding my fists against his muscular back. I'd felt that back while he was on top of me more than once. My pummeling him likely didn't even register.

"I know you can walk on your own," he said before slapping my ass hard with the palm of his hand.

While I watched the downstairs disappear step by step, I couldn't believe he pulled this caveman act on me. If he was any other man, I would have screamed and pitched a fit until he put me down, but something in the way Killian did it so playfully made me not hate it.

Still, I couldn't let him think I liked his prehistorical man routine, so I continued to hit his back to get him to stop. "Are you even feeling any of these punches?"

He laughed before he turned at the top of the stairs to walk down the hall. "Not really. It's sort of like having one of those massager things working on my back. You can hit harder if you want. That might feel okay."

I pulled my arm back and hit him as hard as I could, but still I got no reaction. "Don't make fun of my boxing ability."

"You know I can practically hear you pouting," he said with a chuckle as he opened the door to a room at the end of the hallway. "Head down again."

I dropped my head against his lower back and waited for him to put me down now that we'd made it to a bedroom, but instead, he lifted me off his shoulder and threw me into the air toward the bed. I landed with a thud on the mattress, which thankfully wasn't hard as a rock or I'd be crippled.

Stunned, I looked up as he began lifting his black T-shirt over his head. "I can't believe you tossed me onto this bed like a basket of laundry!"

He poked his head out from underneath his shirt and smiled. "Like clean laundry. Nobody ever tosses dirty laundry onto a bed. That's something."

I opened my mouth to say it didn't matter, but nothing came out. The man had a way of making me speechless. Better for me to just watch him take his clothes off anyway. It was definitely a more enjoyable thing than verbally sparring with him.

Killian tossed his shirt at the foot of the bed and

unbuttoned his jeans before stopping to face me. "Am I the only one getting naked here?"

Shrugging, I leaned back on my elbows. "I was enjoying myself watching you. Feel free to continue."

Enjoying myself was truly an understatement. Killian's body was as close to perfection as I'd ever seen, much less experienced. All this time I'd had so little respect for athletes. Clearly, I'd never considered how incredible all that working out was for their bodies.

My eyes traveled over his broad, defined shoulders that flared into muscular biceps and thick forearms covered in tattoos of images and words I'd never really looked at before that moment. One on his right arm looked like something tribal, and another on his left forearm said something about success, but as I tried to read it, he unzipped his pants and my gaze focused on his washboard abs and his lack of underwear beneath his jeans.

"Do you always go commando?" I asked as he stepped out of them and tugged on my legs to drag me toward him.

He didn't answer my question, instead removing my shoes first. When he moved up to the white capris I'd chosen to wear with my favorite blue T-shirt, he ran his hands over my calves before answering, "No, but I had a plan for tonight, so underwear weren't really needed for this job. I gave them the night off."

As he pulled my capris down my legs, I helped him by wriggling out of them. "A plan? What plan?"

I had no doubt he'd had a plan. The man always seemed to have something planned for me.

Killian lifted his head to look up at me and smiled. His green eyes had a twinkle in them like that first night we got together, and I had a hunch I knew what this plan of his had entailed just by that look in his eyes.

"Well, I was either going to get you to come up here with me, or I was going to spend the night at your penthouse. Either way, I didn't need underwear."

He slid his hands up the outside of my legs and hooked his thumbs through my underwear, tickling me and making me giggle. "That seems pretty presumptuous since I'd told you not more than an hour earlier that I hated you."

In one swift movement, he yanked my panties off and tossed them over to where he'd deposited his shirt. "Loathed. I think it's important to get the sentiment correct."

"Loathed. I remember. Still seems pretty presumptuous."

Pushing my legs apart with his knee, he lowered himself down on top of me. Staring deep into my eyes, he said, "The word you're looking for is confident, remember?"

He thrust his hips forward slowly, and in seconds, his cock filled me completely. Whatever it was called, Killian was that and so much more.

Chapter Sixteen

Killian

T RESSA WRAPPED HER LEGS AROUND my waist and tilted her hips to take all of me on my second thrust into her tight cunt. She moaned sweetly in my ear as I began pumping into her, making my body crave her even more.

For hours, I'd wanted to be inside her. When we were together, I knew we could overcome all the differences she was so sure should keep us apart. All of that meant nothing as soon as she let herself enjoy what we had between us.

I loved fucking her. The icy, distant woman who insisted on being difficult with me melted at my touch, turning me on more than she could imagine. The change between that Tressa and this one who moaned my name and begged me to fuck her harder never ceased to amaze me. After that first time together, I wanted nothing more than to figure out how to get the ice queen who put me through my paces to be the woman who wanted me as much as I wanted her.

As I pushed my hips forward to fill her once more, I thought back to the morning after she bid on me and remembered my fantasy about her riding my cock. Sliding out of her, I rolled her over on top of me. She looked down at me and her mouth made that adorable pout I couldn't deny made me want her even more.

"Why did you do that?" she sulked.

With my hands on her hips, I positioned her over me. "I want you on top."

Tressa pulled her T-shirt off and then removed her bra, tossing them off to the side. Leaning down, she kissed me, sliding her tongue into my mouth before playfully sinking her teeth into my lip.

"So you want me on top? I like a change of pace," she purred in my ear.

My cock nudged up against her ass as my need to be inside her ratcheted up another notch and the thought of my fantasy of her actually coming true made me hard as a rock. She rolled her hips to take me inside her, and the next moment I was filling her completely.

Tressa sat up on me and began to ride my cock like her body was made for me. She looked like a goddess fucking me, her long dark hair teasing my chest just like I fantasized. I watched in awe as her inhibitions disappeared with each time she rocked her hips to take me deeper into her cunt. Her eyes closed, she rode me better than any other women ever had, and I loved it.

When I thought I couldn't handle any more, she looked down at me and smiled in the way only a woman who knew her own power could. Her dark eyes fixed on mine, and I reached up to cup her breasts. She moaned loudly and then leaned forward so I could take one deep pink nipple into my mouth.

I sank my teeth into her tender skin and felt her body contract around my cock as she began to come. She bucked against me with abandon as each wave of her orgasm rolled through her. I stuffed my hands in her hair and tugged hard to force her to still on my cock as my release ripped through me, flooding her pussy as I groaned with relief.

Fuck, this woman knew how to give a man what he needed.

Tressa collapsed on top of me and made a sound like a whimper next to my ear. "That was incredible, Killian."

I ran my fingertips over her back as she continued to recover from coming. "I want you to know that was even better than when I fantasized about it."

Lifting her head, she looked down at me. "What do you mean?"

"I fantasized about doing exactly that the night after the auction before I even formally met you. I told you. I couldn't stop thinking about you from the moment I laid eyes on you."

A slow smile lit up her face. "You're the first man to ever say anything like that to me."

Kissing her, I whispered against her lips, "Trust me. Other men have thought it too. They just didn't have the balls to tell you."

"I'm glad you did."

"That's what you get with a confident guy.

Confidence has its perks."

Closing her eyes, she nuzzled the space between my jaw and my neck and moaned, "Mmmm...I see that."

A few seconds later, she took a deep breath in and moaned again. "I need to know what cologne you wear. You smell delicious. It was one of the first things I noticed about you that night at the auction."

I shook my head and laughed. "I don't wear any cologne. That's all me."

Tressa sighed and kissed my neck. "Mmmm..."

As we lay there naked in one another's arms and me still inside her, it felt like Tressa had been a part of my life forever. I pushed her hair back and glanced down at her face. Her eyes closed, she looked so sweet.

"I wish I'd grabbed our glasses before you went all Cro-Magnon on me," she said with a smile. "I could really go for a drink of something right now."

"Me too," I said as I started to move out from underneath her.

But she stopped me, clinging to my neck and refusing to let me go. "Not yet. I can handle dehydration for a little while. Just stay here."

"Okay."

I wrapped my arms around her and heard her sigh next to me. I liked the fact that I could give her this momentary contentment I doubted she found much of in the rest of her life. Not that I was usually so interested in how anyone I slept with spent their time when I wasn't around. As I lay there while Tressa traced her fingernail over my collarbone, I couldn't remember anyone who'd made me care like she did.

In a quiet voice, she whispered next to my ear, "I think you've hypnotized me or something. I'm guessing it's your eyes. That's how you did it, isn't it?"

Sometimes she could be so cute.

Leaning back, I lifted her head so I could see her face. She looked up at me with a dreamy feel to her eyes like I hadn't seen before in her.

"Why do you think I hypnotized you?"

Tressa drew her eyebrows in toward her nose in an expression that seemed strangely unhappy considering the orgasm I'd given her and that she hadn't wanted me to leave the bed just a minute ago. Confused, I waited to hear her answer as a lick of worry flickered inside my brain over what she'd say.

"Because the Tressa I usually am would have never let you take me away. She would have never spoken to you again after the other night and that premiere. So I can only conclude you've somehow hypnotized me, and the only way I figure that could have happened is with your eyes. I thought they had a hypnotic quality to them when I first saw you up on that stage, so my guess is you did something that night and I've been under your spell ever since. I haven't been able to determine how you keep me under it when you aren't around, though, I have to admit."

I shook my head and tried not to laugh at how cute she sounded trying to understand why she was happy. "I don't think I have that power, honestly. I have a lot of skills, but hypnotism has never been one of them that I know of."

She ran her finger over my cheekbone and pointed at my eye. "Well, there's something going on because I don't run off with men or give them second chances. Ever."

"Don't think about it. Just enjoy it."

Rolling away from me, she turned her head so I couldn't see her face clearly. "I can't help it, Killian. That's what I do. I think. It's just who I am."

"Aren't you allowed to have fun? There's got to be room in your life for that."

I saw the corner of her mouth turn down, and she said, "I think I might be one of those people who can't have fun. Not the way others do."

"What do you mean?"

Instead of answering me, she slid out from under the sheets and walked out of the room, mumbling, "Nothing. I'll be back."

I lay there confused as to how that had all turned bad so quickly and wondering where the hell she planned to go without even a pair of underwear on her body. Looking around, I saw no way there could be a bathroom attached to this room. That must be where she went.

And then a few minutes turned into ten and then fifteen minutes. She had no clothes on. Where the hell had she gone to? And what was that noise that sounded like someone had turned on a waterfall outside in the middle of the night?

A quick walk down the hallway gave me my answers. The door to the bathroom stood open showing the light on, so I peeked in and saw her sitting in the tub, her arms hugging her knees as the water filled up around her.

"Just figured it was time to grab a bath?" I asked with a chuckle.

Tressa looked up at me and gave me a tiny smile. "I came in here to go to the bathroom and just felt like taking a bath. I never do, even though I have that gorgeous tub in my own bathroom. I'm always in such a hurry to get in and out of the shower every day."

Leaning up against the doorframe, I reminded her that wasn't always true. "Not with me. We stayed in there until our fingers got all waterlogged."

"Okay, not always. I just wanted to take a bath."

"Sounds good. Move up," I said as I stepped into the tub and sat down behind her.

The warm water sloshed up around us and over the side of the tub as I stretched my legs out in front of me. Tressa stared back at me in shock.

"What are you doing?"

Gently, I pulled her back so she reclined against my body and wrapped my arms around her. "Taking a bath. Didn't we just have this conversation? I'm beginning to think you have short-term memory loss, you know that?"

Turning her head, she stared up at me. "Do you do this with everyone?"

"Take baths? I can honestly say the answer to that is no. In fact, this might be the first bath I've taken since I was a teenager. I'm more of a shower guy."

"You know that's not what I meant."

I kissed the top of her head and quietly said, "No, I don't, Tressa. I've never chased anyone like I've had to chase you, but I'm not going to let you ruin a good thing because you want to run away."

She sagged against me and closed her eyes. "You'll get tired of chasing me."

Weaving our fingers together, I splashed water against our bodies and squeezed her in my arms. "Then don't run."

"It's who I am," she whispered, like it was a secret I didn't already know all too well.

"Then I'll keep chasing. Don't worry. I'm an athlete. I'm used to working day and night for the prize. A little chasing doesn't bother me at all."

We sat there silently as the bathwater lapped at our legs, hers long and white and mine longer and much tanner, and I knew we'd just told the truth about who we were together. She needed a man to show her he thought she was that prize, and I needed someone worth working for. We'd found what we needed in one another, and even though she wasn't sure about it yet, I was.

Tressa was the ultimate prize, and I had every intention of winning her.

CHAPTER SEVENTEEN

KILLIAN

AFTER TWO DAYS OF BLISSFUL time in the country where Tressa's phone only rang half a dozen times, I knew we had to return to the city and get back to real life. I didn't plan on letting it sidetrack us again, though. I'd had her for two whole days without too many interruptions and without a single reporter screwing up what I was trying to do, and I intended on keeping that progress going.

She'd still run and I'd still chase, but after our time at Darius's house, I believed her running away wouldn't happen as much. Or at least I hoped that would be the case once we returned to the city.

Tressa stood in the entryway looking up at the ceiling and then at the rooms on both sides of the hallway just before we left. With a smile, she said, "This house reminds me of the house I grew up in. I know it sounds strange, but I think I like something old like this more than my penthouse."

Looking at me, she shrugged. "Crazy, right?"

"Not at all. You're an old-fashioned girl. I knew that from the first time we talked."

An expression full of skepticism settled into her face. "I think you're already remembering our history incorrectly, Killian. The first time we talked didn't tell you I was old-fashioned. That phone call told you I was difficult."

I couldn't help but laugh at her insistence to be thought of as something most women would have hated. "Difficult. Old-fashioned. What's it matter? All I knew was you weren't like anyone I'd ever met before. Let's say you were unique."

She considered that description of her for a moment and nodded. "I can go with unique."

Leaning down, I kissed her just as her phone rang. "Do these people not understand I was going for a moment in time there?"

"They have no respect for romance," she said as she quickly opened her bag and rifled through it to find her phone. "This won't take more than a minute. I promise."

When she finally fished it out of her bag, she smiled. "It's just my father. Hang on."

Stepping a few feet away, she said, "Hi, Dad. What's up?"

I watched as her expression changed from happy to serious, and by the time the call had ended, I knew something was wrong. "Hey, everything okay?"

As she put her phone back in her bag, she forced a smile. "I'm sure it will be fine. Do you mind if we take a little detour to my parents' house? I promise it won't take long there. I just want to talk about a few things with my father, and I'd rather do it in person."

Why she thought I wouldn't want to see her father again escaped me. The man was a huge fan of my team. Why wouldn't I want to meet him again?

"Not a problem. You just tell me where and we're on our way."

LESS THAN AN HOUR LATER, we rolled up to a house that looked nothing like the one we'd just left. Darius had purchased an older home with some land. The place where Tressa grew up was an estate complete with security manning the main gate and a home that resembled a mansion.

"I think your description of the house you grew up in needs some work," I joked as the car came to a stop in front of the enormous home.

She looked out the window and then at me. "Your friend's house had a very similar feel to this one, but I get your point. They're both older homes, though, so I was right on that."

I moved to get out of the car, but Tressa clamped her hand down on my forearm, stopping me. Turning back, I saw pure worry in her dark eyes.

"What's wrong?"

She hesitated a few seconds before sighing. "My mother is going to ask you questions about our relationship. I feel like I should warn you. Sorry."

"Why? I'm sure she'll be great."

Tressa screwed her face into a grimace. "Well, it's just

the way she is. My mother's an artist, so she works a lot on the emotional level of things. Think of the exact opposite of me, pretty much."

I leveled a stare of disbelief at her. "You're not emotional? Since when?"

Rolling her eyes, she sighed. "My mother doesn't do icy. I get that from my father. My mother does chatty and feely. I thought you should be forewarned."

"So what do you want me to tell her? The truth or something nice?"

"What's the truth?" Tressa asked.

I smiled before kissing her and said, "That I'm crazy about you and might be a stalker, but that's not entirely my fault because you make it hard on a guy."

She laughed and shook her head. "And the something nice?"

"That I'm new to the city and you're the only woman who will talk to me and that's just because you paid ten grand for me."

A sound like a growl came out of her, and she said, "I don't like either of those choices. Maybe you should just leave the talking about us to me. I know my mother better. I can maneuver around any of her questions."

I shrugged and opened the car door. "For the record, I liked both of those answers, but since this is my first time meeting your mother, I'll let you take the lead this time. But eventually in the future at some point I'm going to let it slip that you played hard to get, but I did the work a man was supposed to in order to have a woman like you."

Looking back at her, I winked and added, "Or I might tell her that I have an addiction to women who are wild in bed and you fit the bill perfectly."

She blushed in that way that looked so cute, and I knew I'd calmed her worries for the moment. When she was like that, Tressa was downright sweet.

FIVE MINUTES AFTER WE WALKED in the door, Tressa and her father hurried off to his office to discuss work, leaving me alone with her mother. It didn't take me long to see Tressa hadn't been wrong about how her mother would want to know about our relationship.

Taking my arm, she guided me to the kitchen as she asked, "Would you like a drink? We have water and iced tea, and there might be soda in the refrigerator. I can look."

"Water or iced tea works, thanks."

She said nothing more and a minute later handed me a glass of iced tea. "It's sweetened."

I took a sip and smiled. "Thanks."

Somehow, the feeling between us had turned, even though she still wore a smile. I couldn't put my finger on why, but I had a sense Tressa's mother didn't like me. I hadn't said much at all since we got there, so I wondered if she'd heard something about my past. It wasn't like any of it was a secret, unfortunately.

"My daughter seems to like you, Killian."

I waited for her to continue, but Nina stopped

speaking and simply stared across the kitchen island at me. In her eyes, I saw a look very similar to Tressa's. She'd been wrong when she said they weren't much alike. I had a feeling behind the kind blue eyes and friendly smile was a sharp woman as bright as her husband and daughter.

So I decided to be straightforward with her as I had been with Tressa and Tristan.

"I hope so. I like her. A lot."

"I'm curious how you got her to warm up to you."

Nina had clearly decided to be frank with me too. Good. I liked people who didn't pull any punches.

"I'm not exactly her type?" I said with a chuckle before taking a sip of sweet tea.

Nina shook her head. Arching a single eyebrow, she said, "Not at all. My daughter is a very serious young woman, and from what I've observed, you're the exact opposite of her. She tends to date equally as serious young men."

From the small amount Tressa had told me about her past, I could only imagine the kind of men she usually spent her time with.

Feeling there was more Nina wanted to say, I offered her a chance. "Observed? I'm guessing you don't mean seeing us together for five minutes today."

"No, I don't mean that. When my husband told me you and Tressa had been dating, I checked out who you were. I'm not someone who follows football like Tristan, so I had no idea who Killian Brenton was. It didn't take long to find out, though. You're someone who photographers love. Picture after picture of you. I could still be looking at them right now there were so many."

I had a feeling charm wasn't going to work on Nina Stone, but I smiled and said what she hadn't. "And most of them with women, right?"

My question hung in the air between us for a long moment before she said, "My husband tells me that quarterbacks are very intelligent athletes. Is this true?"

"I like to think so. I can't speak for all quarterbacks, but I think I'm pretty intelligent."

"My daughter isn't like the women I saw on your arm in those pictures. Tressa is…"

Nina stopped for a moment as if she was trying to think of the right way to describe her daughter, but I knew exactly what she was saying. Smiling, I finished her sentence for her.

"Difficult. At least that's what she says she is. I think a better word for her is unique."

My description of Tressa made Nina's eyes open wide, but then she nodded. "I can't deny that, but I'd say she's challenging. I like that better than difficult. Challenging and unique are exactly what Tressa is."

I leaned forward toward where she stood on the other side of the kitchen island and said, "Well, if I'm being honest here, she puts me through my paces at every step of the way. I told her I'd probably wait to say this until some day in the future, but I might as well say it now because it's the truth. She requires a lot of work, but she's worth every bit of it."

A slow smile lit up Nina's expression. "I like that, and I hope you two do have a future together. I have to admit I never thought I'd see her of all my children so relaxed and happy."

Before I could say making her happy was my only goal, Tressa poked her head into the kitchen. With worry filling her eyes, she asked, "What are you guys doing in here?"

Nina gave me a knowing look before turning to face her daughter. "Killian was telling me about how quarterbacks are intelligent and hard-working."

Tressa stared at her for a moment before turning to look at me as if to get confirmation that was actually what we had been discussing. I nodded and shrugged my shoulders. "Intelligent and hard-working. That's me."

"Well, Dad and I are finished with work, so we need to head back to the city now."

That less-than-subtle hint that she wanted to leave meant my time with Nina had ended, so I took a final sip of my iced tea and held my hand out to shake hers. "It was very nice to meet you."

Instead of shaking my hand, she wrapped her arms around my body and hugged me like we'd known each other for years. I saw Tressa's eyes open wide in surprise at her mother embracing me and smiled at her. I seemed to have won her over.

"It was great to meet you too," Nina said as she stepped back away from me. "I hope this won't be the last time we see each other."

As we all walked toward the front door and Tristan pulled Tressa aside to tell her something he'd just thought of about work, Nina said in a low voice only I could hear, "I can see why my husband and Tressa like you. Just remember that even though my daughter is clearly a fan of yours, she's not the same kind as her father."

Tressa kissed her mother goodbye while I wondered what she meant by that. That Tressa and Tristan weren't the same kind of fan or they weren't the same kind of person?

CHAPTER EIGHTEEN

TRESSA

BY THE TIME KILLIAN STEPPED foot on the field for his first season game as the New York quarterback, we were officially a couple for just over four months. In that time, I'd grown a little more comfortable with the press around him, and although I didn't know for sure, I had a feeling he'd done something to make sure they weren't in our faces twenty-four seven. Like he promised as we sat together in that bathtub at the house in the Catskills, he hadn't stopped chasing me.

Even though I'd tried to run away a few times.

The press tried to make us out to be some high powered super couple, but the truth was we were just Tressa and Killian. I worked my job, and he worked his. I didn't go to see him play, despite my father offering me prime seats in his box for each home game. I didn't feel like I belonged in that part of Killian's world because of how I felt about dealing with the press. I knew he would have loved to know I was there, but I wasn't ready for that just yet.

That didn't mean I didn't watch him play and love

every second of it, even though I had no idea about the rules of football or a clue about any of the other players around him on the field. It didn't matter. I was only watching him anyway.

He had a game in New Orleans on the first Sunday in December, and as I turned on the TV to watch, I thought about doing something I'd considered for the last game he had out of town. I'd been spending more time with Diana over the past few months, so I wondered if she'd want to watch with me.

I knocked on her door and waited for her to answer. When she opened it, she smiled and pulled me inside her room.

"Look who's here!"

I saw Ethan stand up from the couch, and I looked around for any sign of Summer. She hadn't mentioned spending time with Diana this weekend when we talked the other day.

"Am I interrupting? I can come back later," I quickly offered, knowing how close my brother and sister were and not wanting to intrude on their time together.

Ethan waved me toward him and sat down on the couch. "I thought you'd be in the Big Easy this weekend. Isn't that where Killian is today?"

"I don't travel to the cities where he plays. I don't even go to the games here in New York," I sheepishly admitted as I made my way to where he sat.

"Why?" he asked with confusion in his voice that matched his expression. "Isn't that a perk girlfriends of major sports stars get?"

"Maybe. I don't know. I spend very little time in that part of Killian's world. You know how I am about publicity."

Diana hugged me from behind and then joined Ethan on the couch. "We were just hanging out. Come sit with us!"

"Oh. I don't want to intrude. I just wanted to come down and ask you if you wanted to watch the game with me upstairs. It's okay, though. You guys had plans, so it's okay."

Once the words left my mouth, I felt awkward standing in that hotel room. I didn't want to feel that way around my siblings, but it had been a long time since the three of us did anything together, and now that I'd said that, I felt like it might have been a mistake.

Diana and Ethan exchanged glances, and then she turned to face me. "We'd love to! Want me to bring anything?"

Her answer made me genuinely happy. Even though I knew she was only doing it because she had Ethan to come too, it felt like the old days when we all did things together.

"No, I've got stuff to drink, and we can order from the kitchen if we get hungry," I said as my excitement grew for our afternoon watching Killian play.

Ethan stood from the couch and laughed. "I don't know if lobster with clarified butter is really game day food. Why don't we order a couple pizzas?"

As they say, when in Rome, do as the Romans do. I had no idea what to eat as we watched the football game, so I agreed with him since he seemed to know better than I did.

"Okay. We can order pizzas and anything else you guys want."

"Great! Let's go so we can be at your place by kickoff," Diana said, happier than I expected at my offer.

HALFTIME CAME, AS DID THE pizza, and even though I'd had a good time with Ethan and Diana, it was patently obvious I didn't know a thing about the sport Killian played. When my brother mentioned how mobile he was out of the pocket, I couldn't find any sign of anything that even looked like a pocket on his uniform. Diana commented about something involving a screen, but I didn't know what that meant either. At least I was able to figure out what they were talking about when they kept saying he was dropping back.

Ethan tossed a piece of crust into the box on the coffee table and sat back in his chair. "This is nice. I can't remember the last time the three of us sat around and shared some pizza."

"It was that night Mom and Dad went with Aunt Jordan and Uncle Gage to that wine tasting. Remember? We ordered pizza and breadsticks and more soda than the three of us could consume in a year," Diana said as she grabbed her second slice.

I thought back to that night and remembered it

slightly differently. My brother snuck his girlfriend into his bedroom, and when I saw the lights from the car coming up the drive way, he had to practically push her out the window while Diana and I distracted our parents by bombarding them with questions just as they walked through the door.

"What's that face for?" Ethan asked, tearing me from my memories.

"I was just wondering if Mom and Dad ever knew you'd brought your girlfriend over that night. Do you remember how she had to climb out your bedroom window?"

A sly smile spread across his face, and he threw his head back in peals of laughter. "I can't believe you remember that! Damn. We were right in the middle of having some fun when you yelled up about Mom and Dad pulling up the driveway. Poor Shelby. She twisted her ankle climbing down the lattice, and by the time I got down to her, she was in tears. I had to carry her all the way to the back of the estate before we snuck through the fence and she hobbled the four blocks to her house."

"And you had to run all the way back while we kept Mommy and Daddy at the front door talking about wine tasting and how Aunt Jordan and Uncle Gage were doing," Diana said with a giggle. "Daddy kept looking at Tressa and me like he suspected something, but he never asked. Thank God, because he would have seen in my eyes that I was lying."

"Then I would have had to give him my serious face

because he always trusted my serious face," I said. "You still owe us for that, Ethan."

He smiled and nodded. "I know. I owe you guys for a ton of stuff from back when I was a teenager. What can I say? I don't know what I would have done without you two."

For a moment, we all looked at one another like we used to when we were younger, and it felt good. We'd drifted apart in the past few years, but I could never forget that my brother and sister were my first best friends in the world.

And then Ethan, in his usual funny way, looked over at me and said, "Are you ready to start asking questions? Because it's pretty damn obvious you had no idea what was going on in the entire first half of this game."

Leave it to my brother to point out how painfully lacking I was with the one thing Killian excelled at. I lowered my head and quietly admitted the truth.

"I honestly have no idea. Like where is this pocket in his uniform you guys keep talking about? And why can't I see the screen you keep mentioning when he passes the ball?"

My questions were met with silence for a few moments before the two of them burst into laughter. Diana leaned over on the couch and hugged me in my embarrassment.

"Don't feel bad, Tressa. Ethan knows all about football because he played it, and I know a little from those Sundays when I went to the games with Dad. But don't worry. We can help. We have a whole second half for you to ask whatever you want."

I looked up to see both Ethan and Diana eager to help me understand the game. That's what they'd always been deep down, no matter how strained things got among us. They were my brother and sister, and for good and for bad, we were family.

✧   ✧   ✧

THE TOUCH OF SOMEONE'S HAND on my shoulder startled me, and I sat bolt upright in bed to see Killian next to me wearing a big smile and nothing else. While my heart returned to its normal beat, I wiped the sleep from my eyes.

"Sorry. I didn't mean to wake you up. I just got back and came directly here. I figured I'd surprise you in the morning."

"It's okay. How did it all go?" I asked, knowing even in my groggy state that the team had won against New Orleans hours before.

"Twenty-eight, twenty. I had an interception, but other than that, pretty good. We're eight and two and now we're on a bye week, so I'm all yours until next Wednesday."

I stared at him, amazed at how cute he got whenever he talked about football. "I'm sorry I'm not more fun. You're on vacation, and I'm all knocked out."

Killian slid his arm around me, pulling me to him. "Shhh. Go back to sleep. We can talk more in the morning."

My nose pressed against the skin of his neck, and I inhaled, loving how he smelled so clean, like soap and water that had washed away the remnants of his day. Curling up next to him, I sighed, perfectly content to be there with him at that moment. If there was anything like bliss that existed in the world, I experienced it in his arms at times like this.

My eyes fluttered closed as Killian slowly ran his fingertip up and down my arm, lulling me back to sleep.

"BOYD, I'M ON VACATION THIS week, which you and I both know means I only want you to call me if it's an absolute emergency. The fact that there's a strike at a factory in the UK which is going to hold up the reupholstering of the lobby chairs at the London Richmont is not an emergency."

My assistant stared at me in shocked silence, which wasn't surprising since he'd never seen me take a vacation before this and he'd grown accustomed to problems always being emergencies. Both of those were my fault, but now I wanted things done differently.

"Tressa, I'm sorry. I thought you'd want to know about this right away," he said, his eyes wide with fear.

He had every reason to be afraid. The old Tressa all too often found a reason to bark at him for just about anything.

"It's okay. You don't have to apologize. The chairs in the lobby of the London Richmont will get reupholstered when they do. In the meantime, hold down the fort and only call me if there's something you can't handle that comes up. I have faith in you, Boyd. It will be fine."

I smiled because I knew he was as capable an assistant as anyone had ever had. He'd never let me down before, and I believed he'd do a great job this week while I stayed away from the office.

"Thank you, Tressa. I won't let you down."

"I know. I'm sorry I don't tell you that more often, but I've always known."

The fear in my assistant's eyes melted away at my kind words, and he visibly relaxed on the screen in front of me. "Have a wonderful vacation. I'll see you next week."

I ended the call and leaned back against the chair. From behind me, I felt Killian's hands slide over my shoulders, and I looked back at him.

"Did I wake you up with my call? I didn't mean to. It was just Boyd calling about some issue with the lobby chairs in the redesign in London."

"I heard," he said with a smile. Leaning down to kiss me, he added, "I also heard you tell him you're on vacation and not to bother you. Who are you and what have you done with my Tressa?"

"Funny. We've had this time off planned for months. The company can do without me for a week."

He walked into the kitchen and yelled back, "Again, who are you and what have you done with my Tressa? The woman I fell in love with was a hyper Type A who never took time off and worked day and night. Vacation was a four-letter word to that woman."

I sat there in my chair stunned at what he'd said. Love? Neither one of us had ever used that four-letter word before in all the time we'd been together.

Killian returned to the living room and sat down on the couch to drink his coffee as I wrestled with how I should respond. Was I supposed to tell him I loved him too? I did and had for months, but I'd never said the actual words to him. Should I just not say anything and act like I hadn't heard him say he loved me for the first time?

Lost in thought, I didn't notice he'd said something until he tapped me on the knee, tearing me from my mental tug-of-war about what to do. "What? I didn't hear you. What did you say?"

"I asked if you were okay. You looked a million miles away. Something wrong?"

Shaking my head, I tried to think of a good lie so he wouldn't know all I could think of was that he'd said he loved me, but my mind went blank.

He seemed satisfied with my non-answer answer and leaned back against the couch to close his eyes. If only I could relax after hearing those words.

I definitely loved Killian. I had for so long that I just took it for granted that he knew. I didn't know why we never said it before today. There had been hundreds of times in the past months when I could have said it. The man had pursued me when I fought him at every turn.

He made me smile when no one else could, mostly with his stupid jokes and refusal to let me wallow in worry or negativity.

"You're uncharacteristically silent today, Tressa. I'm not sure I like the vacation you. I'm used to the Tressa who talks more. What's going on?"

My brain short-circuited, and I blurted out, "You said you loved me. That you fell in love with me. You've never said that before this morning."

He smiled in that sexy way that never failed to make my stomach flip and shrugged. "I've found that coming at you from a place you aren't expecting usually works best. So I didn't tell you I loved you when I first wanted to. I just decided to work it into a conversation one day. Today happened to be that day."

"I really am that difficult, aren't I?" I asked, sad that the man I loved felt like he needed to sneak his declaration of love into a conversation so I didn't give him a hard time about it.

Killian shook his head and leaned over to kiss me sweetly on the lips. "Not difficult. Unique. You've just got some walls up around you, so I decided to tunnel in instead."

Looking into his green eyes that I'd once thought might have the ability to hypnotize me into caring about him more than I wanted to, I said the words I should have said months before. "I love you, Killian."

He shrugged, and with a smile, made a joke just when he knew I needed one. "I know."

"And you love me."

"Of course I do. I've been in love with you for months. If I didn't think you'd bolt, I would have told you when I first realized it."

I hung my head and quietly said, "I'm sorry for being so…unique."

Kneeling in front of me, he smiled up at me. "Don't be. You keep me on my toes, Tressa. There are men who wouldn't appreciate that, but they're not me. And we didn't have to say the actual words I love you to feel them."

I ran my hand through his soft brown hair, and he laid his head on my thigh as I admitted the truth of how I felt. "I've loved you since that night up in the Catskills, you know that?"

"You run, and I chase you. And even after I caught you, I still chased because you'll always want to run. That's okay, though, because I'll always chase."

That was who we were. I didn't know if it would work with any other man for me or any other woman for him, but it didn't matter. It worked for us.

CHAPTER NINETEEN

TRESSA

REACHING AROUND HIM, I ADJUSTED Killian's tie as I looked at the two of us in the mirror. Just like with his tux, he wore a suit better than any man I'd ever seen. "You clean up nicely," I joked as I finished fixing his tie.

"I do, don't I?" he said with a sexy grin as he leaned forward to admire his look.

"You're so cocky, Killian. You know that?"

He raised his eyebrows in fake surprise and laughed. "Confident. Cocky doesn't have the goods to deliver. I do."

I stepped in front of him and pushed him away from the mirror. "You've done enough fawning over yourself for one night. I need to check myself out to make sure I'm ready."

Rolling his eyes, he walked over to the bed and sat down on the edge as I examined my black dress for any imperfections. I loved Killian more than I could say, but I didn't love some of the things that came with being with a man like him.

Actually, I just disliked one thing. Attending events

with him where there was sure to be press in droves. He loved having his picture taken, as he always had. I still hated it, no matter how much I tried not to. I'd gotten a little better in the time we'd been together, and I didn't freeze in terror at the sight of a camera anymore, but given the choice, I'd avoid any event if I could.

From behind me, I heard him say, "You look incredible. You always do. I don't know why you worry about these things."

I ran my hand over my cheekbones wishing my makeup looked better. "I worry because I want to look good. You should care about that since every picture they take tonight will have me standing right next to you."

"You act as if that would ruin them, Tressa. You're gorgeous. You make me look better, if I'm being honest. You're the real draw anyway since there are a million pictures out there of me by now. Since this is only the fifth event we've done together, you're the one who's the new thing. I wouldn't be surprised if they asked for you and told me to step away."

Spinning around to face him, I shook my head as the mere idea of that happening filled me with terror. "Don't you dare leave me like that, Killian Brenton."

He stood and walked over to me. Taking me in his arms, he kissed me and whispered against my lips, "Uh-oh. She used my full name. This must be serious."

"Promise me you won't step away, even if someone stupidly thinks they should take a picture of me alone."

Killian's expression grew serious. "I won't step away,

Tressa. Not tonight. Not ever. I promise."

I breathed a sigh of relief and the fear subsided. "Okay. Good. Now let me make sure I look perfect since we have to leave soon."

Taking a lock of hair between his fingers, he lifted it away from my head as he walked away. "You're always perfect."

I leaned in toward the mirror and wished that was true. My makeup never lasted for more than a couple hours before it started to look stale. Whipping out the mascara wand from the tube, I gave my lashes a third coat and wished I had gone with the false eyelashes this time. Frustrated, I tossed the mascara into my makeup tray and sighed at the face staring back at me in the mirror.

Why did people need so many damn pictures anyway?

KILLIAN SQUEEZED MY HAND AS the car slowly stopped in front of the Manhattan Room. One glance out the window told me the press had come out in force for the NYCBest! launch party. Dozens of people rushed the car in the few seconds we sat there, and I swallowed hard as fear swirled inside me.

He smiled sweetly and kissed me on the forehead. "This is going to be great. You look beautiful. I've got you. Remember that. I'll have your hand the whole time, so it's just like we're going out for dinner or a few drinks, right?"

Taking a deep breath, I let it out slowly as I tried to calm my nerves and racing heart. "Right. Just like that."

"I love you, Tressa," he whispered as he pressed his forehead to mine. "Thank you for being here with me tonight."

All it took were those few words, and in a second, I relaxed and my anxiety about what awaited us outside that car melted away. I squeezed his hand in return and took another deep breath.

"I love you. Let's go do this magazine launch and show them why it was a good idea to choose you as their cover model."

Killian rolled his eyes. "You sound like Sherilyn now. She's been calling me that for months since she found out they planned to put my picture on the front of their magazine's first edition. I'm not a cover model. I play football."

"I think it would be a cover model and football player as of tonight. Don't downplay this. You love it, and you know it," I teased him, knowing everything I said was true.

He did love it, and even though I still wasn't someone who appreciated the limelight, he did so I supported him.

"Fine. I like it," he grudgingly admitted. "Now let's go out there and have a good time."

A second later, he opened the car door and all I saw were reporters and cameras. Killian held my hand securely in his and helped me out of the car, standing in front of me so I had a few moments to get my bearings. Men and women barked out questions before the car door even closed behind us, but I attempted to block out the noise and focused on keeping a smile on my face as the two of us began walking toward the front door of the club.

They asked the usual questions about how he felt the team was doing and if he thought they'd go all the way to the championship. Every so often, one asked about us and our relationship, but after six months together, very few reporters seemed to focus much on that anymore. I silently thanked God that they didn't because the last thing I wanted to do was be the center of attention at any event I attended with Killian.

He was the star quarterback, the one who enjoyed the spotlight. They should focus on him and his career. We were just two people dating who'd finally said I love you a few hours before. Nothing to see here. Go find some starlet with man troubles to bother about her relationship. We're just two happy people in love.

By the time we walked into the Manhattan Room, my hand hurt from holding onto Killian's so tightly. He didn't seem to mind, though, and when I pulled mine away to stretch out my fingers, he immediately sought it out, even as he made small talk with a man standing in front of us.

When the man turned around, I leaned in next to Killian and whispered, "My hand's cramping up. I guess I was pretty nervous out there. I figured you might like your hand back for a few minutes."

"You sure? I got you. Don't forget that."

"I'm okay," I said as I continued to stretch my fingers out. "Let's celebrate your big night."

We finally made our way into the club to see balloons and streamers in the magazine's blue and red signature colors hanging from the ceiling and tied to every chair in the room. As he said something to me about balloon overkill, Sherilyn hurried over to us and latched onto his arm.

"You have to come over and meet the people who started NYCBest!" she squealed in her usual excited way. "Have you seen the enormous life-sized picture of the cover on the wall over there? Just wait until you see it!"

I'd always found Killian's publicist a bit much for my tastes, but he'd explained even though she did tend to be a little over the top sometimes, she'd been with him since his college days supporting his career in any way she could. She rarely spoke to me, and when she did I had a feeling she had to force herself to, but since I'd had to see her only a handful of times since we started dating, I put up with her and always had a smile on my face when she was nearby.

Killian looked at me and smiled. "Life-sized picture of me. Are you ready for that?" he joked.

As if she just noticed me standing by his side, Sherilyn turned her head to face me and with a big, toothy grin I felt quite certain was forced and may be causing her pain, she said in a far less excited voice, "Oh, hi, Tressa. I didn't realize you were coming tonight. Killian's told me how much you hate these promotional things. I thought you might beg off since this one surely would have more cameras and press than others because NYCBest! is a media outlet."

I didn't need to have spent the last five years at my father's side learning the ins and outs of business to know that hadn't been an enthusiastic greeting. I felt Killian take my hand in his and give it a gentle squeeze, and the desire to explain to his publicist that I supported him no matter how many cameras and reporters were around faded away.

That didn't mean she'd get anything more than the icy Tressa that always existed inside me for just these occasions, though.

"It's so nice to see you, Sherilyn. Are you here with someone or alone?" I asked with my nicest smile in my sweetest voice.

Killian brought my hand to his lips and kissed my finger while I watched her eyes grow big at my comment. I took that as approval for how I'd acted and simply smiled when she said something about being there to work and not socialize before she made some excuse about needing to speak to someone and hurried away.

"Wouldn't all a PR person does be considered socializing?" I wondered aloud as we walked toward the life-sized picture of Killian and the inaugural cover of NYCBest! Magazine.

Pulling me close to him, he leaned down and whispered in my ear, "Most women would want me to say something to Sherilyn, but I like how you handle it all by yourself."

I saw in his green eyes that he had approved of the

way I dealt with her and stood on my toes to kiss him. "I don't need anyone to fight my battles for me, Killian. I don't understand why she doesn't like me, but as long as you like having her as your publicist, I'll have to be around her. She gets from me what she gives, so I promise if she ever becomes nice, I'll be as sweet as pie with her."

"No way. Only I got sweet as pie Tressa," he said in a hurt voice I knew wasn't genuine.

"Well, then she'll get cordial Tressa. How's that?"

"Perfect. Brace yourself. There are about to be two life-sized me's in front of you. Are you ready for that?"

I giggled at his joke and walked with him into the room to see the other version of him that graced the cover of the magazine. I stopped dead as it came into view, surprised to see Killian not in his uniform or in a tux or anything like that. The picture they'd chosen showed him in a pair of jeans slung low on his hips and barely hanging on and wearing nothing else.

Everywhere it seemed was his naked and tanned skin.

His muscular shoulders. His broad chest. His perfect washboard abs.

That spot just below his belly button where I dragged my nails across when I went down on him because it drove him crazy.

I knew it was silly, but seeing him so exposed like that to all those people milling around us felt embarrassing, like they shouldn't see him practically naked right there in life-sized form.

Opening my mouth to say something—anything

about how great it looked—I couldn't get a single word out. They were trapped somewhere between my brain and my mouth, spending time with a fair dose of shock at what I was looking at.

Sherilyn came bouncing toward us with a smile that spread from ear to ear and clamped her hand down on Killian's left arm. "Isn't it great? I know you weren't sure, but at least it's not nude like they first wanted. I personally don't see why you didn't want to do it nude since they were never going to just show all of you on the cover anyway. But this still looks incredible, doesn't it?"

Nude? He was supposed to do that photo shoot nude? He never mentioned that when he told me about it. Granted, that was only a few weeks after we began seeing one another, but I'd remember if he told me the magazine wanted to take a picture of him nude and put it on a cover where millions of people would see him.

I felt my fingers involuntarily squeeze his hand as the thought of Killian on that cover in front of so many people made my head swim. When he'd told me about it, I had in my mind him in his uniform or something classy like a suit or a tux. The man could wear anything and looked fantastic, so naturally I assumed he'd be wearing clothes. Or at least something other than the hint of a pair of jeans that looked like his hipbones were doing their very best to keep them hanging onto his body.

"Nude wasn't ever going to happen, Sherilyn. I told you that the day you pitched me the cover. A pair of jeans worked out fine anyway. The cover looks great."

As my brain grappled with my boyfriend, the man I loved and slept with, being out in the world with practically no clothes on, I had a sense that his statement about how great the cover looked was directed toward me. Looking up, I saw him staring down at me like he was waiting for me to finally say something about that cover.

Opening my mouth, I squeaked out, "It's nice. Very nice."

"Nice? I think you can come up with a better word than nice. It's spectacular!" Sherilyn gushed far too loudly for my comfort. "There's not going to be a woman in this country who doesn't love Killian Brenton after this magazine cover starts appearing everywhere."

I had a feeling my smile had faded and a look of disgust had settled into my face, so I forced the corners of my mouth up high and nodded. "Spectacular. Definitely spectacular. Will you two excuse me? I need to find the ladies' room."

Killian's hand clung to mine, but I tugged my fingers from his hold and hurriedly walked through the crowd hoping to find an exit that wouldn't be clogged with people waiting to take someone's picture. I needed some fresh air and peace and quiet for a few minutes while I convinced myself that the cover of a single magazine wasn't a big deal.

I found a door at the back of the club and pushed it open. Outside there was a small place to stand on top of a set of stairs, so I shut the door behind me and closed my eyes. This wasn't a big deal. I wasn't sure, but I had a feeling many people had seen Killian in various stages of being dressed.

Of course they had. The man had been photographed thousands of times. This wasn't any different.

But all I could see when I closed my eyes was that cover and all of him out there for the world to see.

"You don't own him, Tressa. He's a grown man with a great body. He can show it off to whoever he likes," I mumbled to myself.

But I didn't want him to be showing it off to anyone but me.

"Don't be ridiculous. Everyone knew how he looked before this cover. Not everyone has what you have with him."

I opened my eyes and hoped I wouldn't see anyone standing nearby who could hear me. I knew how stupid my reaction to this cover was. I didn't need some stranger knowing too.

Behind me, the door opened and Killian walked out to join me on that tiny landing. The look in his eyes told me he was worried, but that only made me feel worse. I didn't want to make this about me. This night was about him, not my stupid reaction to some picture because I was possessive and jealous.

"Why did you walk away like that?" he asked as he pulled me to him. "Everything okay?"

I wrapped my arms around him and leaned my head against his chest. "I just needed some fresh air. Nothing big."

"Something's wrong. Tell me."

"No nothing's wrong," I lied, praying to God he dropped this so we could go back into the party.

Killian tilted my head back so I had to look at him. "Tell me what's wrong and I'll make it right."

"You can't make it right because it's me. I'm wrong. Let's just go back in and have a good time. I'm sure people are noticing you're not in there. Sherilyn will be tracking you down any moment now."

He put his hand against the metal door to hold it shut and turned his focus back to me. "No she won't, and I don't care who notices I'm not in there. I'm out there where I need to be. So tell me what's wrong."

There was no way I could avoid telling him what the problem was, whether now or later, so I blurted out the truth. "I've come to realize I'm a possessive woman with a streak of jealousy a mile wide. That's what's wrong."

He smiled and nodded like he already knew what I thought I'd newly confessed. "I'm pretty impressed with how long you took to come to that conclusion. Most women realize that before we get to the second date. It's the cover, isn't it? You don't like it."

Avoiding his gaze, I nodded. "I hate it. The only thing that would make it worse is if you were naked, and I think I'd have to hire a crew to buy up all the copies of the magazine if that were the case."

Instead of being upset at my pettiness, he laughed. "It's an online magazine, Tressa."

"Then I'd have to hire someone who could disable their server."

"Look at me."

I did as he ordered and saw him smiling down at me. "This body is just the outside. It's the stuff that gets on magazine covers. You get to see it all the time, but you get all the inside stuff from me too, and no one gets that but you. That's the important part of me, isn't it?"

"Yes. I know that. I know you're only with me, Killian. I just never realized how the rest of the world looks at you."

"Pretty much like you did the night you first saw me at that auction."

I cringed at the memory of my staring up at him on that stage and thinking of how much I wanted him. "That doesn't help. Not one bit does that help."

Killian cradled my face in his strong hands and gazed down at me like he only did when it was the two of us alone. "I love you, Tressa. I haven't been able to think about anyone else since the night we met. Still to this day, you're all I think about when I'm not out on the field or practicing. I am completely and utterly yours in all the ways that count, and even in the ways that don't count, like how I look on that cover. You have every part of me all to yourself. You don't have to worry what the rest of the world thinks because the only person I care about is you."

I took a deep breath in and felt a sense of calm come over me. Everything he said was right. I'd been jealous and stupid about this cover, but even now he didn't make me feel foolish.

The rest of the world could have their pictures of Killian. I had what mattered.

CHAPTER TWENTY

KILLIAN

I HELD TRESSA'S HAND IN mine as we walked back into the party and began to mingle with the other guests. Her jealousy had surprised me at first, especially since she never showed me any hint that my popularity bothered her like that. As we chatted with some executive at NYCBest! Magazine, I wondered if that's why she hated coming with me anywhere the press was.

She didn't have to worry. Whatever I showed the world in pictures or interviews, no one ever saw the private me. Only Tressa got that.

Out of the corner of my eye, I saw Sherilyn practically running across the room toward us. She didn't have her usual smile on, and by the time she reached me, I wondered if she was in pain by the expression on her face.

Tugging me by the arm, she said, "We need to talk."

"About what?"

"There's an issue we need to handle."

"Whatever it is, I'll handle it tomorrow. Tonight, we're enjoying ourselves. Go get a drink and try to have a good time for once."

Sherilyn shook her head and tugged on my arm again. "No, we need to handle this now."

What the hell was she talking about? The fear written all over her face combined with the fact that my publicist would never consider me passing up a chance to be seen in public told me something serious had happened. But what could it be?

Relenting, I began guiding Tressa toward a quiet spot at the back of the club, but Sherilyn stopped me. "I think this is something we need to handle alone right now. Maybe you should send Tressa home."

Already tired of her cryptic bullshit, I stopped her right there. "No. Whatever's going on, she's part of it, so let's go."

My publicist didn't argue anymore and followed us to the corner where we could talk. I held Tressa's hand and quickly explained Sherilyn had something she needed to tell me.

"I promise this will only take a minute."

Tressa nodded and then Sherilyn pulled me down to her level to say in my ear, "A reporter just asked me for a comment about a story some gossip website released about an hour ago. Eden claims you two were together for a rendezvous the weekend of the LA game."

Eden? My ex-girlfriend Eden Mitchell? Why would she say that?

I waved away my publicist's concerns. "We haven't even spoken since we broke up last February. It's bullshit. Don't worry."

Sherilyn began searching on her phone and a few seconds later held it up for me to see. "She gave them pictures to prove it."

Staring at the screen, I saw some website named Dirt had posted about Eden's claim we were together again. Quickly, I scanned the article that mentioned my relationship with Tressa and said I'd cheated on her with Eden. Scrolling down the page, I saw the pictures they claimed prove we were together. Grainy and slightly out of focus, they showed a man and woman naked in bed together that I had to admit looked a lot like Eden and me.

But that was impossible. I hadn't been with her for nearly a year.

I pushed the phone away and shook my head. "It's a scam. I don't know why Eden would do this, but I'll find out tomorrow."

Sherilyn's gaze shifted from me to Tressa standing behind me. I turned to explain to her about how this wasn't anything important and things like this happened all the time to athletes like me and felt my heart skip a beat when I saw the look of horror on her face.

"It's nothing, Tressa. I'll get this cleared up tomorrow and it will disappear. I promise."

Shaking her head, she held up her phone and I saw she'd read the article already. She pointed at the screen and said, "She says you two were together the night before the LA game. That was in September, Killian."

My heart sank as I listened to her voice crack as she

said those words. She thought I'd cheated on her.

"She's lying. I don't know why, but she is. I'll find out tomorrow. Don't worry. Nothing happened."

Tressa turned the phone to face her and looked at the pictures, enlarging them on the screen. I watched in horror as it became obvious that was me in them with Eden. I didn't know when they were taken or how they'd gotten shots of such an intimate moment between us, but I couldn't deny the pictures were real.

"She says these are pictures taken that night. You cheated on me and had someone there taking shots of the whole thing?" Tressa asked as she continued to stare at those fucking pictures.

I turned to Sherilyn and grabbed her by the shoulders. "I want this handled, so get on it right now. Find out what the fuck is going on and why. I'm taking Tressa out of here, so call me when you have something useful to tell me. Until then, don't fucking call me. Got it?"

By the time I turned back, Tressa had disappeared into the crowd. I barked out a repeat of my instructions to Sherilyn and took off, pushing past people as I searched for her. After looking everywhere at the club, including that little porch thing we'd stood on outside, I rushed out to the street to look for any sight of her, but she was gone.

I knew where she'd run to, so I broke into a sprint down the street and headed to the penthouse. If I was lucky, I'd catch her before she told that damn security guard to keep me out. I didn't have the time or patience to schmooze with him tonight, so if she beat me back to the hotel, I'd just have to use brute force to get past him.

Thankfully, some problem with a hotel patron made slipping past security easy. By the time I reached the penthouse floor, my stomach had twisted itself into a tight knot. I had no idea why Eden was lying, but I saw in Tressa's eyes as she looked at those pictures nothing but pure sadness and pain. She'd always worried about being with me because of my fame, and now that very fear had come back to haunt us.

I opened the door and saw her standing by the window staring out at the city. I practically felt her running away even as she remained in the same room with me.

"Tressa, I want to talk about this."

As I made my way across the floor toward her, she shook her head. "I don't. There's nothing to talk about."

The flatness in her voice made me stop dead in the middle of the room. My chest tightened as the distance between us made me feel like I'd never be able to reach her again.

I couldn't let that happen. Every time she ran, I chased. I never minded doing that. Tressa was worth every step I took to have her, and this time wasn't any different.

"Tressa, this isn't a big deal. I know it seems like it is, but things like this happen all the time with athletes. I have to admit I didn't peg Eden for one of the crazy ones, but obviously I was wrong. I promise I'll get to the bottom of this tomorrow and we'll never have to think about this again. But tonight, I need you to talk to me."

I waited, but no words came. I took a step toward her and slid my arms around her waist as my fears rose inside me that she had already run too far for me to catch her.

"Please talk to me, Tressa. Please."

She shook her head but remained silent. In the window's reflection, I saw her fight back tears, so I hugged her to me, hoping to do something to make her understand I wasn't the man she thought I was.

"I would never cheat on you. Never. I've never cheated on anyone in my life, and I certainly wouldn't start with you. I love you, Tressa. You're everything to me. Please say you know I wouldn't do what that article claims I did."

In an icy voice, she answered, "I think it would be best if you got your things and left."

Turning her to face me, I shook my head in disbelief. We weren't over. I wouldn't let it happen. She fixed her eyes on my chest, refusing to look up at me, and I watched in sadness as she forced herself to not show any emotion at all.

"No, I'm not going. You run, and I chase. It doesn't matter how far you run. I'm going to be right there chasing you. I promised you I'd never stop, and I'm not. We're going to get past this, even if it means I have to chase you around the world."

For a moment, I saw the sadness return to her eyes before she closed them and in a small voice said, "I don't want you to chase me anymore. Whatever we were is over. I want you to leave."

Her words landed harder than any hit I'd ever taken from a defensive end hell bent on leveling me. I felt like I couldn't breathe, like someone had put a five hundred pound weight on my chest and was pushing down on it. I couldn't let this be the end. I had to change her mind.

Dropping to my knees, I looked up at her working so hard to keep the hurt she felt hidden. It tore my heart out that I had any part in it, and I needed to prove to her I'd fix this.

"Tressa, don't do this. I'll find out what this is all about tomorrow and then I'll make sure the truth gets out. I never cheated on you. I don't know what Eden's up to, but I swear to God I wasn't with her any time since we met. There hasn't been another woman since the night I laid eyes on you. Please believe me."

After what felt like an eternity staring up at her and waiting for any sign she'd heard what I said and was still willing to listen, she opened her eyes and looked down at me. The sadness and hurt was gone, and in their place I saw nothing in her deep brown eyes.

No caring about all we had together. No love for me. Nothing.

"What I believe has nothing to do with this. I want you to leave."

"Tressa, don't do this. I know you love me like I love you. Don't let something like this ruin what we have."

I needed her to talk to me. If I could get her to talk,

she'd see we could get past this. I'd be able to make her smile like I always did and we'd be okay. I just needed to get her to talk to me.

But she kept saying those horrible words. I want you to leave.

Standing up, I took her face in my hands and pleaded with her. "Tell me you believe me. Tell me you trust me."

"Whatever I felt is gone, Killian. It left when I saw those pictures. I want you to leave and never come back. Don't send me flowers or bribe the security guard to let you up here. Don't leak something to the press to prove how much you love me. Just leave me alone."

Her words made the weight that felt like it was on my chest disappear, and all of a sudden, my entire body felt like it had been hollowed out. The emptiness of not having her in my life anymore felt instantly unbearable.

"I didn't do this. Please believe me. I wouldn't do this to us. I love you, Tressa. You know that. You run. I chase. I told you I'd never stop chasing you. I won't let this happen. You love me. Don't do this."

For a second, it felt like time stopped as I waited to hear if my pleas had worked. She had to believe me. She ran, and I chased. That's who we were. I accepted it and loved being the man willing to do anything to show her how much she was loved. I never doubted her feelings for me, so how could she doubt mine for her?

She looked up at me with tears in her eyes and said in that emotionless voice that hurt like knives plunging into my heart, "We're finished. Go find another woman to charm, Killian. There are millions out there, so you won't be alone for long."

Then she turned to walk away, leaving me standing there watching as she cut me out of her life like some part she no longer wanted. I couldn't bear the thought of that, so I grabbed her by the arm to keep her there, to keep her talking so I still had the chance to get through to her.

"We can't be finished. What we feel for one another isn't some passing bullshit like others have that can be thrown away like this. We make each other happy, Tressa. I love you. Why won't you admit that and believe I'd never risk losing you. You run. I chase."

Suddenly, she spun around and pushed as hard as she could on my chest. It didn't move me an inch because she was so much smaller, but she kept trying over and over to push me away when I refused to let her.

"Stop saying that! Stop saying I run and you chase. How could you, Killian? How could you do this to us? Do you deny that's you in those pictures? I know every inch of your body as well as you do, and I know those are your legs wrapped up in hers. I know those are your hands holding her. Touching her skin. Pulling her to you like you do with me."

Tressa stopped and drew a sharp breath in as her angry words hung in the air between us. I couldn't deny any of her accusations, even though I hadn't been with Eden for nearly a year.

"I don't know where those pictures came from or how they made it look like I'm in them with her, but I swear to you on my life I didn't sleep with her. I wouldn't do that to you, Tressa."

"So you want me to believe one of your ex-girlfriends who lives in the very city where you traveled to at the exact time she claims you slept together is making all of this up? Why? What reason would she have to do that, Killian?"

"I don't know. Eden and I weren't serious like you and I are. We dated for a few months after friends set us up. I stopped seeing her long before you and I even met. I haven't talked to her since we ended it last February. I don't know why she'd lie like this, but I didn't do this. I swear."

As tears began to roll down her cheeks, Tressa pushed on my chest and sobbed, "You're full of I don't knows, aren't you? I trusted you, even though I broke every rule that kept me safe to believe we could work. I changed for you. I went to those events that terrify me more than you can ever understand because I wanted to be there for you, to make you happy. And the best you can give me after all we've been through is I don't know?"

I felt her slipping away right before my eyes. I grabbed her hands and held her there, knowing I could change this if I just kept her talking. She'd see that I couldn't do this to her. She'd smile at something I said, and I'd get that chance to convince her to let me prove to her this was all a horrible mistake.

"I know I love you more than anything else in this world. I know you love me. I know how much you hated those events and still did them because of how much you love me and how you held my hand so tightly that your fingers cramped because you were scared and needed to feel me there next to you. I know you're not the kind of woman who trusts easily, but you gave me that gift of your trust and I cherish it. I know those pictures hurt you, and I would do anything to erase that pain from your mind. But most of all I know you want to run now, baby, and I don't blame you. It's who you are, and I love you even for that. But you run, and I chase. I promised you I'd never stop, and I'm not going to."

She yanked her hands away from my hold and shook her head as tears flowed down her face. "Stop saying that! That meant the world to me, and you took it away. You ripped it away, and now you want me to keep believing in you. Stop!"

"Tressa, I didn't take it away. I love you and that means if you run, I chase. I never stopped. Right now, as you're running away even as we're standing not two feet away from one another, I'm chasing as hard as I can because that's what I do as the man who loves you."

"You chased someone else, Killian. You chased her all the way to her bed. I can't get over that. You need to go and don't come back."

Right there was the truth I couldn't stop her from believing. I hadn't been with Eden, but until I found out what was going on with her and those pictures, I'd never be able to convince Tressa that I hadn't betrayed her.

I felt the space between us grow by the second as I

stood there watching her cry because of me. My arms ached to hold her, to make her know that the man she loved would fix this and make things better.

But I couldn't reach her, even as she stood close enough for me to touch her. It felt like a unique kind of torture I could only feel with Tressa.

"I won't give up on us. Please don't give up either. I'm going to find out what's going on and who did this. I promise. I don't care how far you run, Tressa. I won't give up on us."

She didn't say a word as I walked away from her, my heart breaking with every step. But I'd be back.

Tressa ran, and I chased. And I had no intention of giving her up to her fears.

CHAPTER TWENTY-ONE

THE IMAGES IN THOSE PICTURES flashed over and over in my brain, each time hurting more than the last. All I wanted to do was forget. Forget what I saw in those pictures. Forget what happened. Forget Killian.

And I couldn't do any of that. I especially couldn't forget him.

I didn't know if I'd ever be able to do that. I'd let down all my defenses for Killian, and now I lay there bare and more vulnerable than I'd ever felt in my life. I didn't know if I should feel stupid or hurt or which was worse.

Stupid stung because I'd promised myself I'd never give so much of me that losing a man would devastate me. Now I was nothing less than that. Devastated and lost without him.

Hurt made me cry at how much I loved him and how hard it was to tell him to go away. My body ached from how much I hurt that I didn't know if I'd ever feel good again. As I lay there in bed hidden under the covers, I couldn't imagine how any good would sneak into me without Killian there by my side.

I lifted the pillow off my head and ran my hand over where he slept every time he stayed there with me all those months. Pulling his pillow to my face, I inhaled in the hope of still being able to smell him. The faint scent of the man I loved still lingered on the cotton pillowcase, and the memory of the last time I saw him lying there when I awoke came rushing back into my brain.

His eyes closed and his dark lashes resting on his cheeks, he'd held me as I fell asleep in his arms, my head on his chest and my ear pressed to the place above his heart so I could listen to its steady beat lulling me to sleep. I'd gotten used to feeling that stability and strength from him, and now that it was gone, I realized how much I needed it as every moment that passed by I felt like my world was crashing down around me and there was no one to protect me.

I didn't want to cry any more. I couldn't understand how I could still have tears left inside me after the hours I'd spent sobbing. But now as I thought about the first day of my life without him, all I wanted to do was cry. I missed him more than I could bear, and all that lay before me in the minutes and hours until I could cry myself to sleep tonight appeared empty without him by my side.

My phone rang for the third time that hour, but I didn't bother to see who it was. Boyd had everything under control at work, so whoever it was calling didn't need me. In truth, they didn't want me in the state I was in. Even if an emergency came up, my assistant could handle it better than I could right now.

I took another deep breath in and smiled even as my eyes filled with tears once more. Part of me loved that I could still smell Killian on my sheets. It made me feel like he was still in my life. But another part of me wanted nothing more than to bleach out the scent of him so I would never experience it and all the memories that came with it again.

Everything in the penthouse reminded me of him. The bed we shared. The couch where we spent hours lying in each other's arms watching films on release days instead of going out to see them. I knew he probably would have preferred going to the movies to see them sometimes, but he never once suggested it. The tub where he'd run me a bubble bath when he saw I'd had a hard day and slide in behind me to wrap his arms around my shoulders so I had someone to lean on when things got rough at work.

There wasn't an inch of my home that didn't remind me of how happy I was with Killian. Now all those parts of the penthouse haunted me with those memories.

As I lay there, I heard a knock at my door. I didn't want to see anyone feeling like I did. Pulling the pillow back over my head, I silently begged whoever it was to leave. Five minutes later, they still insisted on intruding on my misery, so I dragged myself from the bed and slowly made my way to the front door, even as they continued to bang on it.

Stopping to peer out the peephole, I closed my eyes and prayed, "Please, don't let it be him, God. Anyone else in the world but him. I can't do it. I can't see him and tell him to leave me alone again. I don't have the strength."

I opened my eyes and looked out. Standing there was Summer wearing an expression filled with worry. She'd seen the story of Killian and that woman on TV or in the news, no doubt.

Even though I didn't think I could do this, I knew she wouldn't give up. She'd stand out there knocking for hours, if she had to, so better to get it over with sooner than later and not have to listen to that damn knocking for any longer.

I slowly opened the door and looked out at her. "What's up? I'm sick. I think I caught a bug."

Not a single word of that sounded like it could convince a complete stranger, much less the one person outside my family and Killian who knew me best in the world. Summer shook her head and frowned, blowing up my lie without saying a thing.

"Well, come in because I know you want to anyway. Come in and see me at my worst," I said as I stepped back to let her walk past me.

Before I closed the door, I looked out in the hallway, half hoping Killian stood there waiting for me. I knew that was stupid and self-defeating after what had happened, but old habits died hard, and feelings took even longer to fade away. No matter how much I wished I could forget him, one day wasn't enough.

I didn't know if one lifetime would be enough.

"I came by to see if you needed anything," Summer

said in a soft voice like a social worker would use.

"Thanks, but I'm fine."

She held up a paper bag and pulled out a white container. "I brought ice cream. Whenever things go to hell with my romantic life, I find bingeing on ice cream makes me feel better."

"I'll get the spoons."

I returned to the living room to find her sitting on the couch with not one but two containers of ice cream waiting for us on the coffee table. Confused, I handed her a spoon and asked, "Why are you having any? Did something happen with my brother?"

Summer shook her head. "Friends don't let friends overeat ice cream because their love life has gone to shit alone."

I sat down beside her and tried to smile at her lame attempt at a joke. She and Killian were alike that way. Whenever I was down, they always tried to make me feel better.

"Thanks, Summer."

"It's what friends do, Tress. I was there the moment you met him. It's only right I'm here with the ice cream to drown your sorrows in now. I've got Death By Chocolate and Rockiest Road. You choose."

I reached for the quart of ice cream on the table directly in front of me and popped the top off. "Those two names alone tell me my life has gone to hell. Death By Chocolate it is."

Leaning forward, she took the other container and we

plunged our spoons into the delicious dessert. I hadn't eaten anything all day, so as soon as the sugary chocolate taste hit my tongue, my body perked up like someone had given me a shot of caffeine.

"Wow, this stuff is good, but I don't think it's just chocolate. What's in this?" I asked as I ate my second spoonful of ice cream.

"I think it has espresso in it too. Watch you don't eat too fast or you'll give yourself brain freeze."

Dipping my spoon into the container a third time, I dug out a huge mound of ice cream and stuffed it into my face. Seconds later, the brain freeze Summer warned me about hit, and I scrambled to push my tongue up against the roof of my mouth to end it. The trick I'd heard all my life didn't work, and I dropped the spoon onto the table to writhe in pain from the worst headache I'd had in years.

"Why'd you go so fast? I warned you. Brain freeze is a real thing."

I sat hunched over as my headache slowly subsided, leaving me less interested in bingeing on ice cream and as sad as before. Covering my face with my hands, I admitted the truth to Summer as I began to cry again.

"I really loved him," I said quietly.

She put her ice cream and spoon on the table and pulled me into an embrace as I began to sob. "Oh, I know, honey. And if it helps any, he obviously loved you too."

That didn't help because it only made me wonder

why he'd gone with her when he had me. As my body shook from crying, she held me close and let me get it all out.

"Why would he do this, Summer? I loved him. Did he need more? Was I not enough? Did he want someone who adored him like a fan? What did she give him that I didn't?"

Every question that popped into my mind made me feel worse. That last one really hurt. Was she more beautiful? Is that why he was willing to throw away all we had to be with her? Did she have something I didn't that made him happier?

"Don't think like that," Summer said as she rubbed my back. "I'm not even sure men can explain the stupid things they do. You did nothing wrong, Tressa. You loved him. This mistake is on Killian, not you."

I sat up and pushed my hair off my face. Sniffling, I shook my head and wiped the tears from my eyes. "I can't help think like that. He obviously found something in her that he didn't find in me. That's why men cheat. It's rather simple, actually. We just make it more because we want to make ourselves feel better."

"Did he say anything when you confronted him about it? Did he have any excuse? Not that there is an excuse, but did he have anything to say in his defense?"

"I didn't really confront him. I know that must sound surprising, but as soon as I saw the pictures, I ran out of the Manhattan Room where we were at for that party to celebrate the magazine cover he's on. He came here looking for me right after I got back, and he was full of loving words. He loves me. He would never hurt me. All of that. But he never admitted to cheating on me. He tried to get me to believe it was some mistake, but I know it's him in those pictures."

Summer frowned. "Why would that woman say it was him if it wasn't? She's his ex, right? Did they have a bad breakup or something and she's trying to punish him?"

I sighed as my brain tried to process all the questions we had. "I don't know. It makes no sense to me. He says they haven't seen each other since they broke up last February. It sounds strange to me that she'd wait nearly a year to do something to him to retaliate for their breakup. Revenge is a dish best served cold, but that's practically frozen. No, you and I know the truth is far more likely to be the easiest answer."

For a moment, I stopped talking because I didn't want to say the words. When I finally spoke them, they hurt just as much as I knew they would.

"He slept with her when the team had their game in LA in September. For over two months, he's been walking around here pretending to love me when he knew he'd cheated on me."

Then a more horrible thought rushed to the front of my brain. "Oh, my God! Has he been cheating on me all the time since September?"

I tried to remember where he said he was anytime we weren't together. He'd been out of town for games since then, but where? I couldn't remember the damn cities where the away games had been held.

Summer took my hands in hers and gave them a gentle squeeze. "Tressa, don't do this. Look at me. Don't do this to yourself. You'll drive yourself insane thinking about this. You know what you know and you did what you had to do. Don't spend any more time dwelling on what ifs. That's a road you don't want to travel down."

Hanging my head to avoid facing her, I said quietly, "I'm so embarrassed. I thought we were so happy together. How could I have been so stupid?"

"You weren't stupid, Tressa. You were in love."

"I was stupid in love, and now I feel stupid because I still love him."

"It's never stupid to love someone."

No matter how much I wanted to believe she was right, I hated how much regret had seeped into what I felt for Killian. I had been happy, truly happy, and now all that happiness was gone, replaced by sadness and regret.

THE SOUND OF MY FRONT door closing startled me, and I sat bolt upright in bed. Killian still had a key to my penthouse, and even though I hadn't heard from him in the past three days, I didn't put it past him to use it. But I couldn't handle seeing him so soon.

As I sat in bed, frozen in place, I heard a voice say, "Tressa? Are you here?"

A man's voice. It wasn't Killian. It was my father.

I hurriedly threw on a robe and pushed my hair off

my face. Rushing past a mirror as I walked out to meet him, I saw I looked like death warmed over.

"Dad?"

Walking into the living room, I saw him smile at me like he did every morning when I saw him at his office. Was there a problem at work? Was that why he was here to see me?

"I think I got a bug," I lied, hoping it worked on my father better than it had on Summer. I had to look worse than I had two days ago, so maybe he'd buy it.

He nodded and looked around before saying, "I came over to see your sister for lunch, so I thought I'd stop up here to see you."

"Don't worry about me, Dad. I had planned to take a few days off this week, so it's all taken care of at the office. Boyd knows to call me if anything happens that needs my attention. I'll be back in a few days as soon as I get over whatever this is."

My father took a step toward me and smiled. "I'm not here as the CEO of Stone Worldwide, Tressa. I know you have everything handled at work. You always do. I'm here as your father, honey."

Oh, God.

He could have said anything else and I would have been able to keep my emotions under control, but when he said that, I felt all that sadness and hurt I'd been working so hard to keep in check start to unravel inside me.

Covering my face, I sobbed, "Oh, Dad...This hurts

so bad. I loved him."

Strong arms enveloped me as I cried harder than I had since I watched Killian walk out my front door days before. I pressed my cheek against my father's chest, loving the familiar feeling of his dress shirt against my skin as he held me to him like when I was a little girl and he comforted me after I skinned my knee playing tag or fell down roller-skating in the driveway.

Above me, he whispered, "It's okay, honey. Let it all out."

"I loved him, Dad, and I thought he loved me. I thought he loved all the things no other man had ever loved."

There, standing with my father in my living room, I needed the first man who loved me in my life to reassure me I deserved love. For all his coolness, my father had been my knight in shining armor for twenty-seven years, and as he held me while I cried for all I'd lost, his strength helped me feel stronger.

"Of course he loved you, Tressa. I don't know why this happened, but I saw the way Killian acted. He loved you."

That answer only made me cry harder. "Then why did he do this to me? To us?"

Holding me close, my father whispered what I wished wasn't the only answer I had. "I don't know, honey. People make mistakes, and those mistakes can hurt a hell of a lot."

"This hurts so bad. I don't know what to do now," I

sobbed quietly against him. "What do I do?"

We stood there quietly for a long moment before my father answered, "You remember how strong you are. I know this hurts now, but you'll be okay. It just takes time. You've got all of us here for you if you want us to be."

"Is Mom coming up now too?"

He kissed the top of my head and chuckled. "No. You and I know how your mother is. I figured you didn't need all that just yet. She's at the house out in her studio. She has been since she heard about what happened. I suspect the art she's creating will have a heavy touch of anger to it."

Looking up at him, I smiled. My father knew me better than anyone else in the world, and he was right. As much as I loved my mother, she'd want to talk about things, to get them out of my system as she liked to say, but I wasn't like her or Ethan or even Diana.

I was like my father, and when we hurt, we didn't want to talk or lash out. We just wanted someone strong there to quietly remind us that no matter how bad things were, we were loved and we'd be okay.

"Thanks, Dad. Tell Mom I love her and I'll call her when I'm feeling a little better."

"Of course. Now what do you plan to do once you decide to leave the house?" he asked with a smile as he looked down at me and slid the pads of his thumbs over my cheeks to dry my tears.

I attempted to fix my hair after days of lying in bed,

pressing it to my head to smooth it out, but it was no use. Wallowing in heartbreak had a certain sad look to it, and I had it in full force. "I must look like a bus hit me. Well, no leaving today, but maybe tomorrow. Not that I'm looking forward to having to deal with the crowd of reporters I'm sure is camped outside."

My father nodded as he rolled his eyes. "They're still there. I suspect they're going to be there until they figure out you won't be giving a statement."

"You'd think they'd know that already. Anyway, I'll be back at work on Monday like I planned, so you don't have to worry."

"I never worry about work and you, honey. You're just like me in that respect. I hear the London redesign is shaping up to look pretty damn good. Maybe a trip to see how that's going might cheer you up?"

He gave me a sly look like he didn't want to come right out and suggest I leave town to lick my wounds, but beating around the bush wasn't necessary. I'd already thought about what I wanted to do.

"I was thinking maybe I'd move on to the next hotel I want redesigned. The Richmont in Barcelona needs a redo even more than the London location, so I thought I'd head there for a week or so. The designer and I have come to a meeting of the minds after that initial rocky start, so I'll see when she's available and move from there. If she's busy with another project, perhaps I'll still go to the Barcelona hotel and get a feel for what I want to do there."

In truth, I'd known what I wanted for that hotel for nearly a year, but I loved the idea of hiding away in Barcelona where nothing would remind me of Killian, unlike in this penthouse where everything felt like him.

"I like that idea a lot. I'm sure your mother will think it's a splendid plan. I'll probably have to hold her back from jumping on the plane and heading straight to Barcelona herself," he said with a smile.

"It's okay, Dad. Tell her to come visit me if she wants to. I can't hide away alone forever."

He opened his arms to hug me again. "I better go. I'll be sure to tell the rest of the family that you're going to be fine. I love you, honey."

"I love you, Dad. Thanks for coming over and saying all the right things."

After giving me a gentle squeeze, he stepped back and pushed my messy hair away from my face. "You're going to be okay, Tressa. I worry the least about you out of all three of my kids because you're like me. No matter how bad things get, we can handle it. You'll handle this. I know it."

"Thanks, Dad."

I just hoped that would be true this time. I'd made a career out of being able to handle things, but nothing the business world had ever thrown at me had hit me like this.

He turned to leave and then looked back at me. "You know you're always welcome to come back to the house if you don't want to stay here anymore. The carriage house could give you some privacy, and I'm sure if I spoke to your mother, she wouldn't visit too often."

With a wink, he chuckled and added, "Well, I can't promise that, but I can tell you from experience that having your mother around when you feel down is a good thing. She does most of the talking so you don't have to say much, and she has a way of making you see that even in the worst of times, you're not alone."

He didn't wait for me to respond and left me standing there knowing one sure thing. I had the best family in the world.

CHAPTER TWENTY-TWO

KILLIAN

THREE DAYS OF TRYING TO get Eden to talk to me had resulted in nothing but her away fucking message being practically tattooed on my damn brain I'd heard it so many times. I'd spent seventy-two hours watching my world spiral out of control like some kind of goddamned bystander unable to do anything as shit just got worse and worse.

Every minute of those three days I thought about Tressa and what she must have been going through. The gossip and sports channels couldn't talk about Eden's claims enough, running stories and commentary every hour like my personal life deserved the kind of coverage the news gave to real events like wars and elections. I just hoped Tressa didn't watch any of it.

Even the team had gotten in on the act. Not twelve hours after the story broke on that damn gossip site, my coach and owner called me in for a talk. Nothing like having to face people you respected after your bare ass had been displayed across the goddamned world.

And after all of that, Eden still avoided talking to me,

despite the fact that she had no problem lying to that reporter and handing over pictures of the two of us that I still couldn't figure out. I'd stared at the two of us in that dim light in those grainy pictures until my eyes hurt, and I had no clue how she'd gotten me into a picture supposedly taken in September when I hadn't even seen her since February.

I knew they'd been doctored some way, but the bigger problem was she and I never took pictures of us in bed. We'd dated for a few months, had some good times, and then parted ways because neither of us saw it going anywhere. Hell, we'd only slept together not even half a dozen times because our schedules never meshed. In truth, neither of us made much of an effort to get around our scheduling problems, so when I told her I wanted to end it, she didn't put up even the slightest fight. No tears or recriminations at all.

So why the fuck was she doing this to me now?

I paced back and forth through my apartment like a caged animal as the minutes ticked by. I needed to fix this fucking mess, but if I couldn't get Eden to talk to me, that was going to be difficult.

Frustrated, I called Sherilyn for the second time in two hours to see what she'd found out. Usually helpful, she seemed utterly lost with this problem, though.

Her smiling face popped up on the screen in front of me beaming her happiness that had to be for some other client. "Hi, Killian! I didn't expect you to call back so soon. What's up?"

"What's up? What the fuck do you think is up? The same thing that was up yesterday and the day before. The problem that's turned my goddamned life upside down."

That ridiculous smile of hers faded away, and she nodded like she finally understood how pissed I was. "I'm sorry. I was just trying to keep a positive outlook, Killian. I know this has been difficult, but Mike tells me the team isn't upset about the publicity, so you should be fine there. In the end, remember there's no such thing as bad publicity. You just do the honorable guy thing and don't lash out about what's happened and your stardom will only get bigger because of this."

"I don't care about my stardom. All I ever cared about was playing football, Sherilyn. I'll admit I liked being famous and having the press all over me twenty-four seven, but I'm thinking Tressa was right. That life is shit. Look what it's done to me and the woman I love, for Christ's sake. What have you found out about Eden and why the hell she's doing this?"

My head began to feel like it would split open from the stress I'd been dealing with since I first saw those pictures and found out what Eden was claiming. Closing my eyes, I took a deep breath in as Sherilyn yammered on about having a hard time finding her.

I opened my eyes in amazement. "What do you mean you're having a hard time finding her? I've never seen you have a hard time finding anyone. You're a fucking publicist. You've made it your life's work to know where famous people are at all times. Eden is a fucking actress.

Are you telling me it's hard to find an actress now?"

"Well, she's not at her house in Malibu. I checked there. She hasn't answered any of my calls, and her agent says she's indisposed for an indeterminate time."

"An indeterminate time?" I said, repeating Sherilyn's ridiculous words back at her. "She didn't get into a fucking spacecraft and fly to goddamned Mars. She's a famous actress, for God's sake. How hard can it be to find her? I want to talk to her today. Do you understand me? Today! She's not answering my calls, so you better find a way to get in touch with her or…"

I held back the threat to fire her that sat in my brain ready for me to act on. I hadn't appreciated how my publicist treated Tressa, but she'd been useful in other ways and Tressa had told me she could handle whatever Sherilyn threw at her. Now I regretted that. Her usefulness shouldn't have been more important than how she treated the woman I loved.

Love. I needed to make sure I kept that word in the present tense. Nothing had changed for me because of this fucking mess Eden had created, and when I fixed this all, I intended on marching back to Tressa to convince her we weren't over.

Sherilyn's eyes grew wide and full of fear at my unspoken threat to fire her. "Killian, I always do everything I can to help you and your career. You know that, don't you? I've been with you for longer than anyone else. I love you like you're a part of my family."

The sadness in her voice triggered something in me,

and my mind returned to how Tressa sounded that night. Waving away Sherilyn's concerns, I began pacing again.

"Just find Eden and figure out what's going on, okay? I'll be here."

"Okay, Killian. Please don't worry. Everything will work out. This won't hurt your career. I'll make sure of it."

The screen went black as her words rang in my ears. This won't hurt your career. The problem was I didn't give a fuck how this affected my career. My ability to throw a ball and lead my team to the championship affected my career. This affected the rest of my life, the important parts that made everything worth it.

This affected Tressa.

Two hours later, I still paced back and forth through my apartment and hadn't heard back from Sherilyn. A knock on my door broke me out of my thoughts about the mess my life had become, but I welcomed some reprieve from thinking of Tressa and how hurt she'd looked staring up at me like I'd betrayed everything we were.

I opened the door and stepped back in shock at who stood there in front of me. "I have to admit I didn't expect to see you on the other side of this door."

Tristan Stone slowly nodded as his steely gaze studied me. "I think we should talk. May I come in?"

Stepping back out of the way, he walked past me like he owned my apartment, not turning around to face me but looking around like he wanted to inspect where I lived. The man had a presence about him I had no choice but to respect.

He was also the father of the woman I loved and who at this very moment was heartbroken because of me.

"I'm not thinking this is you coming to see me because of how the New Orleans game went," I said as I walked around to stand in front of him.

"No, it isn't. I just went to see my daughter, and now I want to talk to you about what's going on," he said in a low voice that sounded more than a little ominous.

"Did she…" I began to say and then stopped. "How is she?"

Tristan arched a single eyebrow and leveled his gaze on me. "I think you know how she is. She's devastated."

Hanging my head, I wished I could be there to make her smile. "I'm sorry. I never wanted anything like this to happen."

"She loves you, and I believe you love her. Tressa is a private person, and seeing the man she loves in all his glory with another woman for all eyes to see isn't exactly something that makes her happy."

Looking up at him, I needed Tristan to know the truth. "I didn't cheat on her, Tristan. I wouldn't do that. I'm a lot of things, but I'm not a cheater. Tressa means the world to me. I hope you know that."

He frowned and then nodded again. "I do. For what it's worth, I don't see you as a cheater, so that leads me to believe you're being blackmailed. Is that correct?"

"No. That's the crazy thing. Eden didn't contact me about wanting anything in exchange for not releasing the pictures, which by the way are doctored. I don't know how, but I swear to you they are."

Tristan made a low, guttural noise and shook his head. "That doesn't make sense. If she doesn't want money, what does she want? Is she hoping to get you back with this ham-handed ploy?"

"I don't know. I can't even get her to answer my calls so I can ask why she told that website all those lies."

He narrowed his eyes like he didn't believe me, but then he said, "None of this makes any sense. You're telling me no one tried to blackmail you in regard to these pictures before they were released to the public?"

"No. I had someone threaten to go to the press about a month ago with an accusation that I had taken money in exchange for throwing a game in college, but that was total nonsense. I didn't pay them, and nothing ever came of it."

He perked up immediately and reached into his pocket for his phone. As he dialed a number, he said, "By mail, I'm guessing? If you have that letter or whatever they sent you, get it for me."

Then he said to the person on the phone, "Daryl, Tristan. I've got something for you. This is an ASAP situation, so it needs to happen now."

I didn't hear what this Daryl person said in response, but a few seconds later, Tristan stuffed his phone back into his suit jacket and smiled at me. "I've got my guy on this. Anything you can tell me, in addition to giving me what they sent you, can help."

A minute later, I handed him the letter I'd gotten trying to blackmail me. "I don't even bother the police with these things anymore. Nothing ever comes of them, so why would I? I didn't think this would have anything to do with Eden and those pictures, though."

"I don't know if it does, but my guy will find out. I've known him for years. He'll figure out what's going on with all of this. Eden Mitchell has a house in Malibu and one in Idaho, if I'm not mistaken. Have you tried both?"

Surprised to hear someone like Tristan Stone knew anything about my ex-girlfriend, I stammered out, "I only tried the Malibu house. She doesn't stay in the Idaho place after Labor Day."

"Didn't think I'd know about a world famous actress?" he asked with a chuckle.

I shook my head but said nothing, at a loss for words about much of what had happened since he got to my apartment.

"I had you checked out when you started dating my daughter, Killian. I'm a protective father, and just because you're the star quarterback for my team didn't mean I didn't want to know all about you. That's how I was pretty sure this whole thing with your ex wasn't what it seemed. I'll get this letter to Daryl and let you know what he finds out. In the meantime, take it easy. Things might not all be lost yet."

He didn't give me a chance to ask what he meant by

that before he turned and walked out of my apartment, leaving me standing there hoping this guy of his would clear everything up so I could prove to Tressa all of this had been a huge lie.

I SPENT THE NEXT THREE days holed up in my apartment looking at pictures of the two of us and hating every minute I couldn't be with her, couldn't hold her hand and promise her we could get past this. Had she already hardened her heart to the very idea of me so by the time I returned to her with the truth about what Eden had done it wouldn't matter?

Every few hours Sherilyn called to tell me she hadn't found anything out yet, and I listened long enough to be disappointed once more before I ended the call and went back to looking at Tressa and me in better times. These weren't pictures taken by the press since she always looked so stiff and uncomfortable in those that I couldn't help but smile. She'd been so nervous every time we attended those events, but still she was right there holding my hand tightly as the press took picture after picture.

No, the images I loved best of her were the ones I'd taken myself. Some were from quiet moments when we said nothing for long stretches of time and simply sat watching TV, the two of us cuddled together on the couch. I'd take my phone out and snap a picture before she could complain she didn't look good enough or I'd caught her frowning.

Others were of the two of us having fun outside at

Darius's house or relaxing at a secluded beach at one of her hotels or a hundred different times when her smile lit up her beautiful face because I cracked a stupid joke. In each of those, she was happy.

I swallowed hard as I stopped on one of just her out at her parents' estate. My mind flashed back to that day in August right before preseason games began. We walked around the grounds holding hands, and when we reached the fence at the edge of the property, she told me a story about how she'd snuck out to meet a boy from school one night. Tressa had always been the perfect daughter and the perfect student, but that one time she couldn't stop herself from breaking the rules.

She'd blushed in that way I loved as she told that story, so I quickly took out my phone and got a picture of her so adorably admitting to risking everything in her teenage life for some bad boy. I took her in my arms and kissed her after that, charmed by her honesty and vulnerability. She couldn't understand why I liked that story of her so much since in her mind it showed a weakness, but with me, she never had to worry about fearing being weak because I would be strong for her.

And now because of me, all her fears about our differences and how she didn't fit into my world had come true.

The familiar sound of a call coming in tore me from my thoughts, and I looked up to see Darius staring back at me. Our bye week had passed so quickly for me since I'd spent it doing nothing but wallowing in misery and trying unsuccessfully to fix things that I hadn't spoken to him since the shit had started raining down on me nearly a week ago. He looked fresh after the time off, and he'd even shaved.

"Killian, man, what's going on with you? I would have thought you'd call me this week. What's up with that whole story with you and that actress?" he asked in that gravelly voice of his, the only part of him that didn't sound refreshed after nearly seven days off.

"I haven't done much talking to anyone this week. Sorry. The issue with Eden Mitchell is still going on. She unloads her story and those pictures to that bullshit gossip site and since then no one's been able to find her. Nice, huh?"

"Yeah. That's what you get for dating actresses, man. They're the original drama queens," he said, his expression worried as he pushed his blond hair off his forehead.

"Well, if I can get her to admit the whole fucking thing was a lie, I don't plan on dating any actresses ever again. I just have to find her first. I've called dozens of times, but I can't get in touch with her."

"That's just shitty. You know what else is shitty? Looking online for a new jacket and two fucking links later I'm staring at your bare ass."

For a moment, he tried to fight back a smile, but it was no use. He threw his head back and let out a deep laugh I couldn't be angry with. And after days of being miserable, I laughed at this whole thing for the first time.

"Thanks, man. I needed that. Now if I could just get the truth out and get this mess over with, maybe I can get Tressa to take me back."

Darius smiled and nodded like he understood. Of all the people I knew, I had a feeling he did understand how I felt about Tressa. I didn't spend my time telling people how much I loved her because that wasn't what I did with my teammates, but Darius was smarter than most of the men I played with and read people better.

"You know what kills me? It's easily provable that you didn't go with her since the two of us spent the entire night before the game hanging out. Anyone who knows you can attest to the fact that you never break your routine the night before. The idea that you would go off and have some kind of rendezvous with anyone that night is ridiculous."

I sighed, letting the air out of my lungs as the frustration of the whole thing made me want to beat the fuck out of someone. "A picture speaks a thousand words. You know that as well as I do. Ironic, though, that a picture would be the thing that ruins my life. I've always loved getting my picture taken. It was Tressa who hated it. She couldn't understand why I enjoyed it so much. Guess the joke's on me, huh?"

"Well, once your career is over, you could have a second one as a male model. You know the ones who pose nude for art students. You look like you've got the moves down pat," Darius joked.

I laughed again and shook my head at the absurdity of

it all. "Fuck you, man. But thanks for calling. Hopefully when you see me next, this whole thing will be over and done with."

"I'm hoping it is. I'll see you Monday at the field. Call me if you need anything."

The screen turned to black, and I sat back against the couch unsure of what to do. I hoped Tristan's guy would have found Eden by now, but it looked like that hadn't happened, so that left me no better off than before.

Even though I knew I shouldn't do it, I found those fucking pictures Eden had given to that online rag and looked at them closely for the first time. I'd avoided them like the fucking plague all week, but Darius's joking about my future career made me want to see if I could recognize anything that would tell me when they were taken. The fact that Eden had secretly done that still surprised me. I'd been dead wrong about her, for sure.

I stared at the first picture up on the screen and had to squint to make out much of anything through the graininess. That was definitely me and Eden. Nearly six feet tall, her legs stretched even longer than mine on my six foot four frame. They wrapped around mine like two pythons. All that could be seen of me was the back of my head and body, but there was no denying it. It was me.

The picture had been taken in her bedroom at her Malibu home, but I knew that the first time I looked at it. Walking across the room to stand in front of the screen, I tried to make out anything that would indicate when the image had really been taken since September was a lie. I saw nothing except the enormous painting of herself she'd always kept on the wall above her bed. On each side of the image was the bedroom furniture she had the entire time we dated.

Fuck, this was frustrating! Like I wanted to be standing in my goddamned living room staring at a picture of me naked and fucking a woman I never loved and currently didn't even fucking like anymore.

Moving on to the next picture with me sitting up and Eden straddling me in her Malibu house bedroom, my eyes were immediately drawn to that gaudy painting behind us. More than once, I'd looked up at it while we were having sex and wondered why anyone would keep that nearby where they slept. The artist had been talented, but the thing was creepy, like one of those velvet Jesus paintings with eyes that seemed to follow you wherever you went in the room.

I pushed that out of my mind and focused on the two of us for a moment. Eden looked like she always did, at least from behind—long blond hair that curled slightly on the ends as it hit the middle of her back and a nice ass. None of that helped to prove the thing was doctored.

Little of me could be seen since she was perched on my lap with her legs on the outside of my hips and her torso covering up my head and face. In fact, all that could be seen of me were my legs outstretched in front of me and my hands holding her waist.

Squinting even harder, I leaned in toward the image so my nose nearly touched the screen. There had to be something to prove these goddamned pictures weren't taken in September and Eden was pulling some kind of scam. My eyes roved over every square inch of her body and then what I could see of mine.

And then I saw it. Or more truthfully, didn't see it. The tattoo I'd gotten on my right wrist in April after she and I ended things two months before. The one to commemorate being traded to New York. Those two black bands with arrows facing opposite directions were nowhere to be found.

I stepped back as the realization that I could prove these images weren't taken in September washed over me. Proof! But seconds later, the happiness morphed into resignation. I could prove I wasn't with Eden any time during that LA trip with a simple statement from Darius or any other member of the team who saw me at the hotel that night. It didn't matter. As I said to him, a picture was worth a thousand words. My proof didn't matter.

Unless Eden agreed to admit she lied, those pictures would remain the only truth anyone believed.

CHAPTER TWENTY-THREE

As I sat there staring at that picture, Tristan's face popped up in a box at the top of the screen. Compared to the expression he'd worn when he was standing in my apartment three days earlier, he looked excited, so I quickly exited out of the picture of Eden and me and stood up, hoping he had something good to tell me.

"Did you find out anything?" I blurted out, forgetting who I was talking to. "Sorry. Hi, Tristan."

"It's okay. I know you're on pins and needles waiting for news, and I've got some for you." Looking down at his watch, he smiled. "I think you'll want to check out channel eighteen forty. I'm told something interesting is going to appear right about now. I'll wait."

I grabbed the TV remote and punched in the channel number. Eighteen forty. I didn't know what that channel was dedicated to. Hopefully, it was the channel where ex-girlfriends told the truth to the world about how they were lying bitches. I didn't know if there was a huge calling for that kind of thing, but I could definitely get behind it.

Minimized to a square at the top right of my TV, Tristan said, "Watch. I think you're going to like what's coming up."

I waited as some commercial about male pattern balding extoled the virtues of some revolutionary cream that promised to change your life after only a month. Annoyed, I mumbled, "Who the fuck cares about bald guys? Get on with it."

"If you were this impatient on the field, you'd never connect with your receivers," Tristan said in a steady voice. "It's coming. Just wait for it."

If he wasn't the father of the woman I loved, I'd have a few choice words to say about how waiting to see some surprise he sprung on me a minute ago was nothing like my job as a quarterback. Since he was, I kept my mouth shut and hoped this commercial about bald fuckers ended before I exploded.

Then just as I didn't think I had a second's worth of patience left in my entire body, I saw what he'd called about. Eden sat with a dark-haired woman in her Idaho house I remembered her hating in the cold weather and quietly answered questions in what the reporter called an exclusive interview.

Leaning forward, the woman said in a somber voice, "Eden, you agreed to this interview because you wanted to get a few things straight about the article and pictures about you and Killian Brenton. What would you like to say?"

Eden grimaced and then took a deep breath before

letting it out slowly. Turning to look at the camera, she said the words I'd prayed to hear for nearly a week. "I want to say that what that article said was incorrect. Killian and I weren't together in September."

Her admission that she'd lied, as vague as it was, hit me like a truck. I stepped back as the reporter asked her why she said she had been with me long after we broke up and stopped as her answer stunned me.

"I was paid to say that. I realize that was a mistake to take the money now, though."

"Is there anything you'd like to say to Killian?" the dark-haired reporter asked quietly.

For a moment, Eden didn't move and I wondered if the picture had frozen. What could she possibly have to say to me? Sorry for ruining your life? I hope it wasn't too much of an inconvenience? Too bad you lost the most important thing in your world?

When she finally answered the question, her words did little to make up for the damage she'd done. "I'd like to tell him that I'm sorry I made such a terrible mistake. I was misled by a bad person."

Well, Eden never had been the courageous kind. I doubted she cared at all what her lies had done to me and Tressa.

The interview continued, but I had no interest in hearing any more of what she had to say. I turned it off and brought Tristan back to thank him since no doubt his guy had gotten her to admit her lies.

"I'm guessing that guy Daryl found her. How did he

get her to do that interview?"

Tristan smiled and shrugged. "Daryl is very persuasive. From what he told me, though, she wanted to tell the truth about everything once he explained how her lies had caused you and Tressa to break up. You have a bigger problem, though."

"Bigger than the fact that I lost the woman I love because my ex showed the world phony pictures of us having sex? I can't imagine things could get any worse, to be honest."

"Well, they are. Daryl found out who was behind the payment to Eden to get her to lie. You've got a traitor on your team, Killian."

A traitor on my team? No way. He had to be wrong. Every man who played on my team was one hundred percent behind me as much as I was for them.

"He's got to be wrong. From the coach and owner to the water boys, my team supports me. Tell him to look again."

Shaking his head, Tristan said, "I didn't mean the football team. I'm talking about the people you have around you. The person who paid Eden to lie was your publicist, Sherilyn. She's been paying her for over a year."

I stood there in shock. No way. Sherilyn had been with me longer than anyone else. I loved her like a sister, and she loved me like I was part of her family.

"I don't believe it. Why?"

"You'll have to ask her yourself to get those answers."

That's exactly what I'd do, but that conversation

would happen in person. "Thanks for everything, Tristan. Does Tressa know? Did you tell her? I can't wait to see her."

He shook his head slowly and frowned. "No, I didn't tell her, but don't bother looking for her at the penthouse. She flew out yesterday. Give her some time. I'm sure when she finds out the truth that you never cheated on her, she'll come around."

"That isn't how we work. I need to talk to her. Where is she?"

But he wouldn't tell me. He simply repeated his suggestion that she'd come around.

"If you talk to her, please tell her the truth so she knows."

He smiled and said goodbye, and as I stood there wishing I knew where Tressa had gone to, all I could think of was what I told her that night she ended it with me. You run, and I chase.

The problem was this time I didn't know where to find her.

AN HOUR LATER, I STORMED through the front door of Sherilyn's office to find her talking to another client, laughing it up like she hadn't just tried to ruin the best part of my life. I didn't recognize the man on the screen talking to her, but he was better off getting far away from her.

"She'll call you back. Or maybe she won't. I don't fucking care. Find a different publicist because this one's done."

Sherilyn's mouth dropped open, and she began to complain, but I stopped her cold. "I know what you fucking did. Eden did an interview about an hour ago and told the truth. You've been paying her for a year. What the fuck for? To ruin my life?"

She stared at me in shock, like anything I said hadn't been right. "Killian, don't be upset. Everyone benefited. She needed some exposure, and I knew the people she wanted to get in contact with. As soon as I found out Miami was going to trade you, I made sure you two got together. It made for good headlines, so by the time you got here to New York, you were the name on everyone's lips."

"As much as hearing you paid some woman to sleep with me makes me feel like shit, that doesn't explain why you paid her to lie that we were together this September. What did that do for my career or hers, for that matter? Who benefited there?"

Sherilyn came around her desk and stood in front of me to pat my chest, a move she'd done since the very first time she met me. Back then, it made me feel like someone important was looking out for me. Now it sickened me to have her touch any part of me, so I backed away.

"Answer me! Who benefited? Did you? Is that what this is?" I bellowed so loud she jumped.

Her expression hardened, and she suddenly changed in front of my eyes from a forty year old woman who'd helped me to some haggard thing who'd betrayed me.

"You were too involved with Tressa. Your brand is all about sex appeal, Killian. Everything you were was sex. There was no way you'd have any chance at a career in modeling or acting if your brand was tarnished like you seemed intent on doing. The tied-down lovesick guy isn't a huge seller. I was just looking out for your future."

As I watched her explain away the horrible things she'd done, I felt my rage ebb until all that was left inside me for Sherilyn was sadness. She never understood that as much as I loved being in the public eye, it was never about sex appeal or any of that bullshit. All I ever wanted to do was play football and have some kind of happiness off the field.

"You didn't care about my future. You cared about yours. We're done."

She shook her head frantically as she pointed at the pictures of me that covered her walls. "No, Killian, you don't understand. Look around you. You're my most important client. I would never hurt your career. You have to know that."

I looked around at all those pictures of me on and off the field, alone and with ex-girlfriends, and felt nothing for any of them. "You didn't hurt my career, Sherilyn. You hurt the woman I love. Your lies broke us up. Don't you see what that did to me? How can I ever trust you again?"

Hurrying around her desk, she grabbed her phone and held it up as she stared at me desperately. "I'll call her. Right now. I'll call her and tell her it was a publicity stunt. She'll forgive you. I can do it. I'm happy to, Killian. We can get past this and be a team again."

Sad and disgusted at how the person I trusted most for all those years had sold me out, I hung my head and said, "No, we can't. I don't know what's going to happen to you once the authorities find out your part in Eden's lies, but our time working together is done. Goodbye, Sherilyn."

As I turned to leave, she rushed over to grab my sleeve and began to cry. "No, Killian, we can fix this. No one wants you to be successful like me. You know that. Please, don't do this."

I'd heard enough of her plans for my future. Yanking my arm from her hold, I walked out of her office as she sobbed behind me about what she would do for my career.

She didn't get it. I had the career I'd always dreamed of. Now I wanted more, and I didn't care if that meant the world didn't think I was sexy ever again. All I cared about was getting Tressa back.

CHAPTER TWENTY-FOUR

NEARLY EIGHT AND A HALF hours on a plane left me feeling like maybe running off to Barcelona hadn't been my best idea. Actually, I hadn't run off. No running. I'd left on a working trip. That was my job.

You run. I chase.

Killian's words echoed in my head as I tossed my bag onto the couch just inside the door of my penthouse and headed toward the bedroom. I'd hoped to forget all about him, but I forgot how similar the penthouses were in all the Richmont chain hotels. The Barcelona one wasn't the mirror image of this one, but it was close enough that it made all kinds of memories of him come flooding back every day of the past two months.

When I learned the truth of what that Eden woman had done, I almost called him. I stood there in front of the screen and thought about it, but in the end, I walked away. Those pictures of him supposedly cheating on me weren't the entire reason why I broke things off with him. I'd never fit in with his world. I'd tried, and I'd failed. I liked keeping my private life private. I liked staying at home and curling up with the man I loved as we watched movies, just the two of us.

And I liked the idea of a life away from the limelight.

Killian loved being the focus of attention, and I didn't blame him for that. He had the looks and the talent and the personality, so why shouldn't he enjoy his time in the spotlight? I just couldn't be the person by his side in those bright lights.

So I never called. I hid out in Spain far longer than I'd planned, setting up a working office at the Richmont Barcelona and doing my job as I always had. That's who I was. That there probably weren't too many men who would ever appreciate that was something I'd have to learn to accept.

While I lay there on the bed we'd shared, I heard my phone ring out in the living room. Damnit. I hadn't taken it out of my bag when I got home. It might be Boyd, although I sincerely doubted he'd gotten up to call me at six in the morning on a Sunday. I was a slave driver, but even I gave my assistants a day off once a week.

Dragging myself up out of bed to answer the call, I saw it was my father. Instantly, fear rushed through me. He would never call this early in the morning unless something was wrong. A million horrible ideas raced through my brain. My mother had sounded off the last time I spoke to her. Summer had told me she and Ethan were traveling out to Montana to do a photo shoot with some guy and his horses. Had they been trampled? Was something wrong with Diana?

My heart slammed against my chest as my fear ratcheted up in just that brief moment, so I quickly answered and without even saying hello, I asked, "What's wrong, Dad?"

"Nothing. I knew you were getting in this morning and wanted to see how you were doing. Why do you think something's wrong?" he asked in that baffled voice I'd heard him use with my siblings so many times in our lives.

I took a deep breath and tried to calm my nerves. My father needed to learn that calling at six in the morning meant something bad to the majority of the world.

"I'm fine, Dad. Did you see the pictures I sent from the designer? What do you think? I love the Spanish touches she wants to incorporate in the Barcelona location."

"I did, but now's not the time for business. Rest up because I want you to come with me on a trip this afternoon. The plane will leave at two o'clock. I'll have a car come get you at one, so be ready."

My body sagged at the very thought of going on another plane so soon after my flight from Europe hours before. "Dad, can we do this tomorrow or Tuesday? I'm exhausted from my trip back from Barcelona. I just got in."

"No, I'm sorry, honey. It's got to be today. I'll see you at the plane at two," he said firmly.

With a sigh, I accepted my fate. "Okay, Dad. I'll see you then."

I dragged myself back to my bed and set my alarm for noon. My eyes closed a second later, and I fell asleep thankful I wouldn't have time to think about how much I missed having Killian beside me in our bed.

"YOU'RE ALMOST LATE. THIS ISN'T like you, Tressa. Two months in Europe have changed you," my father joked as I walked toward where he sat on the Stone Worldwide company plane.

"I overslept."

Practically throwing myself into the leather seat, I looked over at him and noticed he wasn't wearing a suit. My father always wore a suit for work. Always. As in every day he ever worked since I was born.

"Why are you dressed like we're going out for lunch? I thought this was a work trip."

He winked and gave me a sly smile. "I never said this was a work trip. Just a trip."

So he wanted to be cute. Okay. I liked seeing my father relaxed, so I'd play along. "I know it's not for my birthday because then Ethan and Diana would be coming with us on this little trip, so what's up?"

"You'll see. In the meantime, just sit back and take it easy. We'll be there in a couple hours."

"Be where in a couple hours, Dad? Is Mom coming or is she already where we're going?" I asked, utterly confused by his need to be so secretive.

He shook his head and grinned like a little boy. "No, your mother isn't coming and she isn't going to be with us on this trip. This is just you and me. Now, no more questions or you'll ruin this."

I was too exhausted even after nearly seven hours of sleep to verbally spar with him. Whatever he wanted to do on our father-daughter trip was fine with me. We didn't have enough of these together, just the two of us.

LOOKING OUT THE CAR WINDOW, I wondered why Tampa had bumper-to-bumper traffic on a Sunday afternoon in early February. My father and I hadn't talked much since landing and transferring to the limousine. He seemed deeply involved with some paperwork he'd brought along on our trip. Strange since he claimed this wasn't a work trip, but my father seemed to work constantly all my life, so maybe it wasn't odd.

"This town is as bad as New York in the middle of the week. What's going on here today?" I wondered aloud, hoping he'd take the bait and give me a clue as to what we were doing in Tampa, Florida, of all places.

He didn't look up from his papers but answered, "I used to be part owner of a club down here years ago around the time I met your mother."

"Is that where we're going?" I asked, seizing upon his willingness to talk suddenly.

Lifting his head, he smiled. "No. That wasn't a place to take your daughter."

And that was it. He said nothing more, and I didn't ask another question since I'd get nothing but riddles for answers. My father could be cute that way sometimes.

Still groggy after traveling from a different continent, sleeping far too little, and then sleeping two hours on the flight there, I leaned back and closed my eyes. I'd never liked riding backwards in limos, but my father had insisted I sit opposite him, so being a dutiful daughter, I did as he wanted.

The traffic thinned slightly, and then a few minutes later, the car stopped abruptly. I leaned over and looked out the windows, but the tinting made seeing much of anything difficult since the sun was already setting.

"I guess we're here?" I asked as a feeling of nervousness came over me suddenly. I didn't know why, but something felt off.

I pushed it out of my mind, though. Nothing could be wrong. I was traveling with my father.

He stuffed his papers into a briefcase on the seat next to him and nodded. "We're here. Ready?"

"Ready? I have no idea where I am or what we're doing. And by the way, I feel like I'm overdressed in this skirt and blouse since you're in jeans and a polo shirt, Dad. You want to tell me what's going on?"

The car door opened, flooding the inside with the last remnants of daylight and warmth from the weather outside. I watched as my father got out and then followed him. It only took a few seconds to understand what he'd done.

Instantly, my hands began to shake as nerves overtook my entire body. "Oh, Dad. No. This is a bad idea."

With that little boy grin of his, he shook his head.

"Nonsense. Are you ready for some football?"

I said nothing as every cell in my body screamed, "No!" I wasn't ready for what he'd done.

For two hours, I watched Killian and his team play, still not understanding much of what I was looking at. Yes, I knew what the pocket was, thanks to my brother and sister, but I spent most of the game watching Killian wherever he went on the field, when he moved to the sidelines, and when he ran into the tunnel for halftime. He looked like he always had. So full of life. When they were doing well, he smiled and seemed to command the entire field as if it were his own. When Pittsburgh came back to tie the score in the fourth quarter, his mannerisms changed and he grew serious, like a warrior bent on winning the battle.

And then just as time began to run out, he threw a touchdown to Darius to win the game. The stadium went wild with people cheering, and for the first time, I understood why my father and siblings loved this game.

Even more, I understood why so many people loved Killian. Watching him was exciting, and not only because I loved him. He looked like a god out on that field. No wonder he had so many adoring fans.

I watched as his team basked in the glory of winning their first championship in years because of him. He stood proudly up on the stage rolled out onto the field after the game to accept his MVP award, thanking his teammates for helping him have the best season of his career. He spoke with humility and grace, and I couldn't have been happier for him.

My father sat quietly beside me in the box we now had to ourselves after the owner and his guests left for the post-game trophy presentation, and when it was all over and Killian and the team had left the field, he leaned in next to me and said, "So what did you think? He looked pretty incredible today, didn't he?"

Struggling to hold back the tears from the mixture of pride in Killian and sadness that I couldn't share this important day with him, I nodded and said quietly, "He did. Thank you for bringing me here, Dad."

"You're welcome, honey. I want to talk to Harold Canning, the owner of the team, but I won't be long. You'll be okay alone here for a little bit?"

"Yeah. Go ahead. I'll be fine."

Left to myself, I couldn't deny the strong regret I had that after all that had happened, I wouldn't get to share this with Killian. Did he have a new girlfriend? The mere thought made my chest tighten. Not that he didn't deserve to have a woman to celebrate his big day with. He did. I just couldn't help wish it had been me.

I watched as the stadium emptied out and the workers began to clean where just a short while earlier nearly seventy thousand screaming fans had cheered on the two teams. Every so often, a player would walk out onto the field dressed in his street clothes, and I craned my neck to see if it was Killian.

But it never was.

He had interviews to give and pictures to pose for. Knowing him, he loved every second of that, I thought to myself, smiling at how much an attention whore that man could be.

I stared out at the field wishing I could get just one more glance at him. Behind me, I heard the door open. Reluctantly, I stood from my chair and grabbed my bag, wishing we didn't have to leave yet.

"Did you have a nice time talking to Mr. Canning?"

"Well, he's a pretty big fan of mine right now since I helped bring the championship home to him, but I told him I had someone else I needed to talk to tonight."

My heart skipped a beat. I knew that deep voice so full of confidence.

Stunned, I spun around to see Killian standing there smiling at me like I was the most important part of his day. He looked so good in a simple pair of black pants and a white dress shirt. I'd almost forgotten on incredibly gorgeous he was.

I couldn't find the words to say how happy I was for him, so I stood there simply staring, filling my eyes with the vision of him after so long.

"This reminds me of the first time we met. Remember? You didn't seem to have much to say to me that night either."

I opened my mouth to say congratulations, but suddenly my emotions overwhelmed me and I burst into tears, sobbing, "That night I couldn't stop thinking of how gorgeous you were. Tonight's different because I want to tell you how happy I am for you but the words wouldn't come."

He walked over to me and pulled me into his arms. "I'm so happy to see you, Tressa. I knew you were here, though. I felt it the whole time I was playing."

"My father told you he was bringing me here, didn't he?" I asked against his chest, loving how safe I felt in his arms again.

"No. He kept that a secret until a few minutes ago. I just knew you were here, though. I can't explain it, but I felt it the whole game."

I looked up at him and quickly moved to wipe under my eyes. "I'm sorry for being such a blubbering fool. You know me. I'm not usually like this. I must look a mess. Nice. You win the championship and what do you get? Some woman crying and getting her mascara all over her face."

Killian shook his head. "You look beautiful. I've missed you so much. I thought about calling you every day, but I didn't know where you were. Your father said to give you time, but I want you to know I never gave up on us. You ran, and I wanted to chase but I didn't know where to chase after you. But I never gave up."

"I'm sorry I didn't call you after I found out that whole mess was a lie. I convinced myself we were too different, and you'd be happier living in the spotlight with someone else. But I realized as I watched you today that I don't care about us being different. I love you."

A slow smile spread across his face and lit up those beautiful green eyes of his. "I've waited to hear those words, Tressa. And I have a confession. I thought I loved being famous, but when I lost you, I realized I loved you more than being loved by fans and having my picture taken by the press. When that's all I had, it felt like I had nothing because I didn't have you."

I stood on my toes to kiss him, pressing my lips to his in a kiss I'd longed for since that night I told him goodbye. Like always, he took my breath away, and once more I fell in love with him all over again.

Pressing his forehead to mine, he whispered those words that never failed to make me the happiest woman in the world. "I love you, Tressa."

"I love you, Killian."

He stepped back and nodded in a resolute way that confused me. "I know you'd probably prefer me to do this in private, but I don't think there are any cameras around, so here goes."

Then he took a small black velvet box out of his pocket and knelt down on one knee in front of me. Looking up, he took a deep breath and opened the box to reveal a diamond ring more beautiful than any I'd ever seen. "I've had this for a while now. You know me. Always confident. So, Tressa Stone, will you marry me?"

My mouth dropped open in shock, but I knew my answer. I'd known it since the moment I realized I loved Killian all those months before.

"Yes! Yes, I'll marry you, Killian Brenton," I answered as my emotions overwhelmed me and I began to cry.

He slipped the engagement ring on my finger and stood to take me in his arms. In my ear, he whispered, "You run, and I chase. Forever."

Forever.

CHAPTER TWENTY-FIVE

KILLIAN

TRESSA CURLED UP AGAINST ME on the couch in my living room as we got ready to watch SportsCenter. Although she'd been scared to death to do an interview, she agreed to do her first by my side after we announced our engagement on the network of my choice, so of course, I chose a sports show. I had a feeling that would be easier on her since the reporter would probably spend more time on my career than on gossipy topics like other shows did.

Grabbing my hand, she squeezed it tightly. "God, I'm so nervous. How do you do this all the time?"

I smiled and shook my head at how someone so incredible could be so insecure about this one thing. She'd been spectacular that day as we sat across from the reporter at the television studio. Full of doubt, she held my hand so tightly in the minutes before the interview began that I thought she might hurt herself, but when it came time to answer questions, she was the Tressa I knew and loved. Professional and sweet at the same time, she looked like a natural.

Not that she believed that for a second. Since then, she'd worried about how she looked and if she'd sounded too bossy or too strident. No matter how much I tried to convince her that she'd been perfect, I knew it would take actually watching the interview for her to see she'd done great.

"I told you that day you were perfect. I keep telling you. All these reporters have interviewed me so many times they're going to be knocking down the door to talk to you now. You're the new big thing."

She rolled her eyes at my teasing. "Don't be ridiculous. I just hope my hair looked okay. They did a great job with makeup, but my hair felt a little big. Like country-western star big. Oh, God. Was it big?"

I pulled her close and kissed her to stop her from talking. "It was perfect. You were perfect. I think maybe this needs to be the last interview you do because it's making you go crazy."

A sigh escaped her lips, and her body instantly relaxed. With a smile, she said, "That's the best thing I've heard this week."

I heard the familiar SportsCenter intro music and knew the show was starting. "It's coming on now."

Her hand clamped down on my arm as we watched the host introduce the show and then move into the segment that included our interview. "Oh, God. This is so nerve wracking!"

She had nothing to worry about. Although she didn't believe it, Tressa was a natural in front of the camera.

We watched in silence, and every so often she squeezed my arm when she answered a question or the interviewer asked me about our relationship. Then it came time for my favorite question and answer, so I pulled her close and said, "Listen. I love this part."

"So Killian, I hear you proposed right after the big game. Did you plan it, or was it a spur of the moment thing?"

I watched myself smile and look at Tressa seated next to me before I answered, "I had it planned, but I have to say it went even better than I thought it would."

The interviewer laughed. "Well, she said yes, so that tells me it went great."

Nodding, I smiled. "She said yes and that's all I kept repeating to myself as I hugged her after she agreed to marry me. 'She said yes.'"

A minute later, the interview ended, and Tressa kissed me before letting out a sigh of relief. "That wasn't too bad. I looked okay, and I didn't embarrass either one of us."

"Of course, you didn't."

She pressed my hand against her cheek and leaned into it. "Did you really keep repeating that to yourself after I said I'd marry you?"

I smiled and nodded at her question. "Yep."

Opening her eyes wide in surprise, she asked, "Did you think I'd say no?"

"I wasn't sure, to be honest."

Tressa sat up and looked at me like she couldn't

believe what she was hearing. "What happened to all that confidence you always have about everything?"

"Well, you had told me you never wanted to see me again and then avoided me for over two months. Confidence can only go so far."

My answer made her smile, and she cuddled up next to me again. "That's true. But you never had any reason to doubt I'd say yes, to be honest."

"That's good to know," I said with a chuckle. "Makes all those nerves I had when I asked you seem stupid now."

Hugging me, she sighed. "I run."

I finished her sentence for her. "And I chase."

After a moment, I added, "But if we're being truthful, you technically came to me in Tampa, so you chased when it counted."

Tressa tilted her head back to look at me and smiled. "Okay, then. I chased, and you chased. And in the end, we caught one another."

Pulling her to me, I closed my eyes and let that new reality settle in. I'd caught the elusive Tressa Stone for my own, and one day soon, I'd make her my wife.

That was a future I looked forward to.

The next generation of the Heart of Stone series continues with Silent As A Stone, a STANDALONE featuring Diana and Cole's story!

Innocent. Sweet. Diana Stone, the last of Tristan and Nina's triplets, struggled from the day she was born. Never as confident as her brother or as strong as her sister, she was the brainy Stone child with her eye on one day sitting on the highest court in the land.

Until a horrible accident left her broken and trapped by her fears.

Cole Knight has known Diana for what seems like forever. Her brother's best friend, he's been told by Ethan that Diana is off limits since junior high. But he's been drawn to that forbidden fruit for years.

Once, Diana gave him her heart at a time when he needed it the most. Now, as he looks at her as a man and not a boy anymore, can he give her what she needs most so they can find happiness forever this time?

COMING SEPTEMBER 5, 2019!
PREORDER YOUR COPY TODAY!

About the Author

K.M. Scott writes contemporary romance stories of sexy, intense, and unforgettable love. A New York Times and USA Today bestselling author, she's been in love with romance since reading her first romance novel in junior high (she was a very curious girl!). Under her Gabrielle Bisset name, she writes paranormal and historical romance. She lives in Pennsylvania with a herd of animals and when she's not writing can be found reading or feeding her TV addiction.

Be sure to visit K.M.'s Facebook page at **facebook.com/kmscottauthor** for all the latest on her books, along with giveaways and other goodies! And to hear all the news on K.M. Scott books first, sign up for her newsletter today and be sure to visit her website at **www.kmscottbooks.com**

Books by K.M. Scott:

Crash Into Me (Heart of Stone #1)
Fall Into Me (Heart of Stone #2)
Give In To Me (Heart of Stone #3)
Heart of Stone Volume One Box Set
Ever After (Heart of Stone #4)
A Heart of Stone Christmas (Heart of Stone #5)
Return To Me (Heart of Stone #6)

Forever With Me (Heart of Stone #7)
Heart of Stone Volume Two Box Set
Hard As Stone (Heart of Stone #8)
Set In Stone (Heart of Stone #9)
Silent As A Stone (Heart of Stone #10)

Temptation (Club X #1)
Surrender (Club X #2)
Possession (Club X #3)
Satisfaction (Club X #4)
Acceptance (Club X #5)
The Complete Club X Series Box Set

If I Dream (Corrupted Love #1)
If You Fight (Corrupted Love #2)
If We Fall (Corrupted Love #3)
The Corrupted Love Trilogy Box Set

Crave (Addicted To You #1)
Adore (Addicted To You #2)
Shatter (Addicted To You #3)
Claim (Addicted To You #4)
The Addicted To You Box Set

In The Darkness (Project Artemis #1)
After The Storm (Project Artemis #2)
Behind The Scenes (Project Artemis #3)
The Project Artemis Box Set

Hard Work (Standalone)

K.M.'S BOOKS ARE IN AUDIOBOOK TOO!

Books by K.M. Scott writing as Gabrielle Bisset:

Vampire Dreams Revamped (A Sons of Navarus Prequel)
Blood Avenged (Sons of Navarus #1)
Blood Betrayed (Sons of Navarus #2)
Longing (A Sons of Navarus Short Story)
Blood Spirit (Sons of Navarus #3)
The Deepest Cut (A Sons of Navarus Short Story)
Blood Prophecy (Sons of Navarus #4)
Blood Craving (Sons of Navarus #5)
Blood Eclipse (Sons of Navarus #6)
The Sons of Navarus Box Set #1
The Sons of Navarus Box Set #2

Stolen Destiny (Destined Ones Duet #1)
Destiny Redeemed (Destined Ones Duet #2)

Love's Master
Masquerade
The Victorian Erotic Romance Trilogy